DEATH ON THE ALGARVE

A Bernie Fazakerley Mystery

JUDY FORD

DEATH ON THE ALGARVE

Published by Bernie Fazakerley Publications

Copyright © 2016 Judy Ford

All rights reserved.

This book is a work of fiction. Any references to real people, events, establishments, organisations or locales are intended only to provide a sense of authenticity and are used fictitiously. All of the characters and events are entirely invented by the author. Any resemblances to persons living or dead are purely coincidental.

No part of this book may be used, transmitted, stored or reproduced in any manner whatsoever without the author's written permission.

ISBN-10: 1-911083-16-3
ISBN-13: 978-1-911083-16-0

DEDICATION

To my friend Gill Gilbert, for her advice and encouragement in my writing, and in memory of her husband, Rev. Sidney Gilbert, who made being PCC secretary during an interregnum so much easier than it might have been.

And if our fellowship below in Jesus be so sweet, what heights of rapture shall we know when round his throne we meet!
Charles Wesley (1707-88)

DEATH ON THE ALGARVE

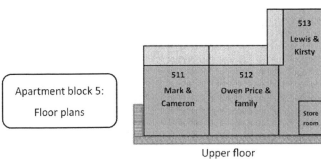

Upper floor

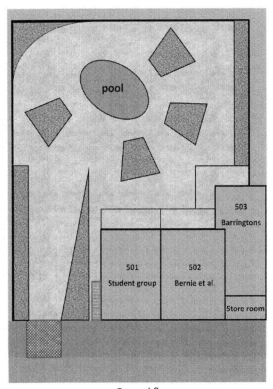

Ground floor

CONTENTS

	Acknowledgements	viii
1	Away my needless fears	1
2	Nobody knows the trouble I've seen	6
3	And kindly help each other on	14
4	Strangers and pilgrims	21
5	Names and sects and parties fall	27
6	Day of sacred rest	34
7	O perfect love	43
8	Like a mighty army	49
9	With succour speedy	60
10	I rose, went forth, and followed thee	71
11	Storms of life	79
12	Now the day is over	91
13	Slow watches of the night	101
14	Crowded ways of life	106
15	Life's little day	118
16	Wounds yet visible	127
17	Manifold witness	139

18	We may not climb	146
19	Lo! What a cloud of witnesses	153
20	The widow and the fatherless	171
21	I cannot tell	176
22	Your captain gives the word	186
23	Who is he?	196
24	The mournful mother weeping	204
25	Brother, sister, parent child	210
26	Fold to thy heart thy brother	220
27	A little child may know	225
28	Forward into battle	235
29	With contrite heart	243
30	Tis Mercy All	255
31	Home! Weary wanders, home	260
	Thank You	264
	More about Bernie and her Friends	265
	About the Author	266

ACKNOWLEDGEMENTS

I would like to thank the authors of a wide range of internet resources, which have been invaluable for researching the background to this book. These include (among others):
- Spinal Injuries Association (http://www.spinal.co.uk/page/living-with-sci)
- Wikipedia (https://en.wikipedia.org/)
- Google Maps (https://www.google.co.uk/maps)
- The University of Oxford (http://www.ox.ac.uk/)

Jonah and Freya both enjoy reading the following books:
- *Hairy Maclary's Bone,* Lynley Dodd, 1984/86, Puffin Books
- *Hairy Maclary and Zachary Quack,* Lynley Dodd, 1999, Puffin Books
- *My Naughty Little Sister*, Dorothy Edwards, 1952, Egremont UK Ltd.
- *It's your turn Roger*, Susanna Gretz, 1985, Dial Books for Young Readers, E.P. Dutton.
- *Dilly the Dinosaur*, Tony Bradman, 1989, 2001, Egremont UK Ltd.

Every effort has been made to trace copyright holders. The publishers will be glad to rectify in future editions any errors or omissions brought to their attention.

1 AWAY MY NEEDLESS FEARS

DCI Jonah Porter was afraid. As the aircraft taxied towards the runway and the cabin crew went through the safety announcements he felt the muscles in his neck tightening and his pulse racing. Yes, he was afraid – not of flying: that would have been absurd. Jonah knew the statistics: he was safer flying to Portugal than crossing the street in Oxford. No. His fear was of something completely different.

He was afraid that the hire car that they had so carefully booked might not, after all, be able to accommodate his state-of-the-art electric wheelchair, which was the key to his independence. He was afraid that the, supposedly accessible, apartment might lack the facilities that he needed – or that it might be awkward for his carers to help him with washing, and dressing, and all the other things that able-bodied people did without even thinking about them. Above all, he was afraid that his presence would spoil the enjoyment of the holiday for his friends, and in particular for sixteen-year-old Lucy, in whose honour it was taking place.

He felt a pressure on the fingers of his left hand and looked down to see that Lucy, who was sitting next to him, had reached out her right arm and taken hold of his first two fingers. She squeezed them gently. Ever since a bullet in the back of his neck had paralysed him seven years previously, these fingers and his left thumb were the only parts of Jonah's body below his shoulders in which he had any sensation. He turned his head to look at Lucy and forced a smile.

'You're not nervous of flying, are you?' she asked. 'I thought you'd been all over the world when your kids were young.'

'No,' he assured her. 'It's not the flying that makes me nervous. I just feel very strange without my chair.'

'It's only for three hours.'

'I know. I realise I'm being stupid. It just makes me feel so helpless. I rely on it so much for everything.'

'I know. You'll just have to put up with relying on us instead for a while.'

'That's right,' Lucy's mother, Bernadette (always known as Bernie or, in recognition of her Liverpudlian origins, *Our Bernie*), chipped in from the seat on the other side of him. 'And mind you ask if you need anything. I don't want to find that you've made a martyr of yourself because you didn't want to be any trouble.'

'And we don't expect any fuss from you when it's time for us to give you your physio to keep your circulation going and stop you getting pressure sores,' her husband, Peter, added from the row behind.

'OK, OK,' Jonah grumbled, feeling just a little less tense as he joined in the familiar banter. 'I'll be a good boy and do as I'm told.'

'We'll have lunch as soon as the seatbelt lights go off,' Bernie suggested. 'That will keep you occupied for a while and we'll be in Faro before you know it.'

'And just tell me if you want to listen to that audio book you brought,' Lucy added, 'and I'll put your headphones on.'

'Thanks Lucy. Later maybe – after lunch.'

Jonah knew that he ought to be grateful for Lucy's attention – and he did recognise how much he relied on her and her parents to get him through ordinary day-to-day life – but he sometimes wished that she did not appear to *enjoy* caring for him so much. He occasionally wondered whether, if some miracle cure were to give him back the use of his arms and legs, she would miss having him dependent on her – like those mothers who regretted that their children were no longer babies. She was justly proud of the skills that she had acquired through seven years of helping his adult carers and clearly took delight in being responsible for his welfare. But surely teenage rebellion should have kicked in by now and she should be starting to resent the amount of time that was taken up with activities of daily living that other people took for granted?

The head steward announced that passengers were now permitted to leave their seats and Bernie got up to reach down a rucksack from the overhead lockers. She took out packets of sandwiches and handed them to Peter and Lucy. Then she turned to Jonah.

'Feeding time! Any preferences between me and Lucy?'

'I know better than to express a preference between two women,' Jonah responded, making an effort to keep the conversation light and jokey. 'You'd better fight it out between yourselves.'

'Here you are then, Lucy.' Bernie handed her daughter another packet of sandwiches. 'You look after the sandwiches and I'll sort out the drinks.'

They were soon comfortably settled, with Lucy on Jonah's left skilfully offering up sandwiches to his mouth at well-timed intervals and Bernie holding a lidded plastic cup in a convenient position on his right so that he could reach to suck from the long straw that stuck out of the top whenever he chose. Jonah started to relax in this familiar occupation and to enjoy the food. Then he looked up and realised that they were being watched. The youngest member of the cabin crew, a slim young woman – by appearances, hardly older than Lucy – with curly black hair and coffee-coloured skin, was openly staring at him. The sight of a grown man being hand fed by a teenage girl was clearly new and fascinating to her. Suddenly realising that he was aware of her interest, she blinked her green-blue eyes – unexpected against her dark complexion and thick black lashes – in confusion and opened her mouth to apologise.

'It's OK,' Jonah reassured her before she could speak. 'I know it looks odd. It's taken me a good few years to get used to myself.'

This was certainly true. Although he always made a point of telling new people that he was not embarrassed about his disability and that they should not be either, he nevertheless had to make a deliberate effort not to feel self-conscious when eating in public. He had tried various techniques and gadgets for enabling him to feed himself, but in the end he had been forced to come to terms with the fact that it was quicker, more efficient and less messy to allow one of his carers to deal with the problem of how to get the food from the plate to his mouth. Therefore, with his customary pragmatism, he tried to push to the back of his mind any idea that it was in some way degrading to submit to this indignity.

'I'm sorry,' the flight attendant replied, still looking anxious. 'I didn't mean to—'

'I know,' Jonah broke in, speaking quietly but emphatically. 'Just forget about it. It *is* difficult not to want to watch, the first time you see it. It doesn't matter – really.'

'Thanks.' The relief in her voice was palpable. 'But I shouldn't have. I'm supposed to be trained to put people at their ease.'

'Well I'm completely at ease now, so there you are! Anyway, you passed the first big test with flying colours.'

'What do you mean?'

'Here we are having a proper grown-up conversation. You didn't talk to me like a child or talk about me to Our Bernie here as if I couldn't speak for myself.'

'Oh. Does that happen a lot?'

'More than I'd like, but I've got all my friends well-trained so they don't respond when they're asked to speak for me, and people generally get the message – or else they just give up and go off. Which is why,' Jonah went on, smiling and tilting his head in Lucy's direction, 'it's down to me to introduce you to Lucy Paige, my left-hand woman …'

Lucy looked up, grinning.

'… and Our Bernie—'

'Your general dogsbody,' Bernie put in, to forestall whatever description Jonah might have had in mind for her. 'I'm Bernie Fazakerley,' she went on, holding out her hand towards the young woman. 'Lucy's my daughter and that's my long-suffering husband, Peter, sitting behind us trying to pretend we're nothing to do with him.'

'Hello. I'm Becky,' came the response, accompanied by a brief handshake. 'I know your name,' she added, turning to Jonah,' because you're on my list of passengers who may need extra help. It's Mr Porter, isn't it? Thanks for not getting offended. I only started last week and I seem to keep upsetting people without meaning to.'

'It's *Jonah*,' Jonah told her firmly, 'and, as you can see, I am well-endowed with helpers of my own, so I doubt we'll be needing your services. Thanks all the same,' he added kindly, seeing Becky's face fall. 'And don't worry so much. You can't please all of the people all of the time and some people *enjoy* being offended.'

'Thanks. Well, if there *is* anything you need, be sure and tell me. Now I'd better go and help with the trolley. It's been nice talking to you.'

She moved off and Jonah settled back to the serious business of eating.

2 NOBODY KNOWS THE TROUBLE I'VE SEEN

The remainder of the flight was uneventful and, just over three hours later, they found themselves waiting in the arrivals area for Jonah's electric wheelchair to be returned to them. It seemed a long time coming. They had been the last off the plane, having waited while the other passengers alighted before a young man (who introduced himself as Pedro) dressed in a high visibility jacket bearing the legend *special assistance* arrived to help Jonah from the plane. Their bags had been waiting for them when they reached the arrivals hall, but there was no sign of the precious chair. Jonah sat in the manual wheelchair provided by the airline to transfer passengers from the aircraft to the terminal building, anxiously looking around, trying to fight down his rising fear as he started to think that it must be lost. Perhaps it had been left behind in Luton – or even stowed in the hold of the wrong plane.

Pedro's mobile phone sounded and they listened as he had a short conversation in Portuguese. None of them understood the language, but his tone of voice and facial expression conveyed a sense of foreboding. Something was wrong, but what?

'Excuse me one moment,' Pedro said apologetically. 'I will be back shortly.'

He strode off rapidly, leaving them looking after his retreating figure wondering what was happening. They could see him talking animatedly with another man, also clad in yellow safety gear, just outside a door marked *Privado*. Both men waved their arms about in excited hand gestures the meaning of which they could only speculate upon, but which, in their current state of anxiety, appeared suggestive of disaster. Then Pedro turned and started back towards them, walking briskly with a look of grim determination on his face.

'He's preparing to tell us bad news,' Jonah said in a low voice, 'and wants to get it over with as quickly as possible.'

He was right. As soon as Pedro reached the little group, he crouched down so that his face was level with Jonah's and addressed him seriously, glancing upwards occasionally to gauge the reaction of the other members of the party.

'I am very sorry, Mr Porter,' he said. 'Your wheelchair has been damaged.'

'What do you mean, damaged?' Lucy demanded, a look of alarm on her face, speaking for all of them as they tried to digest this unwelcome news.

'My colleague is bringing it to you now,' Pedro replied, 'and someone is coming to speak to you about putting things right. They will be here very soon.'

Sure enough, the man whom they had seen Pedro speaking to reappeared shortly, pushing Jonah's bulky, state-of-the-art electric wheelchair, accompanied by a woman in her forties dressed in the livery of the airline. They all watched anxiously trying to assess exactly what damage had been done.

The man stopped in front of them and Pedro pointed down at the left-hand arm of the chair. The control panel, comprising a keypad and small joystick, was hanging loose, with broken wires protruding from it and from the arm of the chair. The chair itself appeared intact, but, without the controller, the power could not be used and Jonah would be completely dependent on his friends to move and steer it. Worse than that, the clever mechanisms for tilting and reclining the chair to prevent pressure sores could not be used and the computer screen attachment that enabled Jonah to compose emails, browse the web and read e-books was useless.

'Good afternoon, I'm Jacqueline,' the woman said, breaking into their thoughts. She held out her hand towards Jonah and then withdrew it hastily when she realised that he could not reciprocate. 'I'm the customer relations manager. First, I'd like to say how very sorry we are for the damage to your mobility equipment and to assure you that we will carry out a thorough investigation into what happened, to try to prevent it happening again. In line with company policy, we will arrange for it to be repaired at no cost to you and we will supply a replacement meanwhile. I'm afraid there are some forms to fill in, so if you wouldn't mind coming with me to the office …'

They all trooped after her, Pedro pushing Jonah in the airport wheelchair, the other man pushing his damaged chair and Bernie, Peter and Lucy all dragging the trolley cases containing their clothes and the equipment that would be needed to care for Jonah for a week.

'It's not as simple as that,' Bernie told Jacqueline, speaking in the aggressive tones of an aggrieved Scouser. 'This is a highly-sophisticated bit of specialised kit. It was purpose-built for Jonah. You can't get a replacement just like that.'

'I realise how difficult it is for you,' Jacqueline replied patiently. 'I can only repeat how sorry we are that this has happened and say that we will do everything we can to put things right.'

'And getting it repaired won't be easy,' Bernie went on,

glad to find an outlet for venting her frustration. She had remained silent during the long wait, knowing that displaying the anger that she felt would only make things worse for the others and not trusting herself to speak without getting angry. 'There probably isn't anyone in the whole of Portugal with the skills and knowledge to fix the electronics.'

They all squeezed into a small office and Jacqueline found chairs for Peter, Bernie and Lucy. Then she sat down behind the desk and nodded to Pedro and his companion, who left the room, closing the door behind them.

Jacqueline looked round at them and apologised again before getting out the paperwork and explaining the options available to them. Having finally been reunited with his chair – albeit in a non-functioning condition – Jonah felt reluctant to put it into the hands of the airline's *damaged items* team for repair. He would prefer to take it with them so that they could be sure that it was safe until the time came to hand it over again for the return flight. He felt like a parent worried about a child's first day at school – or perhaps like the child separated from its mother for the first time.

Jacqueline suggested that they might be able to arrange for a technician to come out to their apartment to fix the chair, but Bernie remained sceptical that anyone locally would understand the workings of the chair's controller.

'I'm going to email Wayne and Dean,' she declared, pulling out her iPad from her rucksack and switching it on. 'They'll be able to send us details of the components that will need replacing. And they may even know of someone locally with the necessary expertise. If nothing else, they can make sure that they have all the spare parts in stock to fix it right away when we get home.'

'They're the guys who designed and built the chair,' Jonah explained to Jacqueline. 'They're the only people who really understand its workings.'

'Why don't you email them a photo?' Lucy suggested, glad to find some way of contributing to the efforts to get them out of the current situation, which she felt was largely her fault. 'That might help them to know how bad the damage is and what we need to fix it.'

'Good idea,' Peter agreed. 'Well done, Lucy.'

Normally Lucy would have been buoyed up by this praise from her stepfather, whose opinion she respected more than anyone's, but under the current circumstances this accolade did not raise her spirits. She blinked back tears, and was glad that the rest of the party were too busy to pay much attention to her.

She felt horribly guilty. This was *her* holiday – a celebration of her having completed her GCSE exams. *She* had chosen the destination, based on photographs of a family holiday that Peter had taken with his first wife and children twenty years previously. *She* had insisted that, now that he lived with them permanently, Jonah was part of the family and must be included in their plans. Despite being vaguely aware that he had misgivings about travelling so far from home where facilities might not match those that he was used to, she had been adamant that she would not enjoy the holiday unless he came with them.

Her parents – and Jonah himself – had urged her gently to consider whether it might be better for all of them to have a break from the routine imposed by his disability. They had argued persuasively that he would be perfectly safe and happy in the care of his son, Nathan, who had volunteered to stay with him while they were away; but Lucy was determined that if Jonah did not go then neither would she. Now all his worst fears were being realised and Lucy was responsible for putting her friend into just the sort of position of total dependency that he hated worse than anything.

She was on the verge of suggesting that they should get back on the plane and return immediately to England: back to their home in Oxford, where everything was arranged to make Jonah's life as easy as possible and where there was a second chair – not quite as sophisticated and versatile as the one they had brought with them, but nevertheless a big improvement on what was on offer here – that he could use while the experts completed their repairs. However, she realised that voicing such a suggestion would only make things worse for Jonah, who was almost certainly already worrying that his predicament was going to spoil the holiday for everyone else, and especially for Lucy herself. So she sat in silence, gazing miserably down at her hands in her lap and praying that somehow things would be sorted out soon.

A little over an hour later than they had hoped, the party was ready to leave the airport for their holiday apartment. Peter, always good at making the best of a bad situation, went off to collect the hire car, leaving the others waiting outside the terminal building. He and Bernie had transferred Jonah into his own chair, fastening the broken control panel to its arm with sticky tape, provided by Jacqueline, to prevent further damage. They all agreed that, although it meant them manhandling the heavy chair, it was preferable for Jonah to be in the chair that was customised to his size and shape rather than a borrowed machine that might impose hidden stresses on his body. Moreover, since he was clearly unwilling to allow the chair out of his sight, now that he had been reunited with it, to accept the offer of a replacement would have meant having to transport both devices, which would have been impractical.

Lucy came and stood behind Jonah and put her arms around his neck, resting her chin lightly on his shoulder with her cheek touching his. She hugged him gently, as she had done so often before during the seven years since his disabling injury.

'I bet you wish you'd never come,' she murmured in his ear.

'Not at all,' he lied. 'It's you and Our Bernie and Old Peter who are going to regret it, what with having to lug me around everywhere instead of letting me go under my own steam.'

'Don't worry about that,' she assured him. 'I've always had a secret craving to be allowed to push you around. I remember, when I was nine, visiting you in hospital and being very disappointed when I was told that you were going to have a wheelchair with a motor. I was hoping to be able to play at being a nurse taking an invalid for outings.'

'Well, it looks as if your wish is going to be granted at last,' Jonah mumbled, trying to sound jocular, but unable to keep out of his voice a hint of resentment. For the second time that day, he reflected on how galling he found Lucy's *enjoyment* of his dependency on her. It was almost as if he were a doll or a pet animal. He recognised the irrationality of this feeling – after all, he would not have wanted her to be miserable – nevertheless it was ... *demeaning* he supposed was the nearest word he could find to describe it. He was very fond of her and was determined never to allow her to know how he felt; nevertheless, he could not deny that it would be reassuring if once in a while she were to make some complaint about the time and effort that she was required to devote to caring for him or the constraints that their caring responsibilities put on the whole family.

Although they spoke in low voices, Bernie heard this exchange and turned from scanning the road in anticipation of Peter's return to look at Lucy and Jonah. She resisted an impulse to put her own arms around them both, as she observed the tear that Lucy could no longer hold back and Jonah's expression of dogged determination not to give way to either panic or self-pity. She felt a surge of mingled love and pride towards them both and hastily turned back again before they had a chance to notice it. Things were going to be quite difficult enough as it was without allowing everyone to get over-emotional.

In less time than they feared, Peter returned with the car, which they had hired through a company that specialised in services for disabled travellers. By now, their expectations were so low that they were surprised and disproportionately pleased to discover that it was exactly as they had ordered. There was a folding ramp to enable them to push Jonah in his chair up into the back of the vehicle, and plenty of space to accommodate all of them and their luggage. Bernie heaved a sigh of relief as she fastened the straps that held Jonah's chair securely in place so that he could travel safely in it. At last, things were starting to go right again!

'You'd better go in the back, Lucy,' Peter ordered. 'I need your mam in the front with me to navigate.'

Lucy climbed up into the back of the car and settled down on a seat opposite to Jonah. Their eyes met and she gave what she hoped was a reassuring smile. He smiled back briefly and then turned away as if fascinated by the view out of the window. Bernie settled into the front passenger seat and took out a map.

'Once you're out of the airport,' she said authoritatively, 'you need to get on the A22, then, according to Google maps, it's only forty-five minutes' drive. You did check that the hire car has the gizmo we need for paying the motorway tolls, didn't you?'

'Yes. It's all present and correct,' Peter confirmed, putting the car into gear and moving off. 'So now the great adventure begins!'

3 AND KINDLY HELP EACH OTHER ON

The aparthotel where they were staying consisted of a collection of two-storey buildings each comprising between six and ten apartments with their own patio area and small pool. A driveway ran along the back of the buildings, with parking and pedestrian access to each block via a path that sloped up from the drive to a tall metal gate, through the bars of which the pool area could be seen. The young woman at the reception desk had explained to them that the gates were left open during the day, but that guests were encouraged to keep them locked at night for extra security.

Peter parked outside building number five and walked up to the cobbled path at the side to check out their route to the apartment. He noted the steep slope and surmised that the cobbled surface would make it difficult to push Jonah's chair up it to reach the paved area around the pool, which gave access to the apartments. He went through the gate and looked round. Their apartment was the middle one of three on the ground floor. Turning to the right, he walked past a group of young men – students he guessed, taking advantage of the cheap flights available between the end of the university term and when the schools broke up – and found the way in. There was a slight ridge at the top of the slope leading from the pool area to the private patio outside their apartment. It would not have been a problem for the electric wheelchair in its working state, but they might have difficulty getting the combined weight of man and chair into the apartment by human effort.

He unlocked the sliding door that led from the patio into the apartment and checked that there was a level surface across the threshold and that the doorway was wide enough to accommodate Jonah's chair. He moved a coffee table to one side to make more space and walked through the living room and dining area to inspect the bathroom. It was not as spacious as he might have hoped, but he judged that it would do. The step into the shower cubicle might be tricky to negotiate, but they would manage. He turned and set off back to help his wife and stepdaughter with the business of getting their friend out of the car and into the apartment.

Meanwhile, Bernie got out, opened the back door of the car and set up the ramp ready for Jonah to descend. Lucy undid the straps securing his chair, and together they manoeuvred it down the ramp and on to the drive. So far so good, but the difficult part was still to come. Peter joined them and together they steered the heavy chair to the bottom of the slope. Then they braced themselves and pushed as hard as they could to propel it up to the gate. The wheels jammed on the cobbled surface and it jerked to a stop. Bernie applied the brake and they repositioned themselves to get a better grip before making another attempt.

'Here! Let us help!' a voice called from above them and a young man of South Asian appearance with a broad Lancashire accent ran towards them, followed closely by three more youths.

Bernie started to protest that no help was needed, but before she could get the words out, a tall broad-shouldered lad with long fair hair and a rather straggly beard had braced his shoulder against the chair and was pushing it with apparent ease up the slope. The Asian youth and a third man with spikey hair dyed an improbable shade of orange joined him. Their companion, an Afro-Caribbean with his right arm in a plaster cast, held back, watching from the sidelines as his friends heaved the chair and its occupant up the rough slope. Soon Jonah and his wheelchair were on the paved area around the pool.

'That's quite a weight to shift,' the blond giant declared.

'It's the battery,' Jonah explained. 'Normally I'm self-propelled, but the baggage handlers vandalised the controls.'

He gestured with his head towards the broken control panel.

'Can't you fix it?' asked the Asian lad.

'It'll be easy when we get home,' Bernie answered, standing the two trolley cases that she had just brought from the car next to Jonah's chair and turning to check that Lucy was bringing the remaining luggage. 'The guys who made it will put it right in no time, but out here …' she shrugged.

'It's specially built for me,' Jonah added by way of explanation, 'and very state-of-the-art, so I'm loath to let just anyone loose on fixing it.'

'Well, if you need another push, you know where to come. We're staying next door to you – in the first ground-floor apartment.' The Asian pointed towards an enclosed patio, similar to the one in front of their own apartment, and an open door leading to a room beyond.

'We've got a lightweight wheelchair in the luggage,' Lucy assured him, staggering up the path with two large cases, determined not to allow these strangers to take over any of her responsibilities for Jonah's care. 'It's easy to push, but no good for in the car and, obviously, the electric one is better when it's working.'

'Anyway,' Peter broke in, anxious that the young men might feel put out at Lucy's evident antagonism, 'thanks a lot for your help. I'm Peter and this is my wife Bernie and her daughter Lucy and our very good friend Jonah.'

'I'm Ibrahim,' the young man responded, shaking Peter's hand with unexpected formality, 'and these are Josh,' he indicated the shock-headed giant, 'and Craig. And this,' he turned and pointed at the young West Indian with the plaster cast, 'is Gary. He fell off a balcony and broke his arm a couple of days ago–'

'I didn't fall; I was pushed!' Gary protested, but with a grin that suggested that he was not particularly bothered about exacting any penalty from his attacker, whoever it might be.

'No you weren't,' Craig contradicted. 'You were drunk!'

'I may have been drunk,' Gary insisted, 'but I know I felt someone push me.'

'You were lucky only breaking your arm,' Peter observed, hoping to divert the conversation away from what looked like being an unproductive argument.

'That what *I* said,' Josh chipped in. 'I said he could just as easily have broken his neck.'

'Not from that height,' Gary retorted scornfully. 'It was less than three metres. And the bushes broke my fall.'

'Well, thank you very much for your help,' Peter said hastily, taking hold of Jonah's chair and pushing it towards their apartment. He did not like the turn that the conversation was taking. Bernie's first husband, Richard, had died after breaking his neck falling from the roof of one of the Oxford colleges and, years before that, her fiancé had committed suicide by jumping from a tall building. This was not the sort of talk with which to start a week of relaxation and reflection.

'Are you sure there's nothing else we can do for you?' Ibrahim persisted.

'Actually there is,' Bernie said suddenly. 'We're later

than we planned to be and it's going to take us a while to get unpacked. Do you think you lot could take our Lucy and show her where to get supplies? We'll need water and milk so we can make a brew and some bread to go with the tinned stuff we've brought for tea.'

'Sure thing,' Josh replied readily. 'There's a supermarket just outside the hotel. And we can show her where all the best clubs and pubs are as well.'

'Just stick to the supermarket if you don't mind,' Bernie said firmly

Lucy went off happily in the company of the young men. Her mother watched her disappear through the gate and down the path before turning to speak to Jonah.'

'It's alright now,' she told him. 'She's out of earshot, so you can let rip if you like.'

'I don't know what you mean.'

'Come off it, Jonah. We all know you've been holding it all in so as not to make Lucy feel guilty about bringing you. You can say what you really think now she's not here.'

'Huh!' Jonah snorted. 'You've really cramped my style now, haven't you? I can't rage against the unfairness of the world or the carelessness of the baggage handlers now that you've given me permission, can I?'

'Why d'you think I made such a point of doing so?' Bernie answered, smiling. 'But seriously. You really don't need to mind us. Shout and swear or burst into tears, whatever. It's water off a duck's back to me and Peter.'

'But while you do it,' Peter added, picking up two of the cases and carrying them indoors, 'we'd better get you out of that chair and on to the bed so we can check you haven't come to any harm being sat down for so long.'

'That's right,' Bernie agreed. 'I'll help with the lifting and then, if you can give Jonah his physio, I'll sort out the Wi-Fi connection and let everyone at home know we've arrived safely. And I'll see if Wayne and Dean have answered my email yet.'

'Sounds a good plan to me,' Peter agreed. 'I suggest

you have the room at the back,' he went on, pushing Jonah through the doorway into the apartment. It's a bit bigger than the other one and it looks out over the driveway, but at a higher level so people can't look in. It'll be a bit more private that the one overlooking the pool.'

'Right you are,' Jonah acquiesced, 'so long as you don't think we ought to wait until Lucy gets back to agree the sleeping arrangements.'

Bernie followed them into the bedroom where there were twin beds, a dressing table and a large wardrobe. She went to the window and looked out. Sure enough, the drive was several feet below them and passers-by would not be able to see into the room even when it was dark and the light was on. Peter manoeuvred Jonah's chair alongside one of the beds and, between them, they lifted him carefully out of it and on to the bed.

'It's a great pity the reclining mechanism doesn't work without the controller,' Peter observed, panting a little at the exertion. 'Maybe that's something Wayne and Dean ought to think of for the next model: mechanical versions of the controls for when the electrics fail.'

'Right,' Bernie said, straightening up. 'I'll leave you boys to get on. I'll be in the living room if you need me.'

Peter nodded and then turned to Jonah.

'Let's get you undressed and have a look,' he said in a matter-of-fact way, gently starting to undo Jonah's trousers. He slid them carefully off, revealing as he did so the plastic urine bag, which Jonah wore attached to his leg when he was in his chair. Peter detached it and checked it for signs of urinary infection – a common problem for people with spinal cord injuries. Good! There was no cloudiness or discolouration.

Peter continued to work methodically, carefully removing his friend's clothes and carrying out a minute inspection of the skin beneath, looking for any signs of developing pressure sores or damage of any kind following the lengthy period with limited opportunity for shifting his weight.

'You look in pretty good nick,' he declared at last. 'Just one or two bruises coming up on your ankles where we had trouble getting you into the seat on the plane, but otherwise, fine. I'll just rub in some more moisturiser on your backside, while we're here and then you can get dressed again.'

He settled Jonah face down on the bed, adjusting the pillow to make sure that his airway was clear, squeezed some cream on to his palms and started to massage his buttocks gently.

Bernie's head appeared round the door of the room.

'The Wi-Fi seems to be quite fast,' she reported. 'I've connected my phone and iPad and your computer, Jonah. Dean has replied to my email and he says they'll check out what needs to be done, and get back to me later. I've sent Nathan an email to say we've arrived. I didn't bother to tell him about the chair, in case he gets worried, but you can give him the gory details later if you want.'

'Better not,' Jonah agreed. 'It'll only confirm his opinion that I'm always trying to do more than I'm capable of and ought to slow down. He'll be back on the, "don't you think it's about time you retired?" line again before we know where we are.'

If the truth were known, his younger son Nathan's opposition to the idea of making the trip abroad had been an important factor in Jonah's decision to come. Nathan did his best to understand his father's determination not to allow his life to be ruled by his disability, but he still felt duty bound to point out potential difficulties and urge caution whenever new ventures were proposed. Jonah was certainly not going to give Nathan the satisfaction of being proved right so early on in the week. He would tell him about the mishap when they were safely back in Oxford and able to laugh about it and make light of the difficulties that it had caused.

4 STRANGERS AND PILGRIMS

Lucy trotted happily along the drive with the four students, who, it turned out were all studying at Liverpool University.

'My mam will be pleased about that,' she told them. 'She thinks Liverpool is the best city in the world.'

'I thought she sounded like a Scouser,' Ibrahim commented. 'But you don't.'

'No. We live in Oxford, but Mam is determined not to become a soft southerner!'

'Do you really call her *Mam*?' Josh asked. It was a term that he had previously only heard in television programmes featuring working class families from *up north* in which, he had assumed, it was used for comic effect.

'Yes,' Lucy giggled. 'She doesn't want me to be a soft southerner either!'

'Are you at uni?' Gary asked to fill the pause that followed this pronouncement.

'No. I've just finished my GCSEs,' Lucy explained. She was used to being taken for older than she was. Her role as one of Jonah's carers, and her upbringing among adult companions, created an impression of maturity that often confused people meeting her for the first time. 'We're taking advantage of being able to go away when most kids are still at school.'

They turned off the drive and took a path between buildings to come to a wide, open area in the centre of the apartment complex. Lucy looked around and took in a large swimming pool, surrounded by sun loungers, a small one with a children's slide, and a play area with swings and climbing frames, surrounded by a gaily-painted fence of wooden palings. A group of young children was being supervised by two young women wearing blues shorts and yellow polo shirts embroidered with the hotel logo.

'That's the bar,' Josh said, pointing to a low building at one end of the large pool. 'They've got a Karaoke night on tonight, if you'd like to come?'

'I don't think so,' Lucy said firmly. 'We usually go to bed quite early,' she added in an effort not to appear either standoffish or critical of the students' choice of entertainment. 'It takes a long time to get Jonah up in the morning, so we need to be ready to get started early.'

'That's the old guy in the wheelchair, right?' asked Josh.

'He's not old!' Lucy said indignantly. 'He's the same age as my mam. And he's a detective inspector in the police. He can do a lot more than you think.'

'I think it's cool the way you're taking him away for a holiday like this,' Ibrahim said warmly.

'It's not like that at all–' Lucy began, but she was interrupted by Craig, who had latched on to the mention of Jonah's police work and remembered having heard about him before.

'So, is that *DCI Jonah Porter*?' he asked, in slightly awestruck tones. 'The policeman who was shot in the back but still carried on working? I've seen him being interviewed on the telly.'

'Yes,' Lucy confirmed. 'But it wasn't as easy as that. It took more than a year before he could go back to work.'

'But how does he manage it?' Josh wanted to know. 'I mean, surely he would need to go out to crime scenes and collect evidence and things?'

'*Usually*,' Lucy explained patiently, 'he can get around wherever he needs to go in his wheelchair. If it hadn't got broken on the flight, you'd soon see how independent he is. And Mam is his personal assistant and goes with him everywhere. And he has constables and sergeants and SOCOs to crawl around looking for clues – just like any other senior police officer does – so he can really do anything he needs to.'

'That's cool,' Ibrahim said in an admiring tone.

They crossed the open area and came to a flight of steps leading upwards between two buildings. Lucy looked around, hoping to see a wheelchair ramp.

'Is this the only way?' she asked. 'Up these steps, I mean?'

'Well, the supermarket is just there,' Gary told her, puzzled at the question.

'But isn't there an accessible route?' Lucy persisted. 'One that Jonah could use in his wheelchair?'

'I suppose you could go round by the side of the bar and out on to the road,' Josh suggested, 'but it's much quicker this way.'

'Could you show me?' Lucy asked eagerly. 'I mean, we can come back down the steps with the shopping, but I'd like to know the way for when we all go out together.'

They retraced their steps and then went along a narrow path between the bar and one of the apartment blocks. Turning left on to the road, Lucy was pleased to see that the supermarket was only a short distance away.

'There's a bigger supermarket further on and to the right,' Craig told her. 'And the beach is up there and then to the left.'

'It's a bit of a walk,' Ibrahim said, 'and rather up and down; but we'll be happy to help push the wheelchair if you want to take your disabled friend down there later.'

'Thanks, but we'll be OK.'

They made their purchases in the supermarket and

Lucy had to admit that it was useful having four fit young men to help carry the large bottles of water and cartons of milk. As they returned down the steps and across the centre of the hotel complex, they quizzed her about Jonah, and Lucy's relationship with him.

'Both my dad and my stepdad were police officers,' she told them. 'They worked with Jonah years and years ago, before I was born. So he was always a friend of the family – coming round to give me presents on my birthday and things. Then, after he got shot, we all helped him to show people that he was still up to the job. They wanted to pension him off, but he wasn't having any of it!'

'That's cool,' Ibrahim commented. 'But isn't it a lot of work for you and your mum and dad?'

'Yes, but we like it,' Lucy said loyally. 'And Jonah does all sorts of things for us too.'

'Like what?' Gary asked in surprise. He had been finding his broken arm more debilitating than he had expected and found it hard to imagine what sort of contribution a man in a wheelchair could make to family life.

'He helps me with my homework sometimes; and he comes and supports my football team whenever he can; and he sticks up for me with Mam when she's being difficult sometimes; and …,' Lucy started to struggle to think of more examples. 'And he talks to me about my dad and things they did when they were working together in CID; and he's just nice to have around,' she finished somewhat lamely.

'So he lives with you – in your house?' Josh asked. 'Doesn't he have any family of his own?'

'He's got two sons, but one's a doctor up in County Durham and the other's a lawyer in London. If he went to live with either of them, he'd have to give up the job. So, now his wife's died, he lives with us.'

'That's really bad luck,' Ibrahim commented. 'I mean getting shot and then losing your wife. That's just unimaginably hard.'

Silence descended on the little party. None of them knew what to say next.

'Have you been staying here long?' Lucy ventured at last.

'Since Wednesday,' Craig told her. 'We're here for a fortnight.'

'But it only took Gary one day to break his arm and get himself plastered!' Josh added.

'You mean,' Craig said, 'he got himself plastered and broke his arm. It was like this,' he added, turning to Lucy. 'There was this group of girls staying in the upstairs apartment at the other end of the row, and they invited us up there for a party. Gary got drunk and stood on the wall of the balcony-,'

'And someone pushed me,' Gary put in.

'And he fell off,' Craig finished.

'I was pushed,' Gary insisted.

'He was pushed – so he says – but he doesn't know who pushed him. Maybe your policeman could investigate and find out who did it,' Josh suggested facetiously to Lucy.

'It's too late for that,' Ibrahim objected. 'The girls have gone home now, remember? They went home this morning,' he added to Lucy. 'There's a couple with a baby up there now.'

'And what about the other two apartments?' Lucy asked, suddenly interested to know about all her new neighbours. She hoped that the baby would not make a noise and keep them awake at night. Jonah tended to get overtired and grumpy when his routine was disturbed. 'Have you met the people who are staying in them?'

'There's an old guy and his wife in the other one on the ground floor,' Josh told her. 'He came round the day we arrived with a leaflet about some church or other. A bit of a weirdo.'

'And upstairs there's two families with kids,' Craig

added. 'They're on the beach most of the time, so if you want to chill out round the pool ...'

'But it wasn't the girls who pushed me,' Gary persisted. 'I reckon it was one of those local guys that they invited – you know, Pedro and Ricardo and, what was the other one?'

'Arnaldo,' Josh answered, 'or was it Armando?'

'Whatever. Anyway, I reckon it was one of those three. They didn't like us being there – especially me.'

'Do you mean it was racially motivated?' Lucy asked seriously.

'Don't take any notice of what Gary says,' Craig said scornfully. 'He's just imagining things.'

They had reached their apartment block by now and conversation stopped as they carried the shopping inside and, under Peter's direction, deposited it in the small kitchen. Jonah was propped in a semi-reclining position on the sofa. The coffee table was drawn up close so that he could see the screen of a laptop computer and manipulate a roller ball mouse with the working fingers of his left hand. He called out a brief expression of thanks to the students as they departed, and they mumbled replies to the effect that they were happy to help and could be called upon any time they were needed.

5 NAMES AND SECTS AND PARTIES FALL

Bernie was returning that evening from a trip to the supermarket in search of fruit, which she had forgotten to ask Lucy to buy on her earlier shopping expedition. Maintaining regular mealtimes and a reasonably consistent diet was something that had become second nature to the little family since Jonah had come to live with them. The lack of communication between his intestines and his brain meant that his bowel movements were out of his conscious control. Regular eating habits helped to ensure that they were confined to appropriate occasions. Peter and Bernie, and Jonah's wife Margaret before them, did their best to keep him in a proper routine, although the demands of his police work – and his refusal to allow his disability to compromise it – often made that an uphill struggle.

As she entered the paved area in front of their apartment, she met three of the students on their way out, evidently off for a night on the tiles. They greeted her cheerily and offered to take Lucy with them, if that was allowed. She declined the offer, trying not to sound too disapproving, but reminding them that her daughter was only just turned sixteen. Passing their apartment on the way to her own, she saw the fourth member of the group sitting alone in a chair on the patio.

'Not going out with the others?' she enquired of Ibrahim. 'You haven't fallen out, I hope?'

'No. Not at all,' he assured her. 'It's just, I don't really go for pubs and clubs – and it tends to get embarrassing explaining to everyone that I don't drink.'

'A man after my own heart,' Bernie smiled. 'My mam was in the Salvation Army and she wouldn't let strong drink in the house, so I grew up the same way. If you've nothing better to do, why not join us for the evening? We're just about to make a brew.'

'Well ...,' Ibrahim hesitated, 'I'm fasting just now so I can't eat or drink until later.'

'Of course! It's Ramadan, isn't it? I'd completely forgotten. Not to worry. If you don't mind watching us eating oranges and drinking tea, you'll be very welcome; and we can offer you a wicked game of scrabble after that.'

'Thanks. I'd like that. I need to go about nine though – for prayers, and to eat.'

'That suits us. We've had a long day, what with one thing and another, so we'll be wanting to get off to bed soon after that anyway.'

Ibrahim followed her inside and saw Jonah sitting in a different wheelchair – one that looked much less substantial than the large electric one from earlier – drawn up to the dining table. He noticed that a bedside cabinet had been brought out of one of the bedrooms and was placed next to the wheelchair with a pile of books and magazines on it that enabled a plastic cup with a straw in the top to come within reach of Jonah's mouth. Bernie pulled out a chair on the opposite side of the table and motioned to Ibrahim to sit down.

'Take a seat while I put the kettle on.'

Lucy and Peter emerged from the kitchen, where they had been doing the washing up, and sat down at the table. Lucy immediately took one of the oranges and started to peel it, cutting the segments into bite-sized pieces with a knife and putting them on a plate. Peter offered an orange to Ibrahim.

'No thank you,' he replied, looking rather embarrassed. 'I'm fasting until sunset.'

'Is it Ramadan?' Lucy asked with interest, at the same time popping a piece of orange into Jonah's mouth. 'I thought that was later in the year. Wasn't it when the Olympics were on?'

'It changes each year,' Ibrahim explained. 'It's based on a lunar calendar, so it gets gradually earlier in the year.'

'This must be about the worst time for it,' Peter observed, 'with the days being so long.' He picked up an orange and started peeling it for himself in a conscious effort to ensure that Jonah was not the only member of the party eating.

'Not as long here as back home,' Lucy pointed out, continuing to feed Jonah while joining in the conversation. 'It was a smart move coming here for a fortnight out of the month!'

'I don't know. I think the other guys think it's a bit of a nuisance having me wanting to keep to different times for meals and stuff.'

'We're used to that' Lucy said. 'It's better for Jonah to keep to strict mealtimes, so we understand about that sort of thing.'

'No need to go into all that,' Jonah intervened not wishing to have the minutiae of his digestive tract discussed with a comparative stranger. 'Ibrahim, tell us about yourself. Where do you come from? And that's not a racist question,' he added hastily, seeing that Peter was giving him a hard look from across the room, 'because I'm guessing it's somewhere on the Yorkshire-Lancashire border – am I right?'

'You are,' Ibrahim answered with a smile. 'Blackburn – or if you know the area at all, Darwen.'

'I thought so! My wife was from Horwich.'

'I've got an auntie who lives in Horwich. When we were kids, we used to go over there on a Sunday and have picnics up at Rivington.'

'Did you really? We always used to go there when we stayed with the in-laws. I remember the first time the boys managed to walk right up to the top of Winter Hill. Nathan must have only been four or five at the time and he was so proud of himself. We haven't been there for years – not since Margaret's mother died.'

'The thing I remember most was looking down from Rivington Pike and seeing the whole of Lancashire spread out below us – right the way to Liverpool and the sea.'

'And speaking of Liverpool,' Bernie said, coming back in carrying a tray loaded with mugs of tea. 'Lucy tells me that you and your friends all had the good sense to choose to go there for your university education. How are you liking it?'

'It's the best city in the world,' Ibrahim answered, deliberately quoting the words that Lucy had used in describing her mother's opinion of her birthplace.

'Of course,' Bernie said complacently, 'that goes without saying, but I really meant the studying. What are you reading?'

'Civil Engineering.'

'Good for you! I know a bit about engineering. I used to be a maths tutor at St Luke's College in Oxford and I taught our engineers calculus in their first year.'

'That's before she chucked it all in to look after me,' Jonah added. 'A strange choice.'

'Not at all. Following you around sniffing out clues and interrogating suspects is much more fun than marking problem sheets – not that students don't have their own charms as well,' Bernie added with a glance towards Ibrahim.

'So do you really go out and investigate crimes?' Ibrahim asked in a surprised tone, turning towards Jonah. 'Lucy said you were a police inspector but I imagined it must be just a desk job – on a computer maybe.'

'Not at all,' Bernie assured him. 'There's not much our Jonah can't do – when all his equipment is working properly. The wheelchair you saw will go most places and we've got an all-terrain version for off-road situations. I reckon it would probably even get up Rivington,' she added, turning to Jonah, 'if you'd like to go back there sometime. I haven't been since they took us all on a primary school trip back in the sixties, but from what I remember, it isn't really that steep.'

'We could go this summer,' Lucy broke in eagerly. 'If you come with us when we go to Liverpool. We could go over there for a day trip, couldn't we, mam?'

'I promised Lucy I'd take her to Liverpool this summer, to see her heritage – and some of her aunts and uncles and cousins before they all die off,' Bernie explained to Ibrahim. 'And yes, Lucy, I suppose we could go over to Rivington for a day if you'd like.'

'And Jonah can show us all the places he used to go with Nathan and Reuben and–'

'I would have thought you'd have stopped wanting to take me away with you everywhere by now,' Jonah broke in, before Lucy could add *and Margaret* to her list of Jonah's family from former times. Two years on from the death of his wife, Jonah was determined not be the grieving widower prostrated with emotion. He made a deliberate effort to speak of her in the same terms that he would have done during her lifetime and encouraged those round him to do likewise. Nevertheless, there were occasions – sometimes at random, sometimes, as now, when he was tired or frustrated with other things – that the memory of her was too much to bear, or at least too much if he were to maintain his composure in front of their guest. 'As we've recently discovered, I can be quite a liability. You'll do a lot better with just your mam and old Peter. And I'm sure you'll find plenty to do re-living Our Bernie's past without trying to capture mine as well.'

Then, seeing Lucy's face fall as she realised that she might have struck a raw nerve, he added, 'Maybe another time.'

'Let me know if you do plan to visit,' Ibrahim volunteered, noticing the awkward gap that followed this exchange and trying to fill it, 'and I can show you around. I expect it's changed quite a bit since the sixties.'

'It's very kind of you to offer,' Bernie said, stowing the tray away against the wall and sitting down, 'but hadn't you better get to know us a bit better first? For all you know we may be the greatest bores in the world and not the sort that you'd want to spend a day with in countryside! Now, since you can't join in eating and drinking, perhaps you'll make yourself useful by setting up the scrabble game. It's on that shelf over there. Get the board out and check that all the letters are in the bag.'

As the game progressed, Ibrahim was surprised to see how good Jonah was at working out combinations from the letters lying on the table in front of him without being able to move them around. Lucy sat next to him, placing the pieces in accordance with his instructions and drawing replacement letters from the scrabble bag. He was soon well out in the lead and, when he succeeded in creating 'exegesis' (a word of whose meaning Ibrahim was extremely unsure) with the 'x' on a double letter score, Peter declared that he didn't know why he bothered taking part when Jonah was playing, because everyone knew in advance who was going to win.

Just then Bernie's mobile phone rang. Seeing that it was their friend, Dean, calling she set it to loudspeaker and put it down on the table in front of Jonah.

'Hi there!' Dean greeted them. 'We've sorted out all the spares we'll need to fix the chair.'

'Thanks,' Jonah and Bernie said in unison.

'And we've booked flights to come out and mend it tomorrow,' Dean went on.

'That's very good of you, but–' began Jonah.

'You didn't need to do that,' said Bernie at the same time.

'What about the business?' Peter cut in, 'If both of you are out here with us?'

'Wayne's dad can keep an eye on the business,' Dean assured them. 'And it'll only be for a few days. We're booked to fly back next Saturday – the same as you. I was ringing to ask for details of your hotel, so that we can find you when we get there.'

'Let me know when your flight gets in and I'll come and get you,' Peter offered.

'Have you got anywhere to stay?' Bernie asked. 'If you haven't booked anywhere yet, leave it to me and I'll see if our hotel has a room.'

All the arrangements were completed in a matter of minutes and Bernie pocketed her phone again.

'That, as I'm sure you've gathered,' she said to Ibrahim, 'was one of the guys who made Jonah's chair. You'll like Wayne and Dean. *They* were engineering students when we first knew them. They designed some kit for Jonah for their third-year project and never looked back.'

'They've got their own business now,' Lucy said eagerly, 'making stuff to help disabled people.'

'And I'm still one of their guinea-pigs,' Jonah added, feeling suddenly less tired and more cheerful, in anticipation of regaining his independence. 'So I get to try out lots of their new ideas before they go into production. It's amazing some of the things they think of.'

An alarm went off on Ibrahim's phone.

'I'll have to go now,' he told them. 'It's time for prayers and then I can break my fast. Thank you for a very nice evening ... and ... I'll see you tomorrow!'

6 DAY OF SACRED REST

'Hello there!'

Jonah was sitting in the morning sunshine outside the apartment while the others cleared away the breakfast things and did the washing up. He looked up from studying a map of the area, which lay on the table before him. There in front of him stood a couple, whom he judged to be in their early seventies, looking over the low wall separating their private patio from the shared pool area. The man who had thus addressed him was tall and thin with white hair, very sparse on top, and pale blue eyes. He was wearing cream-coloured trousers and a pale blue short-sleeved shirt with, to Jonah's surprise, a clerical collar.

'We're your neighbours,' the woman told him, pointing towards the third ground floor apartment. 'We thought we'd come and introduce ourselves. I'm Claire Barrington and this is my husband, Neil.'

Like her husband, Claire was tall and thin, but her hair was blond – probably not its natural colour – and her eyes were dark brown.

'Pleased to meet you,' Jonah said, nodding a greeting towards each of them. 'Jonah Porter.'

'Is this your first visit to the Algarve?' Neil asked. 'We come here every year, so if you need any help finding things …'

'It's the first time for me, but one of the friends who's with me has been before – a long time ago though.'

'Neil helps out at the English-speaking church here for two weeks every year,' Claire told him.

'Ah! That explains the dog collar,' Jonah smiled. 'I thought it was odd that you were wearing it even on holiday.'

'That's right. I wouldn't be wearing it now, only I'm presiding at Holy Communion in a couple of hours. Would you like to come? We don't actually have a church building in the town, but the local Catholic Church allows us to have a service there every Sunday. It's nominally Church of England, but everyone is welcome.'

'We get all sorts,' Claire added. 'C of E, Methodists, Baptists, United Reformed …'

'Well, my father was a Baptist pastor; I became an Anglican after I married; and now I go to a Methodist church. What time is this service of yours?'

'Eleven,' Neil told him. 'Let me give you this,' he added, holding out a glossy leaflet headed *Anglican Chaplaincy of St. Vincent in the Algarve*. 'It has the times of services at all our churches on the Algarve.'

'Just put it on the table,' Jonah instructed him, just too late to avoid an awkward moment as Neil stood waiting for Jonah to take the flyer. 'I'll look at it later.'

'I'm sorry,' Neil flushed red with embarrassment as he realised Jonah's predicament. Of course! He ought to have noticed before the lack of hand and arm movements. It wasn't natural for anyone to sit so motionless.

'Don't be. You weren't to know,' Jonah hastened to reassure him. 'And now, let me introduce you to my friends,' he added, as Peter, Bernie and Lucy appeared from inside the apartment.

'These are our neighbours, the Reverend Neil

Barrington and his wife, Claire,' Jonah announced, 'and here we have an ex-colleague and good friend of mine, Detective Inspector (retired) Peter Johns, his wife, and my principal carer, Dr Bernie Fazakerley, and my beautiful girlfriend,' Jonah paused briefly to observe the reaction to this description of the teenager, 'Lucy Paige.'

'Lucy's my daughter,' Bernie put in hastily, seeing the looks of confusion on the Barringtons' faces. 'Her father and our Peter both worked with Jonah in Thames Valley Police – which is how the storms of life have come to wash us all up together on to, if not exactly the golden strand, at least something like solid ground.'

'He's just joking when he says I'm his girlfriend,' Lucy added, for the removal of any doubt. 'I just help Mam with looking after him, that's all.'

'Mr Barrington was telling me about an English language service this morning,' Jonah told them. 'I was wondering whether we might go.'

'Is it far?' Bernie asked. 'I mean, is it walking distance or would we need to take the car?'

Neil Barrington looked at his wife for confirmation before answering.

'I don't know. We always walk, but ...'

'It takes us about twenty-five minutes,' Claire added. 'We enjoy the exercise, but ...'

'Why not just show us on the map?' Peter suggested. 'Then we can make up our own minds.'

A few minutes later, they had established that the church was a little over a mile away, which would have been well within the capacity of Jonah's electric chair, but might prove a challenge for his friends to push him in what he described as his *unpowered craft*.'

That led on to a discussion of the mishap to the powered chair and mutual criticism of the carelessness of baggage handlers. The Barringtons expressed sympathy and made vague offers of help.

'I reckon we can walk it easily,' Bernie said, bringing

them back to the question of how to get to church that morning. 'There are three of us to take turns to push – or would you rather stay at home?' she asked Peter, remembering that he was not always at ease in churches, especially unfamiliar ones.

'Don't worry, I'm not going to miss out on the opportunity to push a DCI around,' he assured her.

'Is the church accessible,' Lucy asked earnestly. 'I mean – are there steps to get in?'

'Well, yes, there are steps at the front,' Neil said, looking towards his wife again for help in answering. Clearly, he relied on her to take care of such practical details, while he concentrated on the spiritual welfare of his flock.

'That's right,' Claire agreed, 'but the road at the side slopes up, so all you need to do is to walk up there to where it gets to the level of the entrance and then walk back along the outside of the church to the front door. Then there's just one step up, with a ramp at the side for wheelchairs.'

'And what about inside?' Lucy wanted to know. 'Is that all on the flat? Is it pews or chairs?'

'There are moveable wooden benches,' Neil answered, 'and as far as I remember there aren't any steps – except one to get up to the altar, but the congregation don't go up that. I stand on the edge of the step and they come forward to receive communion.'

'We can slide one of the benches across a bit to make room for your wheelchair at the end of it,' Claire suggested. 'Then you can sit with your friends without blocking the aisle.'

'Do you pass the peace?' Bernie asked, suddenly thinking of a potential source of embarrassment for other members of the congregation. 'And, if so, is it an orderly affair or one of those free-for-alls where everyone goes round hugging and shaking hands?'

'Not hugging,' Neil assured her.

'It rather depends who's there' Claire said, speaking at the same time as her husband. 'We get a lot of tourists, of course, and some are more outgoing than others. Is that a problem?'

'Only that people sometimes get embarrassed when they offer me their hand and find I can't take it,' Jonah explained.

'And occasionally people seem to think that, being in a wheelchair means that you don't mind complete strangers coming up and patting you on the shoulder or putting their arms round you,' Lucy added, resentfully.

'Would you like us to brief people?' Neil asked. 'I mean – I wouldn't normally like to draw attention, but if you think it would help …'

'Well, don't go making an announcement from the front,' Bernie said decisively, 'but maybe if you tell your welcome stewards, or whatever you call them, to explain to people as they come in.'

'I'm not sure how that would work,' Neil said dubiously. 'It would be all very well with people we know, but …'

'You know, I wonder if an announcement mightn't be the better option,' Peter said thoughtfully. 'I know what a shrinking violet Jonah is,' he added, grinning in Jonah's direction, 'but wouldn't the simplest way of putting everyone in the picture be to say something along the lines of: *and, as usual, we offer a warm welcome to everyone who is visiting, and today I'm sure you will want me to extend a specially warm welcome to DCI Jonah Porter, whom some of you may have heard of in the news. He's the policeman who bravely fought back from injury and is now working again, despite being paralysed by a sniper's bullet seven years ago. He'll be very happy to talk to you about his experiences after the service, but please bear in mind that he can't shake your hand …*'

'Shut up, Peter!' Jonah interrupted, grinning back at his friend. 'I know you think people always go over the top with the flattery, but there's no need to take the micky like that. 'Old Peter's probably right, though,' he added, turning to the Barringtons. 'But cut out all the *police hero* stuff and just tell them—'

'*I* don't think you ought to single Jonah out at all,' Lucy declared, before he could finish. '*Lots* of people don't like the peace.' She had, for a long time when she was younger, been subjected to unsolicited patting on the head by elderly ladies at church, and felt strongly on the matter. 'Why don't you just explain what happens – 'cos some people may never have come across it before, anyhow – and then say that, if you don't want to shake hands you can just sit down with them in your lap and nobody will bother you?'

'You're right, Lucy,' Jonah agreed. 'That's by far the best way. D'you think you can do that?' he asked Neil.

'No problem,' Neil answered, relieved to have a solution to what was looking to be an awkward dilemma. 'I always have a bit of a preamble to let everyone know that they're all welcome to take communion, whether or not they're confirmed members of the C of E, so I can add that in as well. It's a good idea of yours, young lady!' he added to Lucy, who cringed at being described thus, but had the good manners not to comment on it.

'The other thing you need to remember,' Jonah said to Neil, 'is that it's no good putting the bread into my hand, so you'll have to pretend to be a Roman Catholic and put it on my tongue.'

'And don't tip the chalice too high,' Bernie chipped in. 'He's not used to strong drink!'

'What our Bernie means,' Jonah explained patiently, 'is that you just need to be a bit careful not to pour too much and make me choke. Don't worry about it – it almost never happens.'

After a few more minutes of discussion, Neil and Claire Barrington made their excuses and returned to their own apartment, feeling a mixture of satisfaction at having increased their congregation by four and nervousness that something might go wrong. There seemed to be so much to think about. They wondered how many other disabled people might have felt unwelcome at church services in the past through ignorance or unintentionally inappropriate behaviour on the part of the able-bodied congregation.

At quarter to eleven, the four visitors entered the church. It was light and airy, with white-painted walls and a high vaulted ceiling. As Neil had described, there were two blocks of wooden benches with a wide aisle down the middle and narrower spaces between the bench-ends and the walls. Bernie immediately noticed that one of the benches, about four rows from the front, had been slid sideways leaving a gap adjacent to the central aisle.

Claire was waiting for them just inside the door. She handed hymn books and service sheets to Peter, Bernie and Lucy then hesitated, looking towards Jonah.

'I'll share with my best girl,' he said, in answer to the unspoken question.

Looking relieved, Claire led them down the aisle.

'We've made space for you here,' she said, indicating the displaced bench. 'We thought you wouldn't want to be right at the front, but this won't be far to come up for communion.'

'That will do nicely,' Jonah assured her.

Peter and Bernie sat down on the bench, while Lucy pushed Jonah's chair into the allotted space and applied the brake. Then she sat down next to him and opened the service sheet, which contained a printed order of service and a page of notices advertising weekday events. Bernie looked up at the hymn board and started leafing through the book to see which hymns they were to sing. She leant across to whisper to Jonah.

'I think our Neil must be a Methodist at heart,' she told him. 'We're starting off with *Cwm Rhondda* and finishing up with *And Can it Be?* Will you be singing the bass line?'

'If old Peter will join me,' Jonah whispered back.

Peter gave a sigh of mock resignation, but grinned back along the bench and gave Jonah a thumbs-up sign. He could never decide whether he was being hypocritical going to church when his belief in God was, at best, vague and, most of the time, negligible; but he had to admit that he enjoyed the singing and usually found the company congenial.

At the end of the service, Neil and Claire greeted them at the door and introduced them to some of the regulars – ex-patriots, some retired to homes in the sunshine and relative warmth of the Portuguese southern coast, some running businesses providing English food and football coverage to holidaymakers. Several remembered having seen news reports about Jonah's dramatic injury and subsequent return to the police force. Jonah bore the adulation patiently for several minutes, but then something snapped.

'Stop right there!' he said sharply to a middle-aged woman who had just described him as *heroic*. 'I haven't done anything special. All I did was to get on with things as best I could after something happened that I had no control over. The real heroes are these guys,' he added, gesturing with his head towards Peter, Lucy and Bernie, who were standing in a huddle by the door waiting for him to be free to come home. 'Without them, I'd be nowhere.'

Silence fell and everyone looked around rather sheepishly. Bernie stepped forward, took the handles of Jonah's chair and started to propel it towards the door.

'I think it's time for us to be getting back,' she said, trying to speak as if nothing had happened.

'Yes, of course,' Neil agreed, stepping back from the doorway to let them pass. 'We mustn't keep you. Just one thing before you go,' he added, handing a piece of coloured paper to Lucy, who was closest to him. 'It's on the notice sheet, but this is a bit more information about our monthly healing service. The next one is this Thursday – if you wanted to come along …'

Lucy took the flier in silence and they all moved out into the bright sunshine of the square.

'I'm sorry,' apologised Jonah as they began the steep walk up the street towards the apartments. 'I know I shouldn't have bitten her head off like that, but there's only so much of that nonsense I can stand.'

'So you thought you'd re-direct it at us,' Peter remarked, pretending to be annoyed. He had been taken aback at his friend's outburst and hoped to prompt him to explain what he meant by the accolade.

'At least you deserve it! Like I said, I had no choice about what happened.'

'Neither did we,' said Lucy, bending low to get sufficient traction to push him up the steep hill. The chair might be a lightweight model but, complete with its occupant, it was still a struggle to keep it moving. '*We* didn't want you to get shot any more than you did.'

'Here, let me,' Peter said, taking hold of the handles of the chair.

'It's OK,' Lucy protested. 'I can manage. We're nearly at the top.'

'Lucy, love–' Bernie began.

'Look, Lucy,' Peter said at the same time. 'We said we'd take it in turns, didn't we? You've had your turn; now I want a go!'

Lucy laughed and agreed to hand over the chair to her stepfather, happy that he had avoided any suggestion that she was incapable or not to be trusted.

'I think that's your answer, Jonah,' Bernie said quietly. 'We're not heroes either.'

7 O PERFECT LOVE

As they turned the corner of their apartment block, they collided with a young couple coming down the staircase that led up the outside of the building to the first floor. They were struggling to carry a toddler in a buggy loaded with all the accessories needed for a day on the beach with an infant. The woman, a short, plump twenty-something with black hair forming a long thick plait down her back, very pale skin, in startling contrast, and striking blues eyes, was holding the handles of the buggy. Her companion, a man of similar age with wispy blond hair and nondescript greeny brown eyes, was walking backwards supporting the buggy by the footrest at the front. The occupant of the buggy was a small girl with a thick thatch of flaming orange hair, carrying a plastic cup with a lid and a drinking spout.

'Sorry!' everyone chorused as the young man tripped backwards over Jonah's chair, dropping the buggy and only just managing to prevent himself from falling to the ground.

Fortunately the buggy did not have far to fall and it landed safely with a jerk on the paving stones. The plastic cup jolted against the side of the buggy and the lid flew off, spilling orange juice over the toddler, who opened her eyes wide in astonishment. Then she screwed up her face preparatory to wailing her indignation at the loss of her drink and the coldness of the juice on her legs. Finally, she changed her mind and peered with interest inside the cup, to see what it was like with the lid off, before inverting it so that the remaining contents were deposited over her lap.

'Oh Lily!' the young man said in exasperated tones. 'Don't do that! Here! Give me that cup and let me clean you up.'

While the girl's father was engaged in sponging juice from her clothes, his companion turned to speak to their new neighbours.

'Hi!' she said. 'I'm Kirsty Sumner and this is my partner, Lewis Best. We're in the first floor apartment at the other end of this block – above the God Squad. And this is our daughter, Lily,' she added, turning to face the child in the buggy. 'Say *hello*, Lily.'

'Good afternoon Miss Lily,' Jonah said, speaking to the toddler in the formal way that he always adopted when addressing young children. 'I'm very pleased to make your acquaintance. My name is Detective Chief Inspector Porter, but since I'm on holiday, you may call me *Jonah*. Now, let me introduce you to my friends–'

'I'm Bernie Fazakerley,' Bernie interrupted, conscious that Jonah's speech was liable to go on for some time and aware also of the astonished looks that it was attracting not only from young Lily but also from her parents. Evidently, they were unused to being spoken to in this manner. 'And this is my daughter, Lucy Paige, and my husband, Peter Johns.'

They both nodded and smiled in acknowledgement and Peter bent down to speak to Lily.

'I do like your hair!' He said to her. 'It's very special.'

Peter's own hair had been a fiery red in his youth and he always felt an affinity for redheads.

'I can't think where she got it from,' her mother commented. 'There's no red hair on either side of the family.'

'It's a recessive characteristic,' Lucy told her knowledgeably. 'So you must both be carriers.'

'It's no good,' Lewis said, speaking for the first time. 'I'll have to change her trousers. They're soaked through. I'll take her back and put on some fresh ones.'

He unstrapped Lily from the buggy and carried her back up the stairs.

'We both take an equal share in parenting,' Kirsty told them, as they watched him disappearing round the back of the building, along a walkway that led to the three first floor apartments. 'We think it's important not to reinforce gender stereotypes.'

'Like my mam and our Peter,' Lucy commented. 'Peter's a house-husband and Mam goes out to work.'

'We don't believe in all that husband and wife stuff,' Kirsty told her. 'Marriage is an out-dated patriarchal system designed to subjugate women.'

'I don't seem to have got very far with subjugating our Bernie,' Peter muttered, pretending to grumble. He was highly amused at this young woman's repetition of mantras that he felt sure she had taken verbatim from some feminist publication.

'I know lots of people who are married,' Lucy said earnestly. 'And they're all equal partners. It's got nothing to do with subjugating anyone – not these days.'

'Not for as long as I can remember,' Bernie added. 'My mam never vowed to obey my dad. As Lucy says, it was an equal partnership. Of course, it's only natural that the woman will tend to take the lead,' she added mischievously, 'because we're just better at organisation and managing things, but I'm always careful to let Peter have his say in all the important decisions.'

'Seriously though,' Jonah added. 'Now that you have your daughter to consider, I would advise you to think about getting married.'

'So people won't say she's a bastard?' Kirsty asked scornfully.

'No. I was thinking more of the financial implications if anything were to happen to either of you,' Jonah answered smoothly. 'When my wife died, her NHS widower's pension was a very welcome supplement to my salary – with me having extra costs to cover and so on.'

'And you really discover just how expensive childcare is when you're a single mother,' Bernie added. 'I've been there.'

'I don't know what sort of pension schemes you may be in,' Jonah continued.

'We're both in the NHS,' Kirsty answered, becoming interested in spite of herself. 'I'm a speech and language therapist and Lewis is an orthoptist.'

'Well then,' Jonah replied. 'If one of you were to die then, provided you're married at the time of death, the other will get a pension. It's worth thinking about – for Lily's sake.'

'But we don't believe in marriage,' Kirsty protested. 'Surely, if we've been living together and have children–'

'No. You do have to be legally married,' Jonah insisted. 'At least – well, at least check it out. I suppose you may be able to register Lewis as your partner with the pensions agency or something. I don't know.'

'And there's inheritance tax too,' Peter added. 'That *definitely* depends on being married. I remember working out that, if Bernie had kicked the bucket before we got married, Lucy's home would have had to be sold to pay the tax.'

'I admire the way you're sticking up for your principles,' Jonah continued, 'but don't you think it might be simpler just to hold your nose and take the plunge?'

'It doesn't have to be a big do,' Bernie chipped in. 'Just a few pounds to the registrar and about half an hour of your time and – bingo!'

'I don't like the idea of being given away,' Kirsty argued. 'Like a parcel or something.'

'No need,' Bernie assured her. 'I've been married twice and had one near-miss and there's never been any question of anyone giving me away.'

'Are you sure?'

'Positive. I'm sure I would have noticed!'

At this point, Lewis reappeared carrying Lily, who was dressed in a fresh pair of dungarees. He put her back into the buggy and the little family headed off for the beach. They nodded greetings to Neil and Claire Barrington who were on their way home, having stayed behind at the church to tidy up after the service.

'Hello again!' Neil called to Jonah and his friends. 'I see you've met some more of our neighbours.'

'I suppose they've been boring you with their rather juvenile ideas on marriage,' Claire said scathingly. She clearly did not have much sympathy for Kirsty and Lewis.

'The subject *did* come up,' Jonah admitted with a smile, 'and I think we gave them some food for thought on the matter, but I can't help admiring their sincerity.'

'I'm afraid I can't agree.' Claire was not to be convinced. 'There's too much irresponsibility among young people these days. I was a primary school teacher for nearly forty years and I've seen the way their attitudes have changed. When I started, you expected children's parents to be married before they were born; by the time I retired, it seemed to be the norm for children to be bridesmaids at their own parents' weddings! That is if they bothered to get married at all.'

'I suppose they are entitled to their point of view,' Neil said pacifically. He had noted the lack of rings on Bernie's fingers and the fact that the four members of this strange "family" each had different surnames and had concluded that it was entirely possible that this was another example of a couple who had failed to tie the knot of matrimony.

'It's so bad for the children,' Claire continued, ignoring

him. 'It shows a lack of commitment and generally a poor attitude to responsibility. Even when parents are married, they don't seem to put their children first the way they used to. Take the Prices, for instance. Have you met them yet?'

'They are staying in the other two apartments on the first floor,' Neil explained, seeing their blank faces. 'Major Owen Price and Captain Mark Price are brothers. They've each come for a couple of weeks with their families.'

'In school time,' Claire said with emphasis. 'You'd think that, being in the army, they'd understand about the need for discipline and establishing a good routine, but no! Just take the children off in the middle of term! Never mind the effect on their education …'

'Maybe there's a reason that they can't go at any other time,' Peter suggested mildly.

'Or maybe they just want to save a few pounds,' Claire said dismissively.

'Well, we can't stay here chatting all day,' Jonah said, suddenly feeling very weary, and reflecting to himself that he much preferred Kirsty's rather naïve earnestness to Claire's judgementalism. 'It must be nearly lunch time.'

'I don't see much evidence of female subjugation in *that* marriage,' Bernie whispered as she sliced bread in their small kitchen, after checking that Neil and Claire were safely inside their own apartment.

8 LIKE A MIGHTY ARMY

'Are you coming out to pl–' a high-pitched voice called and then faltered, as its owner realised that she was not addressing the audience that she had expected.

Jonah and his friends were sitting in the sunshine outside their apartment enjoying after-lunch coffee. They looked up to see that their private patio had been invaded by a group of children.

At the head of the little procession was a small girl with short brown plaits, brown eyes and a freckled face, carrying a bright green inflatable turtle, rather larger than herself. She was wearing a pink bikini – which Jonah considered looked rather ridiculous on a girl of seven or eight – and had a pair of fluorescent butterfly hair slides, one above each ear. Behind her stood a boy, one or two years younger, in khaki shorts and tee-shirt, brandishing a large water pistol. He too had brown hair and eyes and freckles across his nose, as did the third member of the party, a smaller girl, hanging back as if nervous of the strangers but not wanting to be separated from her siblings. She was dressed in camouflage-pattern trousers and shirt – hand-me-downs from her brother, Jonah suspected – and was clutching a book to her chest. She gazed wide-eyed at the group of unfamiliar adults from beneath a thick fringe of hair, the same brown as that of her siblings.

'Good afternoon!' Jonah greeted them. 'And who might you be?'

'I'm Holly,' the older girl answered boldly. 'I'm seven and a half. And this is Danny – well, Daniel, really – he's five –'

'I'll be six in five weeks and four days,' Danny informed them, stepping forward to stand next to his sister.

'– and that's Freya,' Holly continued, ignoring the interruption, pointing at the younger girl, who was now pressing herself up against the wall and sucking her thumb. 'She's four.'

'We're very pleased to meet you all,' Jonah told them. 'And to what do we owe the pleasure?'

'Why are you here?' Lucy translated, seeing from her puzzled expression that Holly had not understood the question.

'We came to ask Isabel and Kyle to play with us,' Holly explained. 'We'd forgotten that they went home yesterday.'

'Ah! And Isabel and Kyle were the previous occupants of this apartment, I take it?'

'They were staying here with their mum and dad.'

'I see. Well, I'm sorry to disappoint you. Is there anything we can do for you?'

'No. Thanks.' Holly turned as if to leave.

'Don't go!' Jonah called her back. 'We haven't introduced ourselves yet. I'm Detective Inspector Jonah Porter – you can call me Jonah.'

'And I'm Lucy,' Lucy said quickly, thinking it was high time someone brought the conversation down to a level closer to that of the children, and also wanting to pre-empt whatever description Jonah might be planning to use for her. 'And these are my mam and stepdad.'

'I'm Bernie and this is Peter,' Bernie added.

'Good,' Jonah said in a tone of satisfaction. 'Now we all know each other, are you sure there's nothing we can do for you?'

The children shook their heads and started to back away. They were not used to being spoken to as equals by grown-ups.'

'I like the look of that book,' Jonah said gently to Freya. 'Will you show it to me?'

The little girl hesitated for a moment before taking her thumb out of her mouth and holding the book up in front of her face with both hands. Jonah peered over and read slowly, '*Hairy Maclary's bone*. I like Hairy Maclary. Will you bring it to me so I can see better?'

Freya nodded and then trotted over and stood in front of Jonah, holding the book out towards him, expecting him to take it from her.

'I'm sorry,' he said. 'You'll have to hold it for me.'

'Why?' asked Daniel.

'Someone shot me in the neck, and now my brain can't tell my body what to do any more.'

'Hey kids!' a voice sounded over the wall and they looked up to see a man standing outside looking in. They could see at once, by his thick brown hair, brown eyes and the freckles on his face, which were not quite obscured by a deep tan, that he must be the father of the three children. 'What are you doing in there?'

'We're talking to Jonah,' Holly told him.

'He's been shot,' Danny added, 'in the neck.'

'Afghanistan?' the man asked, looking towards Jonah with interest.

'Oxfordshire.'

'How did that come about?' The man looked puzzled.

'Someone took a pot shot at me through the back fence when I was dead-heading the roses in the back garden,' Jonah told him. 'But that was seven years ago now. I only told your son because he wanted to know why I couldn't move my arms.'

'So you weren't in the forces, then?'

'Not the sort of forces you're thinking of – I'm a policeman,'

'He's a detective,' Danny told his father. 'But how do you look for clues if you can't hold a magnifying glass?' Danny's idea of a detective was based on a picture of Sherlock Holmes, complete with deer-stalker, holding an over-sized magnifying glass up to his face.

'I have other people to do that bit,' Jonah told him. 'I'm just the brains of the outfit – the little grey cells, you know!'

'I'm sorry they've been bothering you,' the man apologised. 'There was another family with kids staying here until yesterday and they've got used to treating this apartment as if it was their own. I'll see it doesn't happen again. I'm Owen Price,' he added, holding out his hand over the wall.

Bernie and Peter got up and each shook hands with him. Jonah nodded an acknowledgement of the greeting and Lucy caught Owen's eye and smiled at him, thinking to herself that he was remarkably handsome – for someone's dad. Owen looked down over the wall at Jonah's folding wheelchair.

'Is that the best the NHS can do for you?' he asked. 'I've seen colleagues – I'm in the army – injured in action who have all sorts of clever bits of kit to help them do things for themselves.'

'Jonah does too,' Lucy told him. 'Except the baggage handlers broke it. You wait till we get his proper chair fixed and then you'll see what he can do.'

'We have a rescue mission on its way, even as we speak,' Jonah informed him with a smile. 'So, with any luck, this time tomorrow you won't be able to see me for dust!'

'Have you found them?' came an anxious voice, speaking in a strong Welsh accent.

They were joined by a woman in her early thirties,

which Jonah judged made her probably ten or a dozen years younger than Owen Price. She had shoulder-length blond hair – although a darker line along her centre parting suggested that this was not her natural colour – and hazel eyes in a tanned face.

'Yes, they're all here, chattering to our new neighbours,' Owen replied over his shoulder. 'My wife, Glenys,' he added. 'Now come along kids, time you left them in peace!'

'Not so fast,' Jonah protested. 'Freya and I were just about to read a book together. You can't leave me in suspense, wondering what happens to Hairy Maclary's bone!'

'Why don't I lift you up,' Peter suggested to the little girl. He stepped forward and Freya permitted him to lift her on to Jonah's lap.

'That's right,' Jonah said to her. Now, you hold the book and I can read it to you over your shoulder. You'll have to turn the pages – can you do that for me?'

Freya nodded happily and settled back with her head resting on Jonah's shoulder. She opened the book carefully at the title page.

'Geronimo!'

The tranquil scene was shattered by a shout from above, as a figure descended amongst them from a first floor balcony. Bernie took a step back as she found a man, very similar in appearance to Owen, dropping down and landing lightly on his feet beside her.

'Mark!' Glenys said angrily. 'I've told you not to do that. It gives such a bad example to the children – and it's so dangerous. You saw what happened to that boy the other day.'

'That was different. He fell off. I just let myself down by my arms and drop gently. It's only a few feet. There's no danger at all.'

For a moment or two, they all stood in silence, taking in this unexpected apparition. He was slim and muscular and looked as if he found it difficult to relax. He was like a coiled spring. It was as if he were poised, ready for a signal to leap into action. He was wearing white shorts and a green and white polo shirt and had canvas trainers on his feet.

'This is my brother Mark.' Owen made the introductions. 'He's staying in the apartment next to ours, with his son, Cameron. And here *is* Cameron,' he added, seeing a teenage boy rounding the corner of the building, having come down from their apartment by the conventional method. Unlike Owen's children, Cameron looked nothing like his father. He was thin, rather than slim, and his face was red, rather than tanned. The skin on his nose was starting to peel, where he had evidently failed to apply sufficient sunscreen. His hair was blond – almost white – and his eyes were a watery shade of blue. Like his father, he was dressed in shorts and canvas training shoes.

'Yes, my son, Cameron,' Mark said in a tone that suggested that he would prefer to be able to disown him. 'No danger of *him* upsetting his Aunty Glenys by doing anything risky. He takes after his mother – no sense of adventure! And she, of course, just encourages him to shy away from everything. She even tried to stop him playing rugby, if you'll believe me.'

'Julie's only concerned that he might get hurt,' Glenys argued. 'It's only natural for a mother to worry about her kids.'

'That's right: you stick up for her. You two always were thick as thieves. I should have named you in the divorce, the way you filled Julie up with fancy ideas.'

'Stop that, Mark,' Owen said quietly. 'Our neighbours don't want to hear all our private family squabbles.'

For a few moments there was silence, broken only by Jonah's voice, speaking low for Freya's ears only, reading her book aloud to her. Lucy, Bernie and Peter were all a little shocked at hearing Mark speaking critically of his son to strangers – especially in his own hearing. It was small wonder that the boy was nervous if his father made a habit of denigrating him in public in that way.

'Why don't you all sit down and I'll make a brew,' Bernie suggested brightly. 'This heat makes me thirsty.'

Peter and Lucy fetched more chairs from inside the apartment and soon the adults were all seated around the white plastic table in the centre of the patio. Holly put her turtle down on the ground and sat on it, while Danny danced around them pretending to take cover behind chairs, then leaping out and aiming his water pistol (which, to everyone's relief, appeared to be empty) at various members of the party.

'Hi Lucy!' Ibrahim's face appeared over the wall. 'We're going down to the beach. Want to come?'

Lucy jumped up eagerly; then she looked at her mother and at Jonah, who was still sharing the story book with Freya. They had reached the end and were now going back studying the details of each picture.

'Is it OK?' Lucy asked doubtfully. 'Will you need me to help with anything?'

'Don't be daft,' her mother replied, smiling. 'This is supposed to be *your holiday*. You go off and enjoy yourself. Just make sure you're back in time for tea, that's all.'

'Hang on a mo!' Lucy called to the students, who had congregated in a huddle around the gate that separated the patio from the communal area. 'I'll get my swimming things and be right there.'

'What about you, Cameron?' Ibrahim asked. 'Would you like to come too?'

'Cameron's got things to do,' Mark said firmly, before his son could answer.

'OK. No problem!' Ibrahim responded cheerfully. He was aware that Mark did not approve of him and his friends and did not trust them, although he was unsure why. Probably he was afraid that students might be into drugs or binge drinking or something, he supposed.

After they had left with Lucy, Mark turned to Bernie.

'Of course, it's none of my business, but I'm surprised you allowed your daughter to go off with that crowd.

'Why?' Bernie asked sharply. She had been seriously unimpressed by Mark's deliberate disparagement of his son in public and she also shared his sister-in-law's misgivings about the wisdom of performing dangerous stunts in front of the children. 'They all seem nice enough to me.'

'They were very helpful and polite yesterday,' Peter backed her up.

'Don't you believe it. We had to complain to the hotel manager about their behaviour last week. Coming in drunk at midnight and holding noisy parties into the early hours! No consideration for people with children wanting to sleep.'

'To be fair,' Owen put in, 'it was the girls who had the parties. You can't blame the boys for going along when they were invited.'

'There was a group of five girls staying in the flat next to ours,' Glenys explained. 'They'd already been here for a while before we arrived and they'd got used to having the whole of the top floor to themselves. We had to tell them off for climbing over from their balcony into ours.'

'Well, I still wouldn't want any daughter of mine going off with that lot. We all know what students are like – sex and drugs and no sense of responsibility.'

'Actually,' Bernie said coldly, 'I do happen to know quite a lot about what students are like. I spent most of my life working with undergraduates and, in my experience, most of them are sensible, hardworking young people who are looking to make the world a better place. And in any case, our Lucy knows better than to let anyone lead her astray.'

'Well, don't say I didn't warn you. You can't be too careful with those people.'

'What do you mean, *those people*?' Bernie demanded belligerently, her Liverpool accent becoming more pronounced as her anger rose. She was coming to the conclusion that she did not like Mark one little bit.

'I mean people who don't share our values. People like that black kid – Gary, isn't it?'

At these words, Peter got to his feet with a thunderous look on his face. He opened his mouth to speak, but then closed it again, not trusting himself to confine his words to language suitable for use in front of three young children. He sat down again abruptly.

'And the Muslim,' Mark continued, apparently oblivious of Peter's movement. 'They come from a different culture from us. They don't understand how we live in Britain.'

'Ibrahim comes from Lancashire,' Jonah said quietly, looking up from Freya's book and giving Mark a hard stare. 'As did my wife. I can assure you that the good folk of Blackburn have very similar values to my own. Of course I can't tell whether they accord with yours,' he added with a hint of threat in his tone.

'I'm not talking about where he comes from; I'm talking about the sorts of things he believes in. You can't trust these Muslims. I've seen how they behave back in their own countries. You think they're on your side and you let them into your secrets and then they betray you.'

'That's enough, Mark,' Owen intervened. 'I know you had some bad experiences in Afghanistan, but you can't go round judging a whole religion on the basis of a few individuals. Just give it a rest, can't you?'

'Yes, stop it Dad,' Cameron pleaded, his face flushing even redder than it already was. He was clearly embarrassed by his father's words and attitudes. 'Ibrahim's alright. You just never give him a chance.'

'I think you should leave now,' Peter said coldly, making an effort to remain calm and to hide the intense anger that he felt towards Mark. His first wife had been a black Jamaican and he was conscious that his two children would both have been classified by Mark as *black kids* and hence, presumably, have come under his censure. Jonah knew this and had deliberately brought his own wife into the conversation as a way of distracting attention and making it less personal for Peter.

'I wasn't planning to stay,' Mark answered cheerfully, apparently oblivious to the hostile atmosphere. 'Come along Cameron, I thought we were playing tennis this afternoon.'

Father and son departed. As soon as they had disappeared round the side of the building, Owen tried to explain his brother's behaviour.

'I'm sorry about that,' he apologised. 'You must try to understand. When he was in Afghanistan, two of Mark's best mates were killed by an Afghan soldier who was working with them. They trusted him and then suddenly … Well,' Owen sighed. 'He ran amok and shot a whole lot of the guys who were supposed to be his comrades. So you can see why he …' Owen's voice tailed off and he shrugged his shoulders.

'That doesn't explain what he said about Gary,' Bernie pointed out, voicing the feelings that Peter did not trust himself to speak about. 'I know he's your brother, but that was racism, pure and simple.'

'I know that's how it comes across,' Owen sighed. 'What can I say? Like you said, he's my brother. I can't defend what he said. I can only say that he's just come out of the end of a nasty divorce and he's not finding things easy at the moment.'

'Well now, Freya!' Jonah said loudly and irrelevantly. 'I think we've just about exhausted this book, haven't we. I mustn't keep you any longer. I'm sure you have lots of more important things to do than entertaining me. Maybe you could come back another day and bring me a new book?'

Freya nodded, slid off his lap and ran to her mother, who took her hand and looked towards Jonah.

'Thank you so much,' she said to him, grateful for what she correctly judged was a deliberate ploy to divert the conversation away from a difficult subject. 'Freya does so love having someone with the time to read to her, but she doesn't usually take to new people so easily. You must have a way with children.'

'It's been my pleasure,' Jonah smiled back. 'Any time.'

9 WITH SUCCOUR SPEEDY

'I'm glad Lucy decided to go out with those lads,' Bernie said to Jonah later that afternoon. 'It's time she started to make some sort of life for herself outside the family.'

They were alone together in the back bedroom of the apartment, where it was more private than in the living room. Peter had gone off in the car to collect Wayne and Dean from the airport. Bernie was kneeling on the floor beside Jonah's manual wheelchair, gently massaging his legs to ensure good circulation of the blood.

'It's flattering that she seems to enjoy our company so much', she continued, getting up and readjusting the cushions to change his position in the chair so that it was less likely that pressure sores would develop. 'But she's never been good at making friends with people her own age.'

'Hardly surprising when she's been surrounded by adults all her life,' Jonah observed.

'I suppose not,' Bernie agreed, 'but I do worry that she feels obliged to be around to help all the time. I mean, I know she loves being allowed to do things for you: it makes her feel important. And it's all brilliant experience for her to talk about when it comes to university interviews, but at her age she shouldn't be feeling tied to home the way she does. She told me the other day that she wants to go to Oxford so that she can live at home and carry on doing her share while she's studying. Goodness knows what she'll do if she doesn't get in.'

'Oxford Brookes, maybe,' Jonah suggested.

'Not for medicine. So I'm going to make sure she has some other realistic choices on her UCAS form when it comes to it – which will be sooner than we think. This time next year we'll be needing to get her around to places so she can make her mind up which to put down.'

'Maybe those lads from Liverpool will persuade her that she'd like to go there,' Jonah suggested.

'That's an idea! I think their medical school's pretty good,' Bernie mused. 'Mmm. Maybe I'll work on that one. She might see it as getting back to her roots. It would do her good to get away – far enough off that even she can see that it wouldn't be feasible to expect to take equal shares with me and Peter – oh! I'm sorry! I didn't mean to make it sound as if it's a dreadful drag having to look after you,' she added, suddenly becoming aware of the implications of what she had just said. 'It's not like that at all. You do know that, don't you?' she asked anxiously, putting her arms round Jonah's shoulders and pressing her cheek against his.

'Oh Bernie!' he sighed. 'What was it you used to keep saying to me during the first year or two after I was shot? You know – whenever I started to feel sorry for myself – you always said: *never think that –*'

'– *you are a burden.*' Bernie joined in, remembering. 'Yes, and I still stand by that. And I know that our Peter and our Lucy agree. And that's why I'm torn over what's best for Lucy, because in a way, what right have I to tell her she can't stay with us and have her fair share of you. Perhaps it's just me being selfish and wanting to keep as much of the fun as I can for myself!'

'I'd have thought you got quite enough of me during

the working day without snatching bits of the nights and weekends as well.'

'Oh, you know me! A glutton for punishment.'

They both laughed and Bernie took Jonah's left hand in hers allowing him to squeeze it gently with his three working digits.

'Anyone at home?' came a cheerful shout from the living area. It was Wayne's voice. 'We've checked in and dumped our stuff in our room and now we're all set to get to work.'

'Just coming!' Bernie called back. She took hold of the handles of Jonah's wheelchair and pushed it out into the passageway that connected the living area to the bedroom and bathroom.

'Am I pleased to see you two!' Jonah exclaimed as they reached the main room and he saw Wayne's bulky form – he had been prop forward in his college rugby team and still looked the part – against the bright light outside the patio doors, and Dean, looking very small and slight by contrast, next to him.

Bernie let go of the chair and embraced the two young men in turn. She noticed that Wayne's fair hair had retreated a little further up his forehead than when they last met. How old was he now? Twenty-six? No, twenty-seven – and looking mature and confident like the successful entrepreneur that he was.

Dean, on the other hand, seemed hardly to have changed from the sensitive undergraduate who had been so keen to take on the challenge of designing some gadgets to help Jonah's rehabilitation during the months following his injury. They had worked together on the project for their final year dissertation and that had been the springboard for starting up their own small engineering firm producing equipment for disabled people. Bernie smiled to herself at the familiar sight of Dean's long unruly fringe of brown hair, which almost obscured his gentle brown eyes and long lashes. As often before, she resisted the urge to offer to trim it back to stop it impeding his vision. Inexplicably, he must like it like that, she reasoned. If it were just that he failed to get round to cutting it, it would not remain always in that same just-too-long style.

'Come and sit down, both of you,' she urged. 'You must be tired after your journey. Put your feet up and I'll make us a brew.'

'A cuppa would be lovely,' Wayne said, knowing that, in Bernie's eyes, hospitality was incomplete without a pot of strong tea. 'But, if it's OK, we'd rather not sit down. We came to do a job.'

'We'd rather get on with fixing Jonah's chair,' Dean agreed, in his soft West Country accent. 'We've brought all the parts and tools we could possibly need, based on the pictures you sent us,' he added, holding up a small toolbox, 'but until we see for ourselves we can't be sure that our diagnosis is correct. It may take a while, so we'd like to get started right away.'

'We want to get Jonah back on his wheels ASAP,' Wayne added, grinning and gesticulating in Jonah's direction. 'We can't have one of our best customers stuck in that old thing. We have our reputation to think of!'

'So – where is the patient?' Dean asked, looking round the room.

'In the bedroom – I'll show you,' Peter said, leading the way, while Bernie disappeared into the kitchen to put the kettle on. Jonah was left alone, feeling very helpless and vulnerable. He knew that he only had to raise his voice to ask and his friends would willingly transport him wherever he wanted to go and help him with whatever he wanted to do, but he had been used to the independence that his powered chair provided and it was frightening to be back in a position of total dependence on others. He strained his ears to hear the conversation going on in the bedroom.

'Let's have a look at you,' Dean said, in the tones of a doctor addressing a child who had been brought into A&E after an accident in the playground. 'You've certainly taken a bit of a hammering there, haven't you?'

He carefully peeled back the tape, which Bernie had used to protect the control panel from further damage during the journey from the airport, and inspected the damage more closely. Wayne knelt down next to him and peered intently at the jumble of protruding wires.

'It looks like major surgery is required,' Dean told Peter, who was watching them anxiously from the doorway. 'But don't worry; we've got everything we need.'

He got up, patting the arm of the chair as he did so, as if reassuring a nervous patient, and turned to the tool case, which he had put down on the bed. He opened it and reached inside, but Peter interrupted him.

'Why don't you bring it into the living room?' he asked. 'The light's better there and you'll have more room to work.'

And Jonah will be having kittens worrying about what you're doing with his precious chair, he added silently to himself. Peter knew how much his friend relied on the chair to give him a modicum of control over his body and his life. It was a lot more than just a piece of kit to help him get about. It was more like an extension of himself.

Dean closed the case and picked it up. Wayne pushed the heavy chair down the passage and into the main room. Peter and Dean followed him.

'D'you think you can fix it?' Jonah asked anxiously.

'No sweat,' Wayne assured him. 'It's a bit of a mess, but we've come prepared. It may just take us a few hours, that's all.'

'Just try and relax,' Dean added. 'We may have to dismantle things a bit to replace the damaged wiring, but we'll have her back in working order by the end of the day, no problem.'

Bernie returned with mugs of tea, which she set down on the coffee table, well away from the chair and its delicate electronics. She did not wish to be responsible for any spillage damaging one of the new parts that Wayne and Dean had taken so much trouble to bring from England for them. She and Peter sat together on the sofa watching intently as the engineers worked.

Half an hour later, the chair was in a hundred pieces – or at least that was how it appeared to Jonah. In actual fact, the main structure was largely untouched, but the casing that protected the complex system of wiring that enabled the controller on the arm of the chair to communicate with various motors, sensors and servos, had been removed and the wires beneath exposed. To do this, some peripheral parts had also had to be taken off and placed carefully in order on the floor beside the chair.

'Not long now,' Wayne assured Jonah, looking up from his work and seeing the apprehension on his face.

There was a murmur of voices outside and Lucy entered the room. Her four escorts could be seen through the patio doors, standing in a cluster at the gate separating their patio from the communal area. They called out cheerfully and waved, but Lucy was intent on what was going on indoors and was oblivious to them. Bernie got up and went out to thank them for offering to take Lucy with them and for returning her promptly at the time agreed.

'Can you fix it?' Lucy demanded, looking impatiently from Wayne to Dean and then back at Wayne again. 'Have you got all the bits you need?'

'No problem,' Wayne assured her.

'We're nearly there,' Dean confirmed, 'although it may not look like it,' he added, gazing round at the components lying on the floor around them. 'We've just got to get this little lot back on and then we'll be in business.'

'Can I help?' Lucy asked.

'The best thing you can do,' her mother told her, 'is to wash your hands and then get Jonah ready to eat. It's obvious they won't be finished before tea time, so let's all sit down while it's fresh and then they can carry on afterwards.'

'Ready when you are!' Peter called from the kitchen.

'It's spaghetti Bolognese – I hope that's OK with everyone?'

'Sounds great to me,' Dean answered. 'Can you just give us five minutes? We're at a slightly crucial stage and it would be good to get this bit finished before we leave it.'

Jonah tried not to show the impatience that he felt over the interruption. He knew that it was his own need for a regular routine that had been the main reason why Peter had not delayed the evening meal until after the repair work was completed. He appreciated that Wayne and Dean must be tired and hungry after their long journey and deserved a break from their labours. His rational mind told him that taking time out to eat now would not delay the time when he would be back in his chair and back in control of his life – or not by any significant amount – compared with waiting for the job to be completed before having their evening meal. And yet ... and yet, he found it very hard not to look across the room from the dining table to the floor by the patio doors where the chair stood, surrounded by the vital components of its control mechanism and to think, *why can't they just get on with it?*

He did not have to wait in this state of heightened anxiety for long. Wayne and Dean seemed almost equally keen to get on and finish their task. As soon as the meal was over, they got down to work again. Bernie and Peter lifted Jonah on to the sofa and propped him up in a reclining position from which he could watch their progress, before returning to the kitchen to wash the dishes. Lucy came and sat beside him, taking a keen interest in the function of each component and how they fitted together.

'Josh Compton's a physio,' she told them, 'or at least he will be when he's finished his degree. 'I told him about you and your company and he was wondering if he could talk to you about it. He's doing a project next year on rehabilitation of people with sports injuries and he'd be interested in hearing about some of the gadgets you make.'

'Bring him on,' Wayne said with enthusiasm. 'Just make sure he knows to get our logo into his dissertation in a nice prominent place where his supervisor can't possibly miss it!'

'Josh is the tall one with the rather feeble attempt at a beard, is that right?' Peter asked, coming in from the kitchen and taking a seat opposite Lucy.

'That's right. He's in his uni rugger team, which is why he's interested in sports injuries. I thought he and Wayne would have a lot in common.'

'Sounds like my sort of guy,' Wayne said, looking across at Dean and giving a wink.

'You always used to say you preferred the small wiry type,' Dean protested, pretending to be hurt by this remark. 'You *promised* me that there was nothing in all that communal bathing and horseplay in the changing rooms.'

'Don't you worry,' Peter told him with mock seriousness. 'He'd never dare to two-time you for fear of what Our Bernie would do to him if she got to know about it.'

'And what's that about *Our Bernie*,' his wife asked, coming in and catching the tail end of the conversation.

'Old Peter was just telling Wayne that you'd give him what for if he was ever unfaithful to his one true love,' Jonah replied with a grin.

'You bet I would!' Bernie agreed. 'You haven't got any plans in that direction, have you?' she added, giving Wayne a hard stare, 'I guarantee that whoever he is, he's not worth it – and you won't be worth anything to him either by the time I've finished with you.'

'Just winding him up,' Wayne assured her with a smile and another wink.

'You'd be out of luck with Josh anyhow,' Lucy informed him. 'He's got a steady girlfriend back home in West Bromwich.'

'That doesn't prove anything,' said Wayne, unable to resist the temptation to continue with his teasing. 'He's probably just hiding in the closet for the right guy to come along. Did you say *West Bromwich*? That's only just down the road from us. Maybe I'll look him up when we get home.'

'If you could just shut up a moment and hold this,' Dean grumbled, 'I'll tighten it up and we'll be ready for a test drive.'

Wayne knelt down and held the control panel in place while Dean attached it to the arm of the chair with two screws. Then Dean climbed in and took hold of the joystick. He touched it with his finger and the chair lurched backwards.

'Watch out!' Peter shouted as it collided with his knees.

'Sorry, Dean apologised. 'I think we must have something connected up the wrong way round. I was intending to go forward.'

He got out of the chair and disconnected the control panel again. He undid some more screws and exposed a network of wires inside. Wayne peered down at it checking each wire against a circuit diagram on his laptop.

'I've got it!' he said at last. 'You're right: we've got these two wires transposed.'

A few minutes later, they were ready for a second attempt. This time, Dean managed to make it move forward and then turn to left and right in response to small movement of the joystick. Finally, he reversed it back to its original position.

'So far, so good,' Wayne muttered. 'Now try out the tilting mechanism.'

Everything seemed to be working perfectly.

'My turn now,' Jonah said eagerly, feeling and sounding like a little boy excitedly awaiting a chance to use a new toy.

Dean got out of the chair and then, standing next to it with his hand on the controller, he made it recline, like a dentist's chair, and then adjusted its height to bring it level with the sofa. Peter and Bernie gently rolled Jonah on to the chair and strapped his left arm in position so that he could use the controls. Soon he had the chair upright again and was manoeuvring it around the apartment, showing off his skill at steering it between the furniture.

The bathroom doorway was too narrow for the chair to fit, but that hardly mattered since they would probably continue to use the smaller folding chair for accessing the shower, delicate electronics and water being a risky combination. They would need to move Jonah's bed further away from the wall to allow the chair to be reclined next to it for transfers between bed and chair, but that was easily done. Lucy was secretly pleased that this would mean bringing Jonah's bed within reach of her own, enabling her to put out her hand to touch him, to check that nothing was wrong, during the night. She had a, largely irrational, fear that he might choke or be smothered in the bedclothes in his sleep.

Jonah steered the chair back out of the bedroom and headed for the open patio doors. He took a turn round the patio and then demanded that someone open the gate to allow him out into the wider apartment complex. Wayne stepped forward, but Bernie stopped him.

'Oh no you don't!' she said, tapping her watch. 'There'll be plenty of time for exploring tomorrow. Right now, it's bed time.'

'Just once round the pool?' Jonah pleaded, like a toddler wanting one more go on the swings.

'No. I don't trust you. Once we let you loose out there, we may never get you back in.'

Wayne and Dean gathered up their tools and left for their own apartment amidst a chorus of grateful thanks. Lucy hugged them each as they let themselves out through the gate. At last, she could relax and stop feeling guilty at having insisted on Jonah coming with them.

'I'll put you to bed tonight,' she told Jonah when the young men had disappeared round the corner of the building. She had been annoyed at having been excluded from much of Jonah's routine care during the past thirty-six hours, on the grounds that she was too young to be allowed to share in lifting him from bed to chair, from chair to sofa and so on. Now that his versatile wheelchair could do the heavy work, she would be able to play an equal part with her mother and stepfather.

Jonah bit back the peevish response that leapt into his mind at this remark and managed to force a smile.

'Whatever you say, Miss. You're in charge.'

10 I ROSE, WENT FORTH, AND FOLLOWED THEE

The family was still eating breakfast when Wayne and Dean appeared at the door of their apartment the following day, anxious to check that the wheelchair was still functioning correctly. Jonah immediately abandoned his bowl of cereal, which Lucy had been diligently feeding to him, and launched into a demonstration of its capabilities. Then, with the eagerness of a puppy let off the lead, he took it outside and drove at speed round the edge of the pool, first one way and then the other. Peter and Bernie could not help laughing at his enthusiasm, but Lucy watched thoughtfully, thinking how easy it would be for him to misjudge a turn and end up in the water.

They decided to leave the washing up for later and to set out straight away to see the town and the beach and to give the wheelchair a thorough test drive. Lucy had taken careful note of the best route down to the beach the previous afternoon and, at first, she led the way; but soon Jonah could not resist the temptation to go on ahead. Downhill, the machine was capable of a good turn of speed and the others found that they were having to trot to keep up.

'Do be careful!' Lucy called out in alarm. 'Some of the pavements are very uneven and lots of the curbs haven't been lowered at junctions.'

'I think I've mentioned before,' Bernie observed to the two engineers, as they hurried along, 'that a governor to limit the maximum speed would be a really neat idea for that thing – seeing as he can't be trusted to behave responsibly,' she added, as they came up behind Jonah, who had stopped at a pedestrian crossing, waiting for the traffic to pass.

'I am completely responsible,' Jonah protested. 'See how patiently I'm waiting for a safe moment to cross the road. Just because you lot are unfit and can't keep up!'

Bernie gave in to the urge to put her arms round his shoulders and hug him. It was so good to see him back on form after the trying time that they had been having in recent days.

'You watch your lip, young man,' she threatened, speaking low in his ear. 'Remember I only have to undo the strap and move your hand off that controller and you are at my mercy – so stop pushing your luck, OK?'

It was not long before they came down to the beach. Lucy led them to the eastern end where the sand was almost level with the road and it was easy for Jonah to steer his chair on to the wooden walkway that stretched along the whole length of the beach. Looking westwards, they could see restaurants and bars dotted at intervals along the path, ready to refresh travellers weary from walking in the heat of the sun, which was now starting to climb high in the sky.

They made rapid progress along the boardwalk and soon reached the far end of the beach, where steep steps prevented them from ascending to continue their walk along the coast. They were just turning to go back, when they heard voices calling their names and, looking up, they saw the Price family descending the steps.

Jonah introduced them to Wayne and Dean and gave a short demonstration of his ability to control the wheelchair, now that it had been mended. Danny immediately stepped forward and asked to have a go. Jonah good naturedly allowed him to try out the joystick and the chair lurched in all directions as the boy discovered that it was not as easy as it looked.

'I've got another book,' Freya announced, standing on tiptoe to look Jonah in the face. 'Will you read it to me?'

'Now Freya,' her mother admonished, 'I'm sure Inspector Porter has lots of other things to do.'

'On the contrary, Miss Price,' Jonah addressed Freya seriously, 'I can think of nothing more delightful than sharing another book with you. Tell me what it's about – another Hairy Maclary?'

'No. It's a very, very old book,' Freya told him solemnly. 'Mummy says that *her* mummy used to read it to her when she was a little girl. It's called *My Naughty Little sister.*'

'Is it really? That sounds like a very interesting book. Have you got it here with you?' Jonah sounded as if he could hardly wait to start reading, although he was in fact very familiar with the book in question, having read it with his own sons, with Lucy, and most recently with his grandchildren, and could probably have recited parts of it without the need for the text.

'Mummy's got it in her bag.'

'Well then, what are we waiting for? Let's find somewhere good to sit and get down to business.'

They made their way down on to the beach, taking care to choose a route across firm sand so that Jonah's chair would not become bogged down, and settled themselves in a secluded corner. Bernie unrolled a rush mat and laid it on the ground to provide a firmer surface for the chair to stand on and to spread the weight so that it was less likely to sink into the sand. Freya watched these preparations with interest and then, as soon as she saw that her new friend was ready for her, she climbed on to Jonah's lap and opened her book for him to read.

Mark got a football out of his rucksack and suggested a game. Lucy and Bernie joined in with a will, although Mark was clearly sceptical of the wisdom of allowing girls to take part. They formed a team with Wayne and Dean. On the other side were Cameron, Mark, Owen and a very excitable Danny, who snatched the ball from Mark's hands and started doing tricks with it, showing off his prowess to impress upon the opposition that the Price family was a force to be reckoned with. Holly declared forcefully that football was a stupid game and Freya was otherwise engaged, so it looked as if there would be two teams of four. Mark looked enquiringly towards Peter, who volunteered to act as referee.

Holly settled down with her back to the game and started purposefully digging a deep hole in the sand with a small plastic spade. Glenys leaned back against a rock and took out some knitting from her bag. Jonah looked up briefly from the book that he was reading and smiled at the preparations for the match. If Mark thought it was going to be easy playing against a team that was fifty percent female, he was in for a nasty surprise. Lucy was a striker in her local girls' football team and Bernie had grown up kicking a ball around the mean streets of Toxteth. He knew which side he would have put his money on, if he were a gambling man.

He was proved right. Lucy might be smaller than Mark, but she was very quick and light on her feet and, once she had possession of the ball, nobody could touch her. Cameron, in goal, was kept busy attempting, usually unsuccessfully, to prevent her from sending the ball flying past him into the gap that he was defending between two upturned buckets. Before long the score was five-one against the Prices, thanks to a very dubious goal from Danny, who had evaded the opposition chiefly because he was so much smaller than everyone else that they were fearful of tackling him lest they inadvertently did him some injury. Wayne, who was guarding a goal delineated by a pile of towels and a small cairn of pebbles, was not expecting an attack so much against the run of play and completely failed to make any attempt to prevent both the ball and Danny from hurtling past him. Or perhaps he decided, in view of Danny's youth, not to allow his efforts to go unrewarded and stepped aside in the interests of restoring some self-respect to the opposing team.

At seven-one, Owen called a halt to the game and declared his intention of going for a swim to cool off. Wayne and Dean excused themselves from the party, saying that they had things to do, and walked off across the sand holding hands. They looked so natural and un-self-consciousness that Owen could not help staring after them. Then he turned to Peter and remarked, 'when you said they were partners I thought you meant business partners.'

'That as well,' Peter smiled.

'You might have warned us,' Mark complained. 'I don't want my boy mixing with the likes of them.'

'It's not contagious, you know,' Bernie told him sharply.

'It all depends what you mean by that,' Mark muttered darkly. 'Lots of youngsters experiment with things that it would be better for them not to know anything about.'

'I'm quite sure your two friends wouldn't dream of encouraging under-age experimentation,' Owen began, trying to calm the situation and divert his brother on to a safer topic. 'They seem like nice lads and –'

'I bet that school caretaker who did in those two little girls seemed like a nice lad,' Mark interrupted. 'All I'm saying is you can't be too careful where kids are concerned.'

'What's that got to do with Wayne and Dean,' Lucy demanded angrily.

'That's what I'd like to know too,' Bernie added, her Liverpool accent becoming stronger and her voice developing a menacing tone. 'Aren't you confusing homosexuality with paedophilia in a rather crass way?'

'How about that swim?' Owen said, with as much heartiness as he could muster. 'Come on Mark - race you to the sea!'

The two brothers ran across the sand towards the waves. Lucy and Bernie, who had been intending to join them, instead borrowed spades from the children and started building a sand sculpture of a boat. Holly and Danny came over and watched. They had never seen grownups doing this sort of thing before. Cameron stood for a moment watching his father and uncle, wondering whether to go with them. Then he shrugged his shoulders and wandered off along the shore, kicking up the sand aimlessly with his bare feet. Peter flopped down next to Glenys and fanned himself with his sunhat.

'Your wife told me you were retired,' she said, making conversation. 'How are you liking it?'

'It's great. After forty-odd years in the police force, I reckoned I'd done enough and it was time for a change. Lucy had just moved up to secondary school, so it gave me the chance to be the one there for her when she came home and so on. I've quite got the hang of being a house-husband now!'

'I wish Owen would leave the army,' Glenys sighed. 'It was all very well when he was younger, but now that we've got the kids … I do worry so, when he goes on active service. He was in Afghanistan for nearly a year. It was supposed to be six months, but then it dragged on. He didn't even see Freya until she was eight months old.'

'It must be difficult,' Peter agreed. 'I don't think I'd ever be able to get used to living apart from my family – although,' he added thoughtfully, 'eventually you do have to accept that the kids are going to move out and then …'

'Do you have kids from a first marriage then? I mean –

that is, I sort of assumed that Lucy's mum must be your second wife.'

'That's right. My own daughter's a nurse in Leeds, and my son has emigrated to Jamaica. They've both got kids of their own now.'

'Do you miss your work?'

'Not any more. It felt strange at first, but, to be honest, I'd stopped getting the buzz out of it that I used to, so I knew it was time to quit. It's a different matter with Jonah – he lives and breathes the police and could never have been happy if they'd succeeded in pensioning him off.'

'That's the sort of thing that Owen says when I suggest he leaves the army. He says: *what else could I do? It's the only thing I know.* And he *is* good at his job – I know that. Do you think there'd be a place for him in the police force, if he did leave? I mean, it would use some of his skills, wouldn't it? But without being so dangerous.'

'The police force is not entirely without danger,' Jonah pointed out. He had come to the end of the book that he was reading to Freya and was eavesdropping on their conversation. 'Our Bernie's first husband – Lucy's father – for example, was killed in the course of carrying out his duty.'

'It's not the same though,' Glenys argued. 'It's not like being shot at day after day, or waiting to hear who has been the latest victim of an IED, or being targeted by an American bomber that's mistaken you for a group of Taliban fighters.'

'No,' Jonah conceded. 'I suppose not.'

'In answer to your question,' Peter added. 'I think that your husband might well be suitable to be a cop, 'but in the current climate, with so many cuts …'

'Oh well!' Glenys gathered up her knitting wool and packed it away in her bag. 'I suppose I'm just being silly. After all, things are supposed to be a lot better now – British troops are just out there in an advisory capacity – whatever that means – so we'll just have to hope he carries on coming back safe every time.'

11 STORMS OF LIFE

'Are you going to go to the healing service?' Lucy asked, idly turning over the leaflet that they had brought back from church.

They had returned to the apartment for lunch, leaving the Price family to enjoy a picnic on the beach. Wayne and Dean were still off elsewhere, doing their own thing. Peter and Bernie were in the small kitchen washing the dishes and making coffee. This left Lucy and Jonah alone together on the patio enjoying the sunshine.

'No,' Jonah said shortly.

'It says it's at seven-thirty in the evening,' Lucy went on. So, on Thursday, we could go there after tea and be back in plenty of time for bed.'

'I said I wasn't going.' Jonah sounded unusually irritable.' Why would I want to go to a healing service?'

'Well ... to be healed, I suppose,' Lucy said, taken aback. 'Don't you believe in miracles?'

'I believe in making the best of things – not sitting around like a lemon while people pray over you and lay on hands. Look Lucy – that sort of thing just isn't my style, OK?'

Bernie came in with two mugs of coffee, which she put

down on the table. Peter followed her with another mug and Jonah's plastic cup. They both sat down.

'I'm trying to persuade Jonah to go to the healing service,' Lucy told them.

'And I've said I'm not going,' Jonah snarled. 'Now give me a break, can't you?'

'But I don't see why you won't try it,' Lucy persisted. 'It can't do any harm and you never know …'

Suddenly something snapped inside Jonah. The resentment that he had been feeling over Lucy's apparent enjoyment of her role in caring for him, his irritation at her refusal to take *no* for an answer, and his underlying insecurity all combined to form an explosive mixture.

'I wouldn't have thought you'd have *wanted* me to be miraculously restored,' he growled. 'You wouldn't be able to play at nursemaid any more – feeding me and dressing me and fussing over me, like a pet animal or one of your dolls.'

For a moment there was a shocked silence. Then Lucy jumped to her feet, knocking the flimsy plastic table so that it rocked, spilling coffee from two of the mugs.

'How could you!' she shouted at Jonah through tears of indignation and distress. 'That's so not true! How could you think …?'

She gave up trying to speak and ran off. Bernie got up to follow her, but Peter pulled her back down.

'Let her go. Give her some space on her own.'

Bernie watched her daughter disappear round the corner of the building. Then she rounded on Jonah.

'What on Earth has got into you?' she demanded. 'There was no call for that.'

Jonah was thoroughly ashamed of himself and knew that he would eventually have to admit to being in the wrong, but he was not yet ready to back down.

'I didn't mean to upset her,' he defended himself. 'I just wanted to get her to shut up about this stupid healing service.'

'By accusing her of wanting to keep you dependent on us so that she could enjoy playing at looking after you?' Bernie exclaimed sarcastically. 'Bit of a cock-up on the logic front there, don't you think?'

'It's all very well for you to talk,' Jonah retorted, resorting to an argument that he had promised himself he would never, never use, namely *you can't possibly know how I feel because you've never been shot in the back and crippled for life.* 'You don't know what it's like having a little Pollyanna around you all the time, being glad that she can do so many things for the poor paralysed man.'

'And you think that gives you the right to go round accusing her of *wanting* to keep you paralysed so that she can have fun looking after you?' Peter asked incredulously. He was the mildest of men and rarely criticised anyone, but he was deeply shocked by his friend's behaviour towards his beloved stepdaughter. 'You really are the most self-centred person I've ever come across. If you're so bloody proud of yourself for making the best of things the way they are, why can't you give us credit for doing the same? Why have *we* all got to go round with long faces complaining about what a drag it is having to devote hours of our time every day seeing to your needs, while you swan around being the brave hero who never lets his disability get him down?'

'And if you seriously believe that Lucy is glad about what happened to you,' Bernie cut in, before Jonah could make any attempt to answer, 'you should have been there when we came back from seeing you in hospital for the first time. You should have been there all those nights that she cried herself to sleep thinking about you. The number of candles we lit for you. The prayer requests she put up on the noticeboard at church. The –'

'Alright, alright, I'm sorry!' Jonah broke in. 'I know. I shouldn't have said it.'

Bernie looked at him. She was still angry and still worried for Lucy, but she was also very fond of Jonah and deep down knew that he must be torn apart by remorse. Her instinct was to put her arms round him and tell him that all was forgiven; but then he could not resist spoiling it all.

'But how was I to know she'd flounce out like that. She should've known I didn't mean it.'

Lucy strode down the road, not bothering to fight back the tears. *How could Jonah have said such things? How could he even have thought them?* Then, because she was a thoughtful and sensitive girl, she started to wonder. *Was there any truth in what he had said? Did she get a kick out of being trusted to look after him? Was there any possibility that she would feel that she had lost something if he were ever to regain control of his own body?*

Without knowing how she had got there, she found herself on the beach. She took off her trainers, stuffed her socks into them and hung them round her neck by the laces. Then she walked across the sand to the edge of the sea, which she noted subconsciously, was significantly nearer now than it had been that morning, and dabbled her feet listlessly in the shallows. Her tears had dried now, leaving salty streaks down her face. *Should she go back? Her mother would be worried about her – and Peter probably more so, although he would pretend not to be. But she was not yet ready to face Jonah. She ought to forgive him ... but ... but, oh! How* could *he have said those hurtful things?*

Walking along through the water, her head bowed, she almost fell over Freya Price, who was crouching down to fill a brightly-coloured plastic bucket with water. She stopped just in time. Looking up, her eyes met those of Owen Price, who had accompanied his younger daughter to collect water to fill the moat of a sandcastle that they had built. He took in her tear-stained face and melancholy expression and immediately asked her to come with him to buy ice creams for the family.

Lucy had no particular desire to discuss her problems with a comparative stranger – or to have to sit with the family making conversation – but she lacked the will to resist and fell in with his suggestion without demur. As they made their way up the beach to one of the wooden huts selling drinks, ice cream and beach toys, Owen gently probed to find out what was wrong. At first Lucy was determined to say nothing about her quarrel with Jonah, but he was so persistent in such a kind and un-pressurising way that she found herself recounting everything that had been said.

'And the worst part,' she finished, as they reached the wooden walkway and turned to head for the ice cream kiosk, 'is that I can't help thinking that maybe he's right. Maybe I would be disappointed not to have him to look after any more. And what sort of person does that make me – wanting him to stay the way he is, just so I can carry on looking after him?'

Owen's first impulse was to tell Lucy how much he admired her; how he and his wife had spoken together, after the children were in bed, about how remarkable it was to see a teenager so devoted to caring for someone who was not even a member of her family. He realised in time that to say these things would have been to fail to take seriously her real moral dilemma.

'I see what you're saying,' he said, after a few moments' thought, 'but it all seems a bit abstract to me. It doesn't make a lot of sense to me to be worrying about how you'd feel in a hypothetical situation that's almost certainly not going to happen. I don't think you ought to be beating yourself up about it.'

'So you don't believe that miracles can happen – ever?'

'I don't know about *ever*, but I've seen a lot of men blown up and shot and none of them have ever been miraculously cured. I mean – try telling a man whose legs have both been blown away by an IED that you're praying for a miracle!'

They reached the ice cream shop and the conversation paused while Owen made his purchases. He handed four cones to Lucy and took two more in each of his own hands.

'Better get these back to the troops before they melt!'

The hours passed very slowly for Bernie, Peter and Jonah. They were all wretched about what had happened and anxious about Lucy. Peter was very angry with Jonah for his treatment of Lucy and worried, both for Lucy herself and for Bernie were anything to happen to her daughter. Bernie felt that she owed it to Lucy to remain angry with Jonah, while at the same time being made miserable at seeing how desperately unhappy the incident had made him. Jonah's guilt feelings were almost overwhelming. Not only was he well aware of the enormity of his behaviour towards Lucy, but also of the impact that it had had on the two friends upon whom he depended so completely.

To make matters worse, that dependence compelled them all to continue with the normal routine of life. Peter and Bernie could not, in all conscience, neglect to do all the things that were so necessary for Jonah's health and comfort, despite feeling that they would very much rather have nothing more to do with him, at least until they were sure that Lucy was safe. Jonah, determined to be as little trouble as possible, made a point of not asking for anything from them. However, this only made things worse, since they now felt obliged to make regular checks to ensure that he had all that he needed.

'Would you like a drink?' Bernie enquired, forcing herself to speak calmly and trying not to sound as if she resented having to ask. 'It's very hot.'

'No, I'm fine,' Jonah assured her, without considering the matter.

'Are you sure?' Bernie insisted. 'You need to keep up your fluid intake.'

'I said I was alright,' Jonah snarled. 'You don't have to treat me like a two year old.'

'I don't see why not,' Peter intervened. 'Seeing as you're behaving like one.'

'Go on then,' Jonah muttered. 'Get me some orange juice if it will make you feel better.'

In silence, Bernie fetched a carton of juice from the fridge and poured it into Jonah's cup, fitted the lid carefully and set it in the holder attached to his chair, turning the straw towards him to be within easy reach of his mouth. Jonah forced himself to drink, aware that he owed it to his friends to look after this health in order not to increase the burdens imposed upon them in caring for him. Everyone relapsed into an uncomfortable silence.

'Do you think one of us ought to go and look for her?' Bernie asked Peter, as she returned from checking the road for signs of Lucy's return, for the tenth time. 'She hasn't even got her mobile with her. I found it on the bed.'

'She'll be back at tea time,' he said, with greater confidence than he felt. 'She knows it's important to stick to regular mealtimes.'

'But she's never gone off like this before. How do we know how she'll behave?'

Peter got up and came over to his wife, who was standing by the wall that separated their patio from the communal area, still gazing out in the direction from which Lucy would return – always assuming that she did return. He put his arms round her and hugged her close.

'She just needs some space by herself for a while,' he reiterated. 'You were saying yourself that you wished she would become more like a normal teenager – now you know what it's like! When Hannah was her age, hardly a day went by without her going off in a huff about something or other.'

'But,' Bernie began. Then she changed her mind. *But Hannah was just a stroppy teenager taking offence at every little thing, determined that her parents were the most unfair in the world, whereas Lucy wasn't like that. Moreover, she had been given real reason to be upset and to want to avoid coming back to face the man who had said those unforgiveable things.* That was what went through her mind, but she realised in time that she had no business criticising either her stepdaughter or, by implication, her husband's parenting skills.

'But I want to have my cake *and* eat it,' she finished at last, in an attempt to lighten the atmosphere by turning the joke on herself. 'I want my daughter to be completely normal and at the same time uniquely perfect in every way.'

'Like every other parent,' Peter agreed. 'Which is why we're all doomed to disappointment.'

Jonah had maintained a miserable silence during this exchange. He knew that he was deeply in the wrong and wished that he could think of a way of putting things right, but any apology now would sound too much like a self-serving appeal from a cripple to his benefactors, on whom he depended for his very life. He would have liked to go out in search of Lucy himself, but realised that to make the suggestion would have been tantamount to ordering Bernie or Peter to accompany him, since they would be sure to feel that he could not safely be permitted to venture out alone in a strange town. Or, if they did allow him out unaccompanied, how was having two of their family astray and in potential danger going to help to decrease their anxiety?

Not being given to self-doubt, Jonah was unused to feeling so totally guilty and he did not know how to deal with it. He needed forgiveness, but he could not think of any way of asking for it that would not sound, to his own ears at least, like a calculated ploy to regain their sympathy. He turned over in his mind various different forms of words, from the humorous, H*ey guys! Lighten up here! It was all just a misunderstanding*, approach through to an abject, *I repent in dust and ashes*, accompanied by a metaphorical beating of the breast. In the end, he decided that any attempt at cleverness on his part would be sure to make things worse rather than better.

'I'm sorry,' he said simply.

Peter and Bernie both turned and looked at him. Bernie, who had been secretly longing to make up, but was determined for Lucy's sake not to be the first to give way, resisted an impulse to hug him. She knew how difficult he found it to admit that he was in the wrong. They said nothing, so Jonah groped around for words to express his contrition more fully.

'I don't know why I said those stupid things. I ought to have known they would upset Lucy ... I mean,' he added, determined not to evade any of the blame, 'I knew it would hurt her, but I went ahead anyway. I shouldn't have done. I really am very sorry.'

All at once, Bernie was there hugging him and kissing him on the cheek. Peter came across and put his hand on his shoulder. He felt warm tears running down his face and was unsure whether they were Bernie's or his own. For several minutes nobody spoke. Then Bernie let go of Jonah and stood up. She blew her nose and then fetched a piece of kitchen towel and helped Jonah to do the same.

'I'll make us a brew,' she declared, heading for the kitchen.

'If Lucy wants me to go to that healing service,' Jonah called after her, determined to make every effort to set things straight. 'I'll go along and let them pray over me and lay hands on me and whatever else they do at that sort of thing.'

'Dead right, you will,' Bernie called back cheerily. 'I never heard such a fuss. Anyone would think it was some sort of ordeal by fire!'

'Yes,' Peter agreed, 'what's the big deal? So, nothing's likely to come of it, but it can't do any harm, can it? What are you afraid of?'

'What am I afraid of?' Jonah repeated. 'I'm afraid that, if a miracle were to happen – and I'm not expecting for one moment that it will – then I'd know that God had some reason for doing it. And then I'd have to find out what his plan was for my life and I'd have to go along with it – whether it fitted in with *my* plans or not.'

'I think I get it,' Bernie said, coming in with three mugs of tea, which she placed on the table. She sat down on Jonah's right and, throughout the ensuing discussion, plied him with small sips from one mug while she herself drank from another. Tea from a china cup was a secret pleasure that Jonah had confessed only to Bernie and which she indulged only on very special occasions. This was her way of making it clear to him that she bore him no hard feelings after the recent contretemps. 'You mean you don't fancy being *a brand plucked from the burning*, like John Wesley.'

Seeing the puzzled looks on both men's faces, she explained.

'When John Wesley was a boy, his father upset his parishioners so much that they set fire to the vicarage. John had to be rescued from an upstairs window. After that, he thought he had been saved for some special purpose. I can see you might be nervous of being expected to ride round the country on horseback leading a religious revival!'

'I still don't see what you're bothered about,' Peter repeated. He was not exactly an unbeliever, but he found questions about God and the supernatural rather pointless. He preferred to stick to the practical world that he could see and touch. 'Surely you don't seriously think that this healing malarkey could actually *work*? And if it did – well wouldn't that just be great for you? I don't see the problem.'

'When I was shot,' Jonah answered, trying to explain, 'people kept on at me to say that I wanted to know *why me?* And I kept saying to them *why not me?* I think they were wanting me to say that I could accept what had happened to me because it was all part of God's plan for my life and that, in the end, I would discover that it had all been for the best.'

'And that isn't what you think?' Peter asked. 'I mean – you keep going to church and praying and all that. I thought, with your dad being a minister and everything, that probably *was* how you saw it.'

'No. And I'm glad that I don't think like that, because if I did, I'd be wondering all the time what lesson it is that I'm supposed to learn from it, and what it is that I'm, supposed to be doing about it. And maybe it wouldn't be just carrying on doing the job I love – maybe I would be obliged to get out there and start up a revival, like Bernie said, or something equally unappealing.'

'Yes. I see what you mean,' Bernie agreed. 'If you can put the responsibility on to whoever it was who shot you, then all you have to do is to try to make the best of things as they are now. Whereas, if you believe that God deliberately arranged for you to be shot, as part of some master plan, then you're obliged to try to fit in with whatever that plan happens to be.'

'Precisely! And that's how it would be if someone came along and laid hands on me and I took up my bed and walked. Then I really would be asking *why me?*'

'So you don't believe in miracles?' Peter asked.

'In the abstract, in principle, I wouldn't want to rule them out; but I have to admit that in any particular case, I'd be sceptical. It all comes down to that *why me?* factor. God can't cure everyone of every disease and rescue everyone from every danger – we all have to die eventually – so why would he do it for a few of his favourites? I can't square that with a just and loving God. So I'd much rather he left the world to run by itself and didn't keep jumping in and fixing things. But then, I can't get away from the fact that he might know better than me and there could be reasons for intervening that I haven't thought of. All I can say is that I'd rather I wasn't one of the ones singled out for special attention, that's all!'

'Not like you to be such a shrinking violet,' Bernie laughed. 'I thought you always loved being the centre of attention.'

'Not at all. I really don't want to be anyone special – it's too much of a responsibility.'

12 NOW THE DAY IS OVER

Peter and Bernie were in the kitchen preparing the evening meal when Lucy finally arrived back at the apartment. She approached quietly and paused for a moment outside, looking in. Seeing that Jonah was sitting alone, apparently engrossed in something on his computer screen, she crept in and put her arms gently around his shoulders.

'I love you,' she whispered in his ear. 'And I'm sorry I got cross and walked out on you.'

Jonah, who had been composing in his mind the humblest of abject apologies, in preparation for Lucy's reappearance, was so utterly taken aback by these words that he could not think of anything to say.

'I've been talking to Owen Price,' Lucy went on, sitting down on Jonah's left and taking his hand between her two. 'He told me about some of the guys he knows who had arms and legs blown off in Afghanistan and Iraq. He said how difficult it is for them to accept what's happened to them. And it made me realise how stupid it was of me to think I understand how you feel. I shouldn't have badgered you to go to the healing service if that's not what you want.'

'And I've just been telling your mam what a prat I was,

saying I wouldn't go, and how I'll go to any number of healing services if you'd like me to. Honestly, I'm the one who ought to be apologising to you. I was well out of order saying all those stupid things about you treating me like a doll. I ought just to be thankful that you can be bothered with me at all.'

'Hear, hear!' Bernie said, coming into the room. 'You really are the world's number one prize pillock, Jonah and I'm delighted to hear you admit it.'

'I do, I do. I'd throw myself at your feet and lick your boots if I could!'

'Here you are, then!' Bernie stood on one leg and held her foot under Jonah's nose. Lucy pushed it away angrily.

'Stop Mam! Don't tease him. It's not fair.'

'After what he put us through this afternoon,' Bernie retorted, 'he deserves all he gets – and more!'

'What are we going to do tomorrow?' Bernie asked as she sat down on the sofa after tea. 'Now that Jonah's properly mobile again, we ought to get out and see things.'

'It's Lucy's holiday,' Jonah said. 'What do *you* want to do?'

'I don't know. Peter! You've been here before. What was the best thing you did then?'

'It was a long time ago. I'm not sure that I remember that much – and anyway things may have changed – but I suppose the one thing I think you shouldn't miss is the sea caves at Ponta da Piedade.'

'Tell me about them,' Lucy urged.

'Well, I remember going on the train – we didn't hire a car when we came before – and walking up to the top of the cliff and then down and down lots of steps to where there were a whole lot of little boats moored, waiting to take us to see the caves. And then the boatman took us round to see all these spectacular rock formations and we went right into some of the caves – in the boat.'

'I think I've seen the pictures you took,' Lucy said

excitedly. 'Lots of tall pillars of yellow and orange stone, and water foaming through between the rocks.'

'That's right. The photos are a bit wonky because the boat was bobbing around so much I couldn't hold the camera straight. You really should go. It's much more spectacular in real-life than in the pictures.'

'That's a good idea,' Bernie agreed. 'How far is it? Will it take all day, or shall we aim to be back here for lunch?'

'I can't remember. It wasn't very far on the train – twenty minutes, maybe half an hour, I think – but then there was a walk at either end. I remember Eddie complaining about how far it was uphill to where we booked on the trip. As I said, we didn't have a car, so I've no idea how long it would take to drive.'

'What about Jonah?' Lucy asked, Peter's words about cliff-top walks and long climbs down steps having just registered with her. 'Is there any disabled access?'

'You mustn't restrict what *you* do because of me,' Jonah put in quickly. '*You* go and bring me back some pictures.'

'But I want us to all do things together,' Lucy protested.

'I won't enjoy the holiday at all if I think me being here is stopping you doing things you'd like,' Jonah insisted. 'I can have a nice quiet day by the pool, soaking up the sun. You've been on about how important it is for me to get more UV exposure to ward off osteoporosis.'

'I don't know,' Lucy said slowly. 'I'd really rather –'

'Jonah's right,' Peter interrupted. 'It's daft thinking we can all do the same things all the time. I think that you and your mam ought to go, and Jonah and I will stay at home – or maybe do a bit of shopping – and I'll cook one of my specials for us all to have for tea when you get back.'

'But then you'll *both* be missing out on the caves,' Lucy argued.

'I've been before, remember,' Peter insisted. 'So I won't be missing out on anything.'

'Well,' Bernie declared decisively, '*I'm* going to the

caves tomorrow, whatever anyone else decides to do. Hand over that rail timetable so I can work out which train to get.'

'And I've been reading about the market that they've got here,' Peter added. 'I thought I'd get us some locally-caught fish and fresh vegetables and cook up a traditional Portuguese feast.'

In their studio apartment on the other side of the complex, Wayne and Dean were also arguing about what to do the following day. Dean, who was a keen but intermittent surfer, suggested a day on the beach, while Wayne favoured browsing around the shops.

'I *must* get something for Dad to thank him for looking after things while we're away,' he argued. 'Anyway, you haven't brought your board.'

'There's a place that hires them out. We could get two. I could teach you to do it properly. I can't believe you still haven't managed to get the knack.'

'I might have done if I'd ever been able to see the point.'

'There isn't one – that *is* the point. It's all just for fun,' Dean shook his head, as if unable to believe his partner's attitude. 'And I thought *I* was supposed to be the boring religious one who takes everything too seriously!'

'You grew up with it,' Wayne argued, returning to the subject of his surfing limitations. 'Where was I supposed to find to go surfing in Halesowen?'

'OK,' Dean conceded. 'We'll go round the shops and find something nice for your dad – and something for your mum too,' he added. Dean was very fond of Barbara Major, who enjoyed spoiling her son-in-law.

'And then, if you really want to, after lunch we could look into hiring surfboards.'

'Tell you what – why don't we book you a lesson at the surf school?'

'Please Mummy! Can we go to the Kids Club tomorrow?' Holly pleaded, as her mother supervised her in the shower prior to getting her into her pyjamas ready for bed. 'They're having a pirate party in the big pool.'

'We didn't bring you away with us so that you could spend your time with a load of other kids,' Owen called from the living room. 'This is supposed to be a *family* holiday.'

'Daddy's right,' Glenys backed him up. 'We only got permission to take you out of school because he's going abroad again next week. This is for you to spend quality time with your father before he goes away.'

'Why does Daddy have to go away?' Freya asked.

'He's a soldier,' Danny told her. 'Soldiers have to go off to fight wars. Like this! Pshaw! Pshaw! Pshaw!' He raised his arm and fired an imaginary gun at his mother and sisters.

'What if someone shoots him?' Freya asked, looking at her mother wide-eyed and anxious. 'Like they did to poor Jonah.'

'Don't worry, sweetheart,' Owen said, coming to the door of the bathroom and looking in. 'No-one's going to shoot me. I'm not going out there to fight – I'm just going to be a military advisor.'

What does that mean?' Freya wanted to know.

'It means he's going to teach other people how to fight,' Danny informed her. 'But what about the Kids Club?' he added, turning to Glenys. 'I want to be a pirate.' The imaginary gun vanished from his hand and became an imaginary cutlass, as he leapt around the room pretending to slit everyone's throat.

'Plea-ease Mummy!' Holly begged. 'Don't you and Daddy want some quality time for yourselves? Chloë's Mum says all parents need time away from the kids to do grown-up things.'

'Oh alright,' Glenys gave in. 'We'll go over there tomorrow and see if there are any places left for the afternoon session.'

In the next apartment, Kirsty and Lewis were also busy with family bedtime, but all was not well with little Lily. She had been fractious all afternoon, but they had put it down to some new teeth that were emerging at the back of her mouth. Then she had been reluctant to eat her supper, and half an hour afterwards had brought it all back up over the sofa. Kirsty picked her up and carried her to the bathroom to clean her up, at which point she discovered that her nappy was leaking spectacularly and both Lily's and Kirsty's clothes were wet with a malodorous brown fluid.

Lewis, whose eagerness to share in the thrills and spills of parenthood did not stretch as far as mopping up vomit and excrement, wandered out on to the balcony and sat looking out over the small pool surrounded by sun loungers. Only two of these were currently occupied. He recognised the man from the next apartment but one – Mark Price, he'd said his name was – and his teen-aged son. The boy had just got out of the pool and was towelling himself down vigorously. The man lay back smoking a cigarette.

There was a sound of voices and a small cluster of young people emerged from one of the apartments below. It was the students from the end apartment on the ground floor. They had a group of girls with them. They walked past Mark and Cameron and stood chatting with them for a few minutes before continuing on their way – off for a night out in the pubs and clubs, Lewis assumed.

'It's OK Lew!' Kirsty called from inside their apartment. 'I've cleared it all up. You're safe to come in now.'

Lewis went back into the living room. He sniffed. The odour of vomit had been replaced by a strong smell of air freshener.

'Don't sit on the sofa,' Kirsty warned him. 'It's still wet, but at least I think I've got it clean.'

'How is she?' Lewis asked, nodding his head towards the bedroom.

'Well, she's gone down OK, but I think she's running a temperature. Maybe we ought to get a doctor to have a look at her.'

'If she's settled, let's not disturb her. See how she is in the morning. Kids go up and down so fast. She'll probably be fine after a good night's sleep.'

'Hi Cameron!' Craig Jenner called out from the little group assembled outside the students' apartment. 'There's a concert and firework display tonight down at the club by the marina. Would you like to come?'

'We need another man!' added the tall girl who was standing next to him.

Cameron looked across at the group and saw that Craig, Joshua and Gary were accompanied by four young women, all dressed as if for a party in off-the-shoulder dresses and high heels.

'Ibrahim's staying in to pray,' Joshua explained. 'So we're one short. Why don't you come along?'

'Can you wait while I get dressed?' Cameron asked, wrapping the towel around his waist and pushing his feet into a pair of beach shoes.

'No you don't,' Mark intervened. 'I'm not having you going off clubbing and drinking and who knows what else.'

'Da-ad!' Cameron pleaded, going red and turning his back on the student group to prevent them from seeing his embarrassment. 'Stop showing me up,' he muttered to his father in an undertone. 'I'm not a kid any more.'

'That's where you're wrong. Until your eighteenth birthday, technically you're still a minor, and I have parental responsibility for you. So what I say goes.' Mark got up and went over to the group of students. 'Cameron won't be coming out with you tonight – or any other night – OK? Have you got it?'

'OK,' the students shrugged and smiled as if quite unconcerned. Mark gave them a hard look before turning back to follow his son, who was making his way to the stairs leading up to the first floor and their apartment.

When he got there, he found that Cameron had locked himself in the bathroom. He could hear the shower running, so he settled himself down on the sofa to wait.

Eventually his son emerged, wet hair standing up on end, wearing shorts and a tee shirt and carrying his swimming trunks. He walked straight past Mark without acknowledging him and went out to the balcony to hang the trunks on the clothes airer. His father got up and followed him out.

'Those girls are way too old for you,' Mark said. Cameron ignored the remark, so he went on. 'And those dresses they were wearing! I've seen tarts showing less cleavage. So you can forget any idea of–'

'OK, forget it, Dad! After the way you showed me up just then, they're not likely to ask me again, are they?'

He sat down on one of the plastic chairs on the balcony, got out his smartphone and pretended to be very busy with it. Mark sat down next to him. For a few minutes, neither spoke.

'Look, Cam,' Mark said at last. 'It's not that I don't want you going out with girls – I just don't want you mixing with girls like that.'

'Like what?' Cameron answered, forgetting that he had intended to ignore his father for the rest of the evening.

'Sluts.'

'Sluts? How do you make that out? You only saw them for five minutes.'

'Anyone can see: the way they dress, their makeup, everything about them just yells out at you, *slut, slut, slut!*'

Cameron relapsed into silence at this, so after a few moments Mark continued.

'And there's the way that brunette was draping herself all over the coloured boy – talk about gagging for it!'

'You're not supposed to say *coloured* any more,' Cameron said quietly, deliberately trying to provoke his father, who could normally be relied upon to respond to such a remark with a tirade about *political correctness gone mad*. Mark opened his mouth to do so and then, with uncharacteristic perceptiveness decided against it. Instead, he tried another approach to win over his son.

'Why don't you ask that pretty blonde from downstairs out?' he suggested.

'You mean Lucy?'

'Yeah. That's right. She seems like a nice girl – and more your age. How about it?'

'No way! She's scary!' Cameron declared decisively.

'Because she's better than you at football?' Mark laughed. 'Is that it?'

'No! She's like … like … like she's not real,' Cameron struggled to explain. 'Like, no kid is like that – not for real.'

'I don't get what you mean.' His father was puzzled.

'Like … OK then, I told her I was in the lower sixth and she was like, *aren't you worried about taking time out in term time in the middle of your A level course?* And then she says she'll be disappointed if any of her GCSE grades aren't A's or A-stars. And she's going to go to Oxford uni to become a forensic pathologist and cut people up when they're dead. And I was like *isn't that a bit gruesome?* And she was like, *no, I've been to a post-mortem and it was cool.* And she meant it, too: she really has watched some friend of her stepdad's cutting up this guy who drowned in the Thames. And she's been like helping to look after that guy in the wheelchair ever since she was nine. And … like I said, she's just scary. She knows so much more about everything than I do.'

Downstairs, in the smallest apartment on the ground floor, Claire and Neil were planning their day.

'I'd like to go to Silves again,' Claire said. 'The cathedral is well worth another look. And there's the Moorish castle too.'

'Good idea,' Neil agreed. 'It says here,' he pointed to his iPad screen, that it's going to be hotter tomorrow. We'd better go in the morning. As I remember, it's quite a pull up to the castle, so best not to leave it until the heat of the day.'

'Then in the afternoon, I was wondering if we should offer to look after Mr Porter – to give the family a bit of a break.'

'I don't know,' Neil said dubiously. 'I'd like to help them too, but you need to be very tactful with offering help. Often relatives are very protective of disabled people. We can't expect them to trust us when they've only just met us.'

'I was only thinking we could offer to sit with him so they could go off on their own for a while – down to the beach, for example, or shopping. I feel sorry for that young girl. It can't be much fun for her'

'Well, let's see how things go. Maybe, if we stay around here in the afternoon, we'll get a chance to talk to them – to get to know them better.'

13 SLOW WATCHES OF THE NIGHT

Jonah found it difficult to get to sleep that night. He lay staring at the pattern of light made by the street lamp outside filtering through the lattice of the window shutters. He tried to find calming things to think about to quieten his mind, but nothing could prevent the same thought coming back: *how could you have said those things to Lucy?*

A clatter of feet on the cobbles and a murmur of voices signalled the return of the students to the next-door apartment. It must be past midnight now. The plumbing gurgled as they prepared for bed. Then silence again. *You should have known she would be upset. You* did *know, didn't you? But you went ahead anyway. Why did you do it? You are a worm, a monster ...*

An alarm went off. It was Lucy's phone signalling to her that it was time to turn Jonah over into a different lying position to protect him from developing pressure sores. She reached over from her own bed and touched him gently on the shoulder.

'Are you awake?' she asked softly. 'It's time to turn you. Close your eyes and I'll put on the light.'

She got out of bed and padded round on bare feet to inspect the urine bag attached to the side of Jonah's bed. It was not full, but she judged that it might not last out until the morning.

'I'd better change this while I'm up,' she told him, bending down to disconnect it. She worked systematically, going through a familiar routine. A few minutes later, she returned to her own bed, having re-connected Jonah's plumbing and repositioned him in the bed so that he was now lying on his left side facing towards her. She switched off the bedside light, noticing that daylight was starting to penetrate through the shutters. She lay down on her right side and looked towards Jonah. Their eyes met in the gloom and she smiled at him.

That was too much for Jonah in his current state of exhaustion and remorse. The full enormity of his behaviour towards her the previous day pressed down like a weight on his mind and he was unable to stop the tears welling up. He blinked fiercely to disperse them and hide them from Lucy, but she was immediately alert to his distress.

'Jonah! What is it?' she put out her hand and rested it gently on his shoulder. 'You're not still worrying about the healing service are you?' she asked anxiously. 'It really isn't a big deal, if you'd rather not go.'

Jonah made a great effort and managed to compose himself.

'No. It's not that at all. I said I don't mind going, if that's what you want. Mind you,' he went on, trying to lighten the mood by adopting his usual joking style, 'I'm not expecting anything to come of it, so prepare to be disappointed.'

'I don't know what to expect either. I just thought … I've never been to anything like that before and … well … you never know do you? It can't do any harm to ask, can it?'

'I think it would be a bit ungrateful of me to ask for anything more from God when he's already given me you and your mam and old Peter.'

Lucy opened her mouth to protest at this statement, then changed her mind and leant over to give Jonah a quick peck on the cheek.

They lay in silence for a few minutes.

'Jonah!'

'Yes.'

'*Do* you believe in miracles? I mean, you do hear stories, don't you, about people who got better when all the doctors said it was impossible.'

'I don't know. All that necessarily means is that the doctors didn't know everything – and they'll all admit that there are plenty of things that they don't know about how the human body works. I was married to one for thirty years, so I should know.'

'But you believe in God – and the Bible – don't you?'

'I suppose,' Jonah said thoughtfully, 'I believe that God *could* intervene and do something that goes against the laws of nature – or at least our understanding of them – but whether he ever actually *would* is another matter altogether. I suppose I believe in the possibility of miracles in principle, but I'm deeply sceptical every time anyone claims to have witnessed one.'

'Don't you even believe in the miracles in the Bible? There are lots of stories about Jesus healing people.'

'And there are lots of reasons why it's impossible to tell what really happened. I never like re-opening a case years after the event because it's just impossible to get trustworthy evidence.'

'But you read the Bible every day. Don't you believe what it says?'

'Come on, Lucy, you know it's not as simple as that. I believe in the Bible as what it is – a collection of all sorts of different writing that has somehow got handed down from generation to generation because it's somehow important. None of it even claims to be an accurate historical account. It's no good trying to treat the gospels, for example, as if they were the sort of witness statement that I'd try to get if I was investigating a crime. We only have one side of the argument, for a start. And none of it was written down until years afterwards. I know from experience that people's memories often get things wrong after even a few days. We see what we are expecting to see instead of what was really there, or we think about what we saw and try to rationalise it to fit in with our expectations, and what we remember changes. And, on top of all that, the people who wrote the gospels viewed the world differently from us – and so did the people they were writing for – so it's difficult for us to interpret what they really meant.'

'You mean things like demon possession being what we'd call mental illness these days?'

'Yes. That sort of thing.'

'I've been thinking,' Lucy said, after a long pause. 'After Owen told me about his friends who'd had arms and legs blown off, I was thinking about what would happen if one of them went to the healing service.'

Jonah looked at her keenly but said nothing.

'I mean, *no-one* would think that they could be healed, but plenty of people would think that *you* might be. So why can we believe that God might miraculously re-grow your spinal cord, but not someone's leg?'

'Put like that, it makes me think that probably none of us really believes in miracles – only in things that we can't explain yet.'

'That's what I thought, but …'

'One way of thinking about it,' Jonah suggested, 'is that God can't work any miracle that would be so blatantly supernatural that it would force everyone to believe in it. He always leaves the door open to a natural interpretation.'

'That sounds too much like telling kids that Father Christmas won't come if they stay awake to watch for him,' Lucy said, wrinkling her nose. 'Or, *don't tell anyone what you wished for when you blew out the candles, or it won't come true.*'

'I know,' Jonah admitted. 'It's not a very good explanation, but it's the best I can come up with at this time in the morning.'

'Sorry. I didn't mean to keep you awake.'

Lucy kissed Jonah on the cheek again, then turned over and settled down to sleep with her back to him. He lay watching her yellow curls and the gentle rise and fall of her breathing beneath the covers. Then he closed his eyes and offered up a heartfelt prayer of thanksgiving.

14 CROWDED WAYS OF LIFE

Bernie and Lucy set out immediately after breakfast the following day.

'We'll go on the train,' Bernie told Peter and Jonah, 'then you'll have the car if you decide to go anywhere while we're out.'

'Just make sure you're back for tea,' Peter told her. 'I don't know what it'll be yet, but it'll be something special and I don't want it spoilt.'

'Don't worry, we know the rules,' Lucy assured him, standing on tiptoes to kiss him goodbye.

They walked off down the cobbled path and out into the drive, their rucksacks on their backs and stout shoes on their feet. Peter stood watching them go.

'I'm sorry you're stuck back here with me,' Jonah said from behind him, thinking that Peter was wishing that he had been able to go with his wife and stepdaughter.

'I'm not,' Peter said turning to face his friend. 'Too many memories. I'd hate to spoil their day with thinking about Angie.' He sighed and then smiled. 'I remember, it was quite funny when we went there,' he went on, picturing the scene in his mind. 'We booked our trip with a Portuguese woman who had a little girl with her – must have been only two or three. The kid can't ever have seen a black person before, I suppose, and she stared at Angie and the kids as if she couldn't believe her eyes. I remember there was a long queue of people waiting for a boat to be free, so we sat down on the steps and the little girl came up to have a closer look. Her mother was busy telling tourists about the boat trips and didn't notice she'd wandered away. Hannah was going through a rebellious phase and she wouldn't let anyone do anything with her hair – though goodness knows, Angie tried to persuade her to have it cut short if she didn't want to have to look after it – so it was just a great mass of frizzy curls, all standing out round her head. Well, this little girl was fascinated by it and she crept up and patted it with her hand.'

He paused and Jonah wondered whether he ought to say something, but was unsure what. Peter did not often talk about his late wife, except to Bernie, who had been Angie's special friend and was godmother to their two children.

'I don't know how she did it,' Peter went on, 'because she didn't speak any Portuguese and of course the little girl didn't understand English, but somehow Angie managed to make friends with her. She showed her how her own hair was braided to keep it tidy and then she opened her mouth to show that she was pink inside even though she was dark brown outside. She had a knack of getting to know people in a matter of minutes. I never quite worked out how.'

'I think your Hannah must take after her,' Jonah said, searching for something to say that would make his friend feel comfortable about exposing his feelings in this way and encourage him to continue with his reminiscing. 'She always seems very good at putting people at their ease.'

Peter did not answer. He was proud of his daughter, who had followed in her mother's footsteps to become a nurse, and whom Peter would have been the first to declare was closer to being her mother's match than any other woman in the world; but nobody else knew – unless perhaps Bernie had an inkling – how much Peter longed for someone to say – as they never did – that one of his children took after their father. Surely, they must have inherited some characteristics from him? But nobody ever seemed able to pinpoint anything.

Jonah had another go at prompting him to talk more about his wife.

'I'm sorry that I never got to know Angie,' he said. 'I can tell from the way you and Bernie talk about her that she was a very special person.'

'Yes. Well. What say you we go out in a bit and see what the market has to offer?' Peter said, changing the subject abruptly. 'It says in the guide that it closes for a siesta in the afternoon, so we'd better go this morning if we're going to get something for tea.'

'Right you are. Whenever you're ready.'

'Give me half an hour to sort out a few things and then we'll go.'

Peter went back inside the apartment while Jonah drove his chair out on to the paved area round the pool and positioned himself between a sun lounger and a raised bed planted with some reddish-coloured succulents and white daisies with large yellow centres. Claire and Neil Barrington greeted him as they walked past on their way out for their trip to Silves, a small town situated on the Arade River a few miles inland from the coastal fishing port of Portimão that lay at the river mouth.

'Lovely day!' Claire called to him. 'But it's going to be hot this afternoon.'

'Yes,' Jonah smiled back at them, 'lovely.'

They walked off and Jonah turned his attention to his emails, which were displayed on the computer screen attached to his chair. It was not long, however, before he was interrupted by the appearance of a small head bobbing about just outside his line of vision. He looked down and saw Freya looking up at him and waving another picture book.

'Look,' she said, 'I've got *Hairy Maclary and Zachary Quack*. It's about a duck.'

'Really?' Jonah smiled down at her. 'I'm afraid, Miss Price, that I'm not at liberty to read it with you this morning because we are going out. However, this afternoon–'

'We've got to go to the Kids Club after lunch,' Freya told him, looking disappointed. 'We're going to be pirates.'

'Are you indeed?'

'I'm sorry,' Glenys came up behind Freya. 'Is she bothering you?'

'Not at all.'

'Only she doesn't understand that people don't always want her pestering them. Come along, Freya, let's take you all over to Reception and get you booked into the Kids Club.'

She took Freya's hand and led her away. Holly walked on her other side and Danny dashed after them in short bursts of energy as he ran from one piece of cover to another, brandishing his (thankfully still empty) water pistol. After they turned the corner of the building to go out through the gate, he reappeared briefly to take aim and fire an imaginary bullet towards Jonah before leaping back out of sight.

Owen, who had come down with his family, sat down on the sun lounger next to Jonah.

'Glenys has decided we need some time on our own,' he told Jonah. 'So she's packing the kids off to the holiday club this afternoon.'

'You don't sound as if you approve.'

'I suppose she's right, but I always feel that I see little enough of my kids as it is.'

'I know what you mean,' Jonah agreed. 'When my boys were young, something always seemed to crop up at work just when I most wanted to be at home with them. And now, when I look back, I sometimes feel that I missed a lot of their growing up. But then, I really enjoy the job and I knew I was doing something worthwhile, so it was always a hard decision to know what ought to come first.'

'That's exactly how I feel. Glenys keeps on at me to jack in the army and sometimes I think maybe she's right, but then, at other times ...'

'Thank you for giving Lucy a shoulder to cry on yesterday,' Jonah said, remembering what she had told him about Owen's contribution to her change of heart. 'I behaved like a cad of the first order and she had every right to be upset.'

'I'm just glad she happened to run into us. She's a great kid. I just hope my Holly might turn out something like that eventually. At the moment she's far too cocky.'

'Not as cocky as I was at her age,' Jonah laughed. 'In fact, Peter would probably tell you that I've never properly got over my congenital cockiness. Poor old Peter! In many ways he's a better policeman than I am – more systematic, more disciplined, more caring, even, and he'd been in the force eight years longer – but I got promoted to Inspector ahead of him and then he'd only just caught up when I made DCI. I used to accuse him of being a plodder, but I realise now that plodding is often what gets the job done in the end. I suppose there were too many other people with my attitude when it came to the promotion board.'

'I know the feeling,' Owen nodded. 'Mark's a year older than me, but somehow he never gets the breaks I do. He rubs people up the wrong way without meaning to and then ...'

'Hey Jonah! How're you doing?' Wayne strode up the path and across to where Jonah was sitting.

'And how's the chair?' Dean added, hurrying up behind him.

'Both tickety-boo,' Jonah assured them.

'Are the others inside?' Wayne asked, looking around.

'Peter is. Lucy and Bernie have gone off on a boat trip to see some sea caves.'

'Sounds like fun,' said Dean. 'But wouldn't they let you on? I thought tourist attractions were all supposed to be accessible now.'

'I rather fancy that knocking down half the cliff to make a ramp falls outside the scope of *reasonable adjustments*,' Jonah laughed. 'Don't you worry! Peter and I are going to have some quality male-bonding time together, without any of those irritating feminine interruptions.'

'I get it,' Wayne grinned. 'You're talking about the way women don't understand things like the off-side rule and how to bowl overarm?'

'That's the sort of thing I had in mind,' Jonah grinned back. 'We're two poor hen-pecked blokes who need a bit of time out occasionally.'

'And talking of bowling,' Wayne went on, turning to Owen. 'After the thrashing we gave you lot at football, I won't ask for a return match, but how about some beach cricket? The five of us against the seven of you – and Jonah here can be umpire.'

'I don't know whether Holly will co-operate,' Owen replied, 'and the kids are all being booked into the Kids Club for this afternoon, as we speak, but how about tomorrow? I'm sure Danny would love it and it would do Cameron good to mix a bit more.'

'OK then,' Wayne said heartily. 'It's a date!'

'What's that about?' Mark's voice sounded hostile. Nobody had seen him arrive, dropping down soundlessly from the balcony above into the patio area belonging to the students and then vaulting lightly over the wall to join them beside the pool.

'We were just discussing a friendly game of cricket on the beach,' Owen answered, 'to give us a chance to get our revenge after the rout yesterday. Our kids are going to the Kids Club this afternoon, but we thought maybe tomorrow – if you and Cameron would like to join in.'

'I don't think I want my son mixing with your type,'

Mark said bluntly to Wayne.

'Brummies, you mean?' Wayne answered with an innocent grin that conveyed quite clearly that he was well aware of what Mark really intended to imply. 'I'm sorry you feel that way, but Dean can vouch for it that I don't let it affect my behaviour.' He reached out and put his arm around Dean, drawing him forward and presenting him to Mark.

'You know full well what I mean,' Mark growled.

'You know, I'm not sure that I do,' Wayne answered, still speaking in tones of innocent wonder, while at the same time hugging Dean close.

'Jonah! Will you read my book now?' Freya's cry interrupted what seemed to be developing into a standoff between Mark and Wayne. She raced across the flagstones and threw herself at Jonah, gripping him around the knees. Glenys hurried after her with Holly and Danny trailing behind.

'I'm so sorry,' Glenys apologised. 'I don't know what's got into her. Usually she's quite shy with strangers.'

'But we're not strangers any more, are we, Miss Price,' Jonah said, addressing Freya solemnly. 'However,' he went on, 'I fear that I will have to disappoint you, because we will be going out soon. Perhaps you could bring your book to me after you finish your piratical adventuring this afternoon?'

Freya looked puzzled, not quite sure of the import of Jonah's words.

'That would be nice,' her mother answered for her, 'wouldn't it, Freya? Inspector Porter's offering to read to you after you get back from the Kids Club.'

'Yes,' Freya nodded, brightening up. 'Yes please!'

'It will be my pleasure,' Jonah assured her.

Cameron sauntered round the corner, having come down from his apartment by the more conventional method of the stairs. He joined the cluster of people around Jonah's chair, positioning himself unobtrusively between his aunt and his young cousin, Holly, who was standing with her hands in her pockets looking rather sulky.

'We were just talking about maybe having a cricket match down on the beach tomorrow,' Owen said, in an attempt to bring Cameron into the conversation. He worried that the boy was becoming introverted and thought that it would do him good to engage with more young adults. It was not for him to say, but in his opinion, Mark was too controlling and ought to allow his son more independence. 'You'll help us to show this lot what we're made of, won't you?'

'I already told you, I don't want Cameron mixing with these people,' Mark cut in before Cameron could answer.

'What do you mean *these people*?' Cameron asked, showing more spirit than Owen expected.

'I mean that I don't want you mixing with a lot of mincing perverts. I want you to learn what it means to be a proper man.'

'Like you, you mean?' Glenys asked sharply. 'The sort who takes his frustrations out on his wife by knocking her around?'

'I never touched her. She fell down the stairs. You can ask them at the hospital – that's what she told them.'

'Well, it's not what she's saying now.'

'She just made it all up to stop me getting access to my son. But the judge saw through her, didn't she? Said I had a right to take him away for two weeks' holiday every year and access every other weekend. She wouldn't have done that if she believed I was violent, would she? But, of course, you and Julie always were thick as thieves. You'd believe anything she said about me, wouldn't you?'

'I think we'd better be making tracks,' Dean said as soon as there was a lull in Mark's outburst. 'Let Jonah know what you decide about the cricket.'

The two young men walked off arm-in-arm, rather ostentatiously, Jonah thought as he watched them go.

However, he did not blame them. He admired the way that they had stood their ground without becoming defensive and laying themselves open to accusations of over-sensitivity or being provocative. This very modest display of gay pride was surely irreproachable.

Peter came out at that moment, dressed ready to go out, with a sunhat to protect his fair skin, and a small rucksack on his back for their anticipated purchases. He greeted the Price family briefly before turning to Jonah.

'You've just missed Wayne and Dean,' Jonah informed him. 'They came by to check that their repairs were still functioning OK.'

'They're going to play cricket with us tomorrow,' Danny added eagerly.

'So are you,' Jonah told Peter. 'I hope you don't mind. I've volunteered to umpire.'

'Don't worry – I know my place. No point expecting to have a say in what goes on in this family! Now, I'm ready for the off – how about you?'

'All set to go. I fear,' Jonah added, addressing Freya, who had somehow managed to manoeuvre herself on to his lap while no-one was paying her any attention, 'that you will have to get down now. We have an important mission to undertake. We have to visit the market to get provisions for the hungry wanderers when they return.'

Freya pulled a face, but slipped obediently down to the ground and went over to stand by her mother. Peter and Jonah turned to go, but their exit was blocked by the huddle of students who had come out of their apartment and were standing arguing about their plans for the day. They called out cheerily to the group by the pool and invited Cameron to come with them to sample some of the water sports on offer.

'He's staying with me,' Mark told them coldly. If we want to go jet skiing or kite surfing we'll do it on our own, thank you very much.'

'Actually, Dad,' Cameron said tentatively at first but

then sounding more confident. 'I was thinking of going to the market with Jonah and Peter. I'd like to see what it's like and I might be able to help ... you know ... to carry things or something.'

'We'll be glad to have you along,' Jonah said heartily, 'if you don't mind spending the morning traipsing round with a couple of middle-aged police officers. I'm sure I'd have had much more exciting things on my mind at your age.' He was surprised and pleased at Cameron's boldness in defying his father, and impressed by his mature judgement in choosing to do so in a way that would make it hard for Mark to raise any objection.

'I suppose if that's what you want,' Mark agreed grudgingly. 'So long as they really don't mind.'

'Not at all.' Peter had not been privy to Mark's snubbing of Wayne and Dean, but he sensed that Jonah was keen to allow Cameron to join them and assumed that there must be good reason. 'You never know when an extra pair of hands may be useful.'

They set off down the road towards the town centre, with Jonah setting the pace, as he had done the day before. Twenty minutes later they reached the market, where there were stalls arrayed with locally caught fish and locally grown fruit and vegetables. Peter was soon engrossed in trying to decide what to buy. He had heard that salt cod was the mainstay of Portuguese cuisine, but that would need soaking overnight, so should he buy some now to cook in a few days' time? They were staying in the Sardine capital of Europe – or so he had been led to believe from the tourist board website – so perhaps fresh sardines would be a good choice. Potatoes and kale seemed to be the most popular vegetables, and onions were always useful. He wandered around the stalls planning in his mind a menu for the week ahead.

At first Jonah tried to follow, but it soon became clear that his bulky wheelchair was a liability in the narrow spaces between the stalls, where often baskets piled high with oranges or melons obstructed his path. He decided to accept his limitations and stationed himself in an out of the way corner between a stall selling brightly coloured scarves and a display of artisan cheeses.

'Don't feel obliged to stay to keep me company,' he told Cameron, who was standing rather awkwardly next to the chair. 'Go off and have a look round – see what you can find to take home for your best girl!'

'If only!' Cameron said with a wry smile. 'But I suppose I ought to get something for Mum. I wonder – do you think she'd like one of these scarves?'

'Difficult to say without knowing your mum. I'm sure a lot of women would be delighted with one – my wife, for instance – but it's a matter of personal taste isn't it?'

'I thought Bernie was *Peter's* wife,' Cameron said in surprise.

'That's right. I was meaning my late wife, Margaret. She loved a bit of colour. Those red and green ones would have been just up her street – or maybe that purple design with the swirling pattern. But you need to think about your mum. What sort of things does she wear?'

'I don't know. I've never really noticed. I remember once, she put on a red dress that was rather tight round the hips and showed a lot of leg, and Dad told her she looked like a tart. Apart from that, I dunno. I think she mainly wears jeans around the house.'

'If she still has the red dress, maybe you could get something to go with that,' Jonah suggested.

'And what would go with red?'

'Now you're asking! I think Margaret would have gone for that cream-coloured one with the red pattern on it – if that's the right colour red, of course – or maybe that black one with the sparkly pattern. That might be safer. It's quite expensive,' Jonah added cautiously. 'Are you sure you've got enough money?'

'No problem. Dad gave me some spending money, but he never gives me a chance to go anywhere to spend it.

He'll be like, *what d'you want to waste your money on that for?* when he finds out I've spent it on Mum,' he added triumphantly, reaching in his pocket for his purse.

15 LIFE'S LITTLE DAY

After lunch, Peter and Jonah went outside to sit on their patio. Peter positioned himself at one side, so that the wall dividing their apartment from the one occupied by the students cast some shade over him. Jonah, mindful of the need to give his body the opportunity to absorb the ultraviolet rays and manufacture vitamin D, had consented to allow Peter to replace his usual trousers with shorts and had slightly reclined his chair so as to expose maximum skin surface area to the bright sunshine. He had the pages of a detective novel displayed on the screen in front of him and was attempting to read, but the heat made it difficult to concentrate and he found himself dozing off. In the end, he abandoned his book and leant back watching the scene outside the patio.

Kirsty and Lewis walked past, pushing Lily in her buggy. They greeted Jonah as they passed and he nodded acknowledgement.

'How's Lily?' Peter asked. He had heard that the little girl had been ill.

'We're just back from the doctor,' Lewis answered. 'He said it's just a twenty-four hour bug, but he's given her some antibiotics to be on the safe side.'

'She seems a lot better already,' Kirsty added. 'We weren't sure whether to bother with the doctor, but with kids it's always so difficult to know …'

'That's right,' Jonah agreed, deciding against treating them to his late wife Margaret's standard lecture on the over-use of antibiotics. 'It's always better to err on the side of caution. And you'll be able to enjoy the rest of your holiday better, knowing that it's not something more serious.'

The young couple headed back up to their apartment, almost colliding with the Price children, who were on their way out to the Kids Club.

'Come along, Holly!' Glenys called. 'It was your idea. What's taking you so long?'

'I told you,' her daughter grumbled, 'I didn't know that German boy was going to be there. He's gross! What if they make me be in his group?'

'Well, it's too late to change your mind now. We've booked. So come along. If you get there early, you'll have a better chance of choosing who you go with, won't you?'

They disappeared round the corner of the building, hurrying after Danny, who was running on ahead eagerly, waving an imaginary cutlass in his hand and shouting out piratical orders to a non-existent crew of cut-throats. Freya stopped briefly to peep through the bars of the gate at Jonah and favour him with a broad smile and a wave. He nodded back.

'Until this evening, Miss Price!'

A few minutes later, Ibrahim appeared. He came over to speak to Peter and Jonah.

'Had enough of water sports?' Peter asked conversationally.

'Not exactly. The others have gone off on a banana boat, but I needed to come back for mid-day prayers.'

'Surely Gary isn't going on a banana boat with his arm in plaster?' Peter asked incredulously.

'Well, no – they wouldn't let him in the end. He

thought it'd be alright after he wrapped it up in plastic bags, but they said *no way*. So he's just watching, and hoping to see Craig or Josh fall off so he can get a good picture to put on Instagram.' He grinned. 'Actually, I think I'm quite glad to have an excuse to pass on that one. I don't think getting soaked through with cold water and having a picture of you looking like a drowned rat posted all over the internet is such great fun really!'

He vaulted nimbly over the low wall dividing the communal area from the patio in front of his apartment and disappeared inside to prepare himself for prayer.

For about fifteen minutes, all was still. Jonah became aware of the high-pitched trill of warblers in the trees that lined the driveway on the other side of the apartment building. Then the murmur of more voices came to his ears. It was the Barringtons, arriving back from their sightseeing, looking tired and hot. They flopped down at the side of the pool in the shadow of one of the gaily-coloured umbrellas placed there to provide shade. Neil reached into the bag that he had been carrying and took out a guidebook, from which he started to read aloud. Claire lay back on her sun lounger listening and making occasional remarks, comparing the descriptions in the book with the reality as they had seen it.

A few minutes later, she seemed to remember something and she picked up the bag and headed for their apartment. Neil continued to turn the pages of his book, pausing every so often to insert a piece of paper to mark places that he wanted to talk about when his wife returned.

'I'm going to get another glass of water,' Peter said, getting up. 'Shall I get one for you? Or some juice if you'd rather. We need to be careful about dehydration in this weather.'

'Water please. And I think I'd better have some more sunscreen. It's so strong I'm afraid of burning.'

'Right you are! Won't be long.'

Peter turned to go, but before he reached the door, an

unexpected noise made him turn back and stare in disbelief. Everything seemed to happen very quickly. An inarticulate cry was followed by a rustling sound and then a sickening thump of a heavy object hitting the paving. Jonah too, wide-awake now, was staring wide-eyed with his mouth open. There, in front of them, lay a human form, crumpled and twisted from the impact with the paving and the wall dividing the apartment from the communal area. It lay in the corner, hard up against the wall that separated their apartment from the next – a man, bare to the waist and barefoot, dressed in khaki shorts. Clearly, he had fallen from the balcony of one of the first floor apartments.

For Peter, the scene brought back a grotesque feeling of déjà vu. This was just like the occasion, nearly seventeen years previously, when his great friend and colleague, Richard Paige, had fallen to his death from the roof of an Oxford college while in pursuit of a suspect. As he ran back to discover what had happened, images of that incident flashed across his mind. Richard's dying words – *tell Bernie I'm sorry* – were seared into his memory, as was the dreadful moment at the hospital afterwards when they heard the devastating verdict *dead on arrival*.

Peter ran back and knelt down by the body, thankful that he had kept up his Basic Life Support training after leaving the police force. He recognised at once the handsome features and thick brown hair of Owen Price. His apartment was immediately above theirs. He must have fallen over the edge of the balcony, but what could have caused him to fall?

'What happened? Can I help?' Neil Barrington was there beside him, reaching out as if to take hold of Owen by the shoulder to turn him to face them.

'Don't touch him,' Peter instructed sharply. 'You may do more harm than good.'

Then, seeing the look of shock on Neil's face, he regretted speaking so abruptly.

'The best thing you can do,' he went on as calmly as he

could, 'is to get help – fast. We need an ambulance right away. Get over to Reception – they'll know what to do.'

Neil nodded and headed off at a brisk walk. Peter turned back to Owen's motionless body, quickly checking for vital signs. No breathing. No pulse. Could he have had a heart attack? Could that be what had made him topple over the balcony wall? He lay on his side facing the wall. Peter gingerly turned him over on to his back to start the routine of breaths and chest compressions that might just keep him alive until help came. He hated having to deal with victims with suspected spinal injuries. Any movement might cause irreparable further damage and consequent avoidable permanent disability, but any delay in providing life support could result in death. He noted in his mind the presence of something small and hard clasped in Owen's right hand, but did not have time to think about what it might be.

'Hey!' Mark's voice, coming from above, sounded loud in the stillness. 'What's going on?'

Peter did not reply. He was too busy working on the task of keeping Owen alive until the ambulance arrived. There was a slithering sound and Mark was standing beside him.

'Owen?' he gasped in tones of disbelief. 'But how?'

'Might be a heart attack,' Peter panted through his exertions.

'He fell from the balcony,' Jonah told Mark. 'Do you have any idea what could have made him do that?'

'No,' Mark shook his head and continued to look around as if bewildered by what had happened. 'Did he hit his head? Why's he unconscious? It's such a short fall! Here – let me do that,' he added, pushing Peter out of the way. 'It's alright. I know the drill. It's not the first time I've been here.'

They were so busy attending to Owen that they did not notice Cameron walking across the paved area, dressed in his swimming trunks and carrying a towel. He saw his father kneeling down on the ground jerking rhythmically and Peter scrambling to his feet and stretching his limbs, which felt surprisingly tired. He could not see what it was that Peter and Jonah were looking at so intently – something lying on the ground, hidden behind the low wall.

'What's going on?' he asked, coming across to the wall and looking down over it. He gave a rapid intake of breath as he recognised his uncle's body, looking very strange as his father repeatedly pumped at his chest and breathed into his mouth. The face was an unnatural grey colour and the lips were blue. Peter took charge.

'You'd better sit down over here,' he told Cameron, taking the boy firmly by the shoulders and steering him towards one of the sun loungers. 'Your uncle's had an accident. He fell from the balcony.'

'Like Gary?' Cameron asked, still looking around with a puzzled expression on his face. 'But he only broke his arm. Uncle Owen looked so …'

His voice trailed away and he looked up pleadingly at Peter, waiting to hear more.

'I don't know exactly. I think he may have had a heart attack before he fell – or else maybe he hit his head and it knocked him unconscious – or …' Peter hesitated to voice his worst fears.

'Or?'

Peter took a breath and tried to think what to say. A siren wailed in the background. He decided to be honest. There was no point in raising false hopes that might soon be dashed.

'Look, Cameron, I have to admit it's not looking good. Whether his heart stopped and that made him fall, or he fell and the impact stopped his heart, he's been unconscious and not breathing for a few minutes now. We'll just have to hope the ambulance is here soon. Meanwhile, tell me, where's your aunt Glenys?'

The siren became louder and then stopped abruptly.

'She – she – look! She's here now.' Cameron pointed towards the end of the building and Peter looked up to see Glenys rounding the corner. When she saw Peter and Cameron looking towards her she quickened her footsteps, but she was overtaken by two uniformed men who strode efficiently past her carrying bags. Peter stepped forward and directed them to where Mark was still desperately administering CPR. Then he turned to Glenys, who had now reached the scene and was staring down over the wall at her husband's body. Peter took her arm and gently persuaded her to come with him and sit down next to her nephew. They were soon joined by Jonah, who, satisfied that everything possible was now being done for Owen, had come out to the poolside.

'What happened?' Glenys asked in a trembling voice.

'Your husband fell,' Peter told her. 'We don't know exactly how it happened,' he went on, trying to find words to prepare her for the worst, 'but we think he may have had a heart attack.'

'But that's impossible! He's so fit. He'd only just had a medical – they'd never have passed him if there was anything wrong with his heart.'

'Sometimes these things come out of the blue,' Peter said. 'But you may well be right. That was just my theory. The other possibility is that it was the impact that –'

'What are you trying to tell me?' Glenys demanded, jumping to her feet as if to go back. She almost collided with one of the paramedics who had come over to speak to them.

'I am sorry,' he said slowly, speaking in strongly accented English. 'There was nothing we could do for him.'

'What do you mean?' Glenys shouted in a voice of mingled anger, distress and terror. Then, seeing the look of compassion on the man's face, she pushed past him and ran across to see for herself. Cameron stood up and made to follow her, but Peter pushed him back down and sat down next to him. The ambulance man stood for a few moments looking down at them with a rather helpless expression.

'Excuse me,' he said at last. 'I go to help my colleague.

'What's happened? Where's Neil?' Claire's voice broke the silence that had descended on the little group by the pool. 'I heard an ambulance. He isn't …?'

'No,' Jonah reassured her. 'Neil's fine. He'll be back any minute. He went to Reception to call the ambulance.'

'So who …?'

'It's Owen Price. He fell from the balcony.'

'He's dead.' Cameron added baldly in a strange flat voice.

'Surely not?' Claire looked from Jonah to Peter for reassurance.

'I'm afraid so,' Jonah confirmed. 'It looks as if he must have broken his neck when he hit the ground.'

'Or he could have had a heart attack or a stroke or something before he fell,' Peter added. 'We just don't know.'

'Poor Glenys!' Claire exclaimed. 'And the poor children! Were they there when it happened?'

'No. Fortunately they're all at the Kids Club this afternoon,' Jonah told her. 'But Glenys is here. I wonder,' he added, seeing Claire's anxious-to-do-something-to-help expression, 'if you could look after her? She's in shock and needs someone with her.'

'Of course.'

Claire hurried over to where Glenys was standing, looking down at her husband's body. Mark attempted to put his arm around his sister-in-law's shoulders but Glenys shook him off and moved so that one of the ambulance men was between them. Jonah watched as Claire approached her and gently persuaded her to sit down in one of the plastic chairs on the patio.

Then everything suddenly seemed to become very busy. The ambulance crew brought a trolley to take

Owen's body away. Neil returned in the company of the manager of the aparthotel, who looked very flustered and red in the face and kept reiterating to anyone who was listening that nothing like this had ever happened here before. Ibrahim emerged from his apartment and stood gazing over the wall that separated his patio from the next with an expression of amazement on his face. Kirsty and Lewis appeared on their balcony and called down to know what was going on. Mark walked over to where Cameron was sitting, staring around in a daze. He put his hand on his son's shoulder, but Cameron shrugged it off and moved away. For the first time, Jonah felt a small measure of sympathy with Mark, who seemed to be doing his best to comfort his family and was facing rebuff on all sides.

The paramedics worked quickly and efficiently and it was only a matter of minutes before Owen Price's body had been loaded into the ambulance and driven away. Glenys leapt to her feet as they wheeled the trolley across the paved area towards the cobbled path and hurried after them, angrily pushing aside Claire's restraining hand, as if she expected to accompany her husband in the ambulance. Claire and Mark followed her to the ambulance and stood with her, watching as the crew closed the doors and drove away. Then Claire took her arm and led her back to join the group at the poolside. Up above, Kirsty and Lewis turned from the scene, satisfied that there was nothing they could do to help, and went back into their apartment.

Glenys sat down, still looking dazed.

'I don't understand,' she murmured. 'How could he be dead? How could such a short fall kill him?'

16 WOUNDS YET VISIBLE

Claire sat down next to Glenys and took her right hand in both of her own. She sat gazing anxiously at her, saying nothing. Neil came over to them and stood, looking uncomfortable, as Glenys repeated, 'it was such a short fall. How can he be dead?' He cleared his throat and Glenys looked up.

'I tried to contact the British consulate for you,' Neil told her, 'but, would you believe it? They only open on Mondays, Wednesdays and Fridays! Would you like me to call them first thing tomorrow? They'll be able to help with things like registering the death and funeral arrangements – I assume you'll want to take him home for that?'

'Yes, I suppose so,' Glenys looked rather bewildered. 'I just still can't believe this is happening!'

'I know.' Claire patted her hand. 'It'll take a while to sink in. Just try to take things a bit at a time, and let us help. Now,' she went on gently, 'the first thing to think about is the children–'

'Oh my God!' Glenys cried, with a sharp intake of breath. 'The kids! What am I going to tell them?'

'It's very lucky they went to the Kids Club this afternoon,' Claire said, still speaking in a very calm, deliberate way. 'That means we have time to think about that. What time does it finish?'

'I booked them in till four thirty.'

'Good that gives us plenty of time. Now, let's get you off–'

She broke off at the appearance of two police officers in the uniform of the Polícia de Segurança Pública. The hotel manager introduced them, reiterating his statement that nothing like this had ever happened before.

'Apart from that boy, who fell off and broke his arm last week,' Mark commented aggressively.

'What boy?' demanded the manager, his red face turning rather white. 'I know nothing of this.'

'One of the students in Apartment 501,' Mark told him. 'They were at a party upstairs and one of them fell off the balcony and broke his arm.'

'Why was I not told about this?' the manager asked, looking all round at the assembled company. 'It should have been recorded and investigated.'

'Certainly it should,' agreed the leading policeman, 'but let us leave that for another time. Please. We would like to speak to everyone who was here when the unfortunate gentleman fell to his death today.'

The hotel manager hastily rearranged chairs and sun loungers into a rough circle, and the police officers sat down to address the whole group. They expressed their condolences to Glenys and then the older man proceeded to ask a sequence of questions, while his assistant took notes. Peter felt a rising tide of irritation at the officer's persistent habit of speaking to him over the head of Jonah, whom he evidently considered incapable of contributing to the discussion. However, in a foreign country and in the presence of a shocked and grieving widow, he decided against making any sort of complaint. He was pleased to see that Jonah appeared to be adopting the same approach and was contenting himself with taking his own notes of everything that was said on the computer connected to his versatile chair.

The police officers took their leave with a few formal words to Glenys and departed. Claire turned to Glenys with the intention of urging her once more to return to her apartment and lie down, but she was interrupted in her resolve by the arrival of Bernie and Lucy.

'What's up?' Lucy asked, looking round at the group of people assembled at the poolside. 'What were the police doing here? Has something happened?'

'There's been an accident,' Peter told her. 'Owen Price fell off his balcony.'

'Was he badly hurt?' Bernie asked anxiously, looking towards Glenys and fearing the worst.

'Fatal,' Peter answered. 'That's why the police were here. I'll tell you all about it later.'

Claire looked down at her watch.

'The Kids Club will be closing soon,' she said to Glenys. 'Would you like me to collect the children for you? I think you could do with a lie down.'

'No! I want to do it. They'll be expecting me.' Glenys leapt to her feet and then swayed involuntarily as her head began to swim. She sat back down heavily. 'I'm sorry. I'll be alright in a minute,' she apologised.

'No. You've had an enormous shock,' Claire said gently but firmly. 'Let me take you back to your apartment so that you can have a rest. Then Neil will stay with you while I go and collect the children.'

'But they don't know you,' Glenys protested.

'Tell you what,' Jonah suggested. 'Why don't I go along with Mrs Barrington? I promised Freya to read her book with her later, so they won't be surprised to see *me*.'

'Yes. I suppose that would be OK,' Glenys agreed, sounding very weary. 'Alright, but please – don't mention what happened to their dad. I *have* to be the one to tell them.'

'Right you are. I understand.'

Jonah and Claire waited until Glenys and Neil turned

the corner of the building on their way to the stairs. Then they set off to collect the children from the large pool in the centre of the apartment complex. Peter led Bernie and Lucy indoors to explain to them what had happened. Ibrahim stood alone for a moment and then followed them in. Seeing how shaken he looked, Bernie immediately declared the intention of 'making a brew.' Then she remembered that Ibrahim was not allowed to eat or drink until sunset and wondered whether there was anything else they could do to help settle his nerves. She had a vague idea that illness permitted the breaking of the Ramadan fast and Ibrahim certainly looked unwell, but she did not like to make the suggestion. After all, it was *his* conscience that had to be satisfied.

They sat round the table while Peter briefly described what he and Jonah had witnessed and his (and Mark's) fruitless endeavours to revive Owen after he had fallen. When he finished there was a long silence as Lucy and Bernie took in the story.

'I don't understand,' Ibrahim said nervously. 'I mean – Gary fell off because he was standing up on the balcony wall, but how did it happen to Owen? Do you think he did it deliberately?'

'Suicide, you mean?' Peter asked sharply. 'No chance! He wouldn't have been such a fool. The chances of a fall like that being fatal must be absolutely tiny. Think about it – he knew that Gary fell and only broke his arm, and his brother was forever dropping down from the balcony just for the hell of it.'

'Perhaps he was trying to do the same as Mark,' Ibrahim suggested.

'Maybe that's what he was planning to do,' Peter conceded, 'but if so, he must have fallen before he started coming down or he wouldn't have fallen head first the way he did.'

There was a confusion of voices outside, announcing the return of the rest of the student party, talking excitedly about their trip on the banana boat. Ibrahim looked towards Peter, who immediately understood and went out to break the news to them. Ibrahim followed and soon all the students had gone inside their own apartment to chew over the unexpected happening. Peter returned and all three sat drinking tea in silence. There seemed to be nothing more to be said.

The silence was soon broken, however, by the return of the young Prices, in high spirits following their afternoon of piracy. Freya was ecstatic at having been permitted to ride all the way back on Jonah's lap. Danny was dashing around with his usual exuberance, running twice as far as everyone else and shouting out random nautical phrases. Holly walked sedately beside Claire Barrington, showing off her superior maturity and telling at great length how the despised German boy had got his comeuppance in a game involving teams competing to throw the opposition off balance and into the water.

At the sound of their voices, Bernie got up and went outside. She watched as they rounded the end of the raised bed that separated the path leading to the steps to the first floor from the cobbled slope down to the driveway. There was a brief argument with Freya, who was reluctant to get down from Jonah's chair, before the children all disappeared again down the side of the apartment building accompanied by Claire. Jonah saw Bernie waiting for him and headed over towards her.

'I hope Glenys Price understands that it won't help to keep the truth from the kids,' he said in a low voice as they made their way inside to join Peter and Lucy. 'I know it's her right to be the one to tell them, but I can't help wishing she'd let us do it.'

He need not have worried. Glenys had thought about the possibility of Owen's untimely death on many occasions when he had been on active service in war zones in the Middle East and in Afghanistan. Ever since Holly had been a toddler she had gone over in her mind alternative ways of explaining why Daddy would not be coming back, and now she delivered her prepared speech in a calm, almost impersonal tone while sitting on her bed in the apartment. The children fell silent and looked at her wide-eyed. Holly was the first to speak.

'You mean Daddy's dead?' she asked, trembling a little but determined to be brave, as befitted the eldest of the family.

'Yes.' Glenys nodded.

Freya threw herself at her mother, who gathered her up into her arms and held her tight against her chest with one arm while patting her back gently with the other hand.

'How?' Danny wanted to know. 'Did someone shoot him?'

'No, of course not!' his mother told him. 'It was an accident. He fell off the balcony. I kept telling you all not to lean over the wall, didn't I?' she added, unable to resist the maternal instinct to drive home the oft-repeated safety message.

'But Gary fell off and only broke his arm,' Danny argued.

'I know, Danny,' Claire put in gently. 'We don't know exactly how it happened. Your dad must have fallen awkwardly and ... we think he may have broken his neck ... or maybe hit his head on the wall.'

Freya started to cry quietly and Glenys rocked her back and forth, as if she were a baby, glad to have something to occupy herself at last. Claire took the older children into the kitchen and set them helping her to prepare a meal for the family. Danny protested, first at being made to wash his hands and then at the idea of a boy being expected to participate in domestic tasks. However, a look from Claire quelled his rebellion and he was soon busily washing strawberries and arranging them in four bowls, while Holly took on the responsible task of stirring a tin of baked beans in a pan on the hotplate.

Downstairs, Peter remembered his planned culinary masterpiece and banished the others from the kitchen while he worked on a simple dish of fresh sardines. The kale and Chouriço sausage stew that he had intended for today would have to wait until there was more time. Lucy set the table, while Bernie cleared away the tea mugs and replaced them with glasses and a jug of iced water.

'Peter!' Jonah called from the living area. 'What did you make of those marks on his back?'

'What marks on whose back?'

'*These* marks, on Owen's back.' With a slight movement of his index figure, Jonah caused the computer screen attached to his chair to swivel round towards Bernie and Lucy, who crowded round to look.

'They look like cuts or scratches,' Bernie said, peering closely at the photograph displayed on the screen. 'When did you take this?'

'Just after he hit the ground – before old Peter turned him over to start CPR. And this is the one I took a few moments later.' Another small movement of Jonah's finger produced a second photograph, almost identical to the first. 'Notice how that dribble of blood has elongated? Those wounds must have been recent – the blood was still fresh and runny. Moreover, it looks as if the bleeding started while he was upright – see how the blood goes very slightly *down* his back from the wound and then changes direction when he's lying on his side on the ground.'

Peter put the tray of sardines into the oven, rinsed his hands at the sink and came over to have a look.

'Distinctly odd, don't you think?' Jonah asked him.

'You're right,' his friend agreed. 'Those two,' he went on, pointing, 'look almost like stab wounds. And each of them has got another mark next to it – like a bruise, maybe. Any idea what made them?'

'None at all.' Jonah shook his head. 'But whatever it was, it must have been something hard and sharp and it must have been done from behind him.'

'By someone else, do you mean?' Bernie asked.

'Or could he have hit something as he fell?' suggested Lucy.

'As you so astutely point out,' Jonah answered, 'those are the key questions. Have any of you been in any of the upstairs apartments? Is there anything up there – spikes round the edge of the balcony to repel borders, for example – that could have made these?'

The others all shook their heads.

'Why didn't you tell the police about these?' Peter asked.

'I was going to, but I thought I ought to be polite and wait my turn to be asked – and they evidently didn't consider that the poor cripple could possibly have anything to contribute, so I didn't get the chance. Of course, what they failed to comprehend is that I was the one person who wasn't too busy faffing about, trying to save the poor chap's life, to notice things.'

'Still – you ought to hand over these photos,' Peter insisted, wondering to himself how often, during his own long police career, he might have inadvertently alienated a witness and thus unintentionally impeded an investigation. 'They're evidence.'

'Yes. I know – and I will, when, and if, there's a proper investigation. Those two weren't detectives; they were just asking routine questions so that they could file a report about another unfortunate accident to a tourist. And, after all, there's every possibility that it *was* just an unfortunate accident; I'd just like to know what happened to make those marks, that's all.'

'Won't the pathologist pick them up at the PM?' Lucy asked. 'Then they'd have to investigate, wouldn't they?'

'I'd hope so,' Jonah replied, 'but the blood will be dried by then – or it could even have all been wiped off on to the patio when Peter and Mark were trying to revive him. So the danger is that they assume the wounds were done earlier and have nothing to do with his fall – or else that they happened on the way down.'

'Couldn't that have been what happened?' Bernie asked.

'Not by my reading of it,' Jonah insisted. 'It's the way the blood seems to have run *down* his back that makes me think they must have been *before* he pitched forward off the balcony. Now,' he went on, changing the picture on his computer screen with a few small movement of his finger. 'There's something else too. What do you think this is?'

The others peered at the screen and saw a close-up of the dead man's hand. There was something clasped in it. For a few moments, none of them could see what it was. Then Lucy gave a cry of recognition.

'It's a toy dinosaur,' she exclaimed. 'Danny's got a whole collection of them. I've seen him playing with them.'

'Yes,' Bernie agreed. 'You're right – a triceratops, I think.'

The alarm on Peter's phone went off, signalling that the meal was ready. For the next few minutes everyone was occupied with getting ready to eat. It was not until the serious business of demolishing the first course was completed that conversation resumed.

'If you're really keen to find out the lie of the land on the upstairs balcony,' Bernie said to Jonah as they waited for Peter to serve the pudding, 'I could pop up to see how Glenys is doing – as a friendly gesture – and have a recce at the same time.'

'A bit devious, don't you think?' Peter observed as he handed round small bowls of serradura – a Portuguese dessert consisting largely of whipped cream, which he had prepared and put in the fridge before the drama of the afternoon drove thoughts of food from their minds.

'Not at all: she could probably do with some visitors to prise her out of the clutches of Claire Barrington – who, being the archetypal vicar's wife and primary school teacher combined, is very much a force of nature!'

'Maybe the Reverend Neil ought to exercise his healing ministry with an attempt at raising the dead,' Jonah whispered to Lucy mischievously, recalling their conversation of the previous night.

She giggled and then, remembering that someone had actually died, she straightened her face again and blushed guiltily.

'Are we allowed to share the joke?' Bernie asked, seeing the looks that passed between Jonah and Lucy.

'It's nothing,' Jonah told her. 'We were just remembering a little discussion we had in the early hours about the inconsistency of expecting God to cure us of things that could conceivably get better by themselves, but not of things that obviously couldn't – such as amputation or, in this case, death itself.'

'Based on what you were saying yesterday,' Bernie observed, 'you wouldn't *want* to believe in it even if you saw it happen with your very eyes.'

'That's not fair,' Jonah protested mildly. 'I didn't have a problem with it happening to other people; I just don't want the responsibility of it being me – and I don't like the idea of God doing favours for his chosen few.'

'You know,' Peter said thoughtfully, 'I've been thinking, since you said all that stuff yesterday. Bernie – do you remember when Hannah was ill with scarlet fever?'

'Mmm.' Bernie nodded. 'I remember you were both very worried about her.'

'Well, there was one evening when she was running such a high temperature that it was making her delirious. Angie had gone out to the church prayer meeting and I was holding the fort with Hannah age three and Eddie still just a baby. I remember pacing around Hannah's bedroom rocking Eddie in my arms trying to get him back off to sleep and watching her tossing and turning and crying out nonsense ... and then, all of a sudden, she just lay back, calm as anything, and looked up at me and smiled ... and then she went off to sleep, and by the time Angie got back you'd hardly have known there was anything wrong with her.'

'Children do go up and down tremendously quickly when they're ill,' Jonah remarked.

'No, but, that's not the point,' Peter replied. 'The thing is, when Angie and I compared notes, it must have been at just the same time that the people at the prayer meeting started praying for Hannah.'

There was a long silence. Then Lucy spoke.

'What I don't understand,' she said, frowning in puzzlement, 'is why that didn't convince you that God's out there listening to our prayers.'

'I don't know,' Peter shrugged and sighed. 'I suppose I have to admit to there being something more out there than we can see and touch, but somehow it seemed more to do with all those friends of Angie's being concerned about us than ... Actually,' he went on, brightening up and grinning across at his wife, 'based on what Jonah was saying before, it seems to me that it's *easier* for me to believe in the power of prayer to change things than it is for him, with his idea that, if God did something for him, he'd have to do something in return!'

'That isn't what I said,' Jonah objected. 'But I think you've got something there. I suppose, it isn't just about the person whom God heals with a miracle, but just as much about the people who were praying for it to happen.'

'Now that,' Bernie said, putting her spoon down in her empty bowl and pushing it away from her, 'is a very biblical attitude.'

'What do you mean?' Lucy asked.

'I was thinking about the man born blind. The disciples ask him why he was born blind and Jesus says it was so that the glory of God could be revealed, or something along those lines – in other words, it was all for the benefit of the people around who were going to see the miracle.'

'It's a bit tough on the blind man, isn't it?' Peter

muttered.

'Yes,' agreed Jonah, 'but I do see what you're getting at – and you need to remember what the actual question was. The disciples wanted to know whether it was the man himself or his parents who were to blame for him being born blind, and Jesus said that it was neither. I agree with you that it's not acceptable to imagine that God deliberately caused a baby to be born blind, but I suppose he could have used the naturally-occurring situation to make a point by curing him of his blindness in a dramatic way.' He paused for a few moments in thought. 'Or,' he went on, remembering that he had vowed not to give Lucy any encouragement in the idea that the Healing Service might produce miraculous results, 'it may be just a dramatic story to make the point that we shouldn't assume that people's misfortunes are punishments for things they've done wrong.'

17 MANIFOLD WITNESS

The next day, Bernie and Lucy got Jonah up while Peter prepared breakfast. A tapping sound attracted his attention and he looked up to see Kirsty Sumner standing outside the patio doors looking rather nervous. He went over and let her in.

'I'm sorry,' she began. 'Is it too early? I can come back later …'

'No need, we're early risers ourselves. Now tell me, what can I do for you?'

'Well, it was your friend I was hoping to talk to really,' Kirsty said, looking around as if expecting to see Jonah hiding somewhere behind the furniture. 'With him being a police officer and everything, I thought he might be able to give me some advice.'

'He'll be through in a few minutes. Why don't you sit down and have a cup of tea while you're waiting?'

Kirsty sat down at the table and Peter poured tea for her before going into the kitchen to get another cup.

'Good morning, Ms Sumner!' Jonah greeted Kirsty, gliding out from the bedroom and positioning himself facing her across the table. 'And what brings you here at this early hour?'

'I was hoping you might be able to give me some advice,' she repeated. 'You see, I was on our balcony yesterday ... and I saw something ... and I wondered if I ought to tell someone about it.'

'You interest me strangely,' Jonah said with a smile. 'Tell you what: why don't you tell me and then we can decide whether anyone else needs to know?'

'That's what I wanted. You see ...' Kirsty seemed to be finding it difficult to find the words to tell her story. She stopped. Then she took a deep breath and continued. 'Our apartment sticks out in front of the others.'

'Yes, I'd noticed,' Jonah said encouragingly, looking intently at Kirsty as she hesitated again.

'And that means,' she went on, 'that, from our balcony, you can see people at the front of the other two balconies. Yesterday afternoon, I noticed that Owen Price was sitting up on the wall of his balcony – with his feet in the flowers, just like his brother always does – and I thought it was strange, because I'd never seen him do it before.'

'I see. Go on.'

'And then ... Well, you know the pole thing that you have for pulling down the awning over the balcony?'

'No, I'm afraid I don't. We don't have a balcony or an awning down here.'

'Well, it's like a long wooden pole, with a metal hook and a ring on the end of it.'

'Really?' Jonah looked across at Peter who nodded briefly in acknowledgement that he had grasped the significance of this description.

'Anyway,' Kirsty went on. 'The thing is ... while I was looking, wondering what Owen was doing up there, I saw the end of the pole prodding him in the back, like this.' She stretched out her arm rigidly in front of her and poked Lucy, who was next to her, in the back with her forefinger. 'And then he fell forward and I rushed back in to get Lewis, but he was changing Lily, so by the time we got back outside you were all there with the ambulance men and everything.'

'I see,' Jonah said thoughtfully. 'When you say that the awning pole prodded him, obviously awning poles don't move by themselves …'

'No, but I could only see one end of it,' Kirsty explained. 'Whoever was holding it was further back, out of my line of vision. And, come to think of it, they were probably lower down too – I think the pole was sort of sloping up to reach his back, if you see what I mean. They could have been crouching down to make sure no one could see them. That's why I didn't say anything to anyone else. I thought there was no point, seeing as I couldn't say who it was. But Lewis and I talked it over and we decided that we ought to let someone know, but we didn't really know who. So that's why I came to you. I thought that, with you being in the police …'

'I don't have any jurisdiction over here,' Jonah told her. 'It's the Portuguese police who will need to investigate this.'

'I know.' Kirsty looked down at the table and nervously twisted her hands in her lap. 'But I wasn't sure what to do about it – and – and we were worried about getting involved in a police enquiry. Do you think we'd have to stay here until it's over? I mean, we've both got jobs we need to go back to.'

'I'd have thought you'd be allowed home as soon as you've made your statements,' Jonah told her. 'But then, I imagine you'd have to come back again for the trial – if there is one – but that could be a long time off.'

'I see.' Kirsty appeared dissatisfied. 'You couldn't … well … look into things yourself, could you?'

'As I said, it's the Portuguese authorities that are responsible. I can't do anything to impede their investigation.'

'I see. Well … do you think you could tell whoever needs to know? I mean – I don't know how to go about it.'

'Alright,' Jonah agreed, secretly delighted to have been

given an excuse to get involved. 'We'll tell the police what you've told me and then they can take it from there.'

'Before we do,' Peter put in quietly. 'Don't you think someone ought to warn Glenys Price? It'll come as a terrible shock to her if the first she knows is when a police officer comes knocking on her door telling her that her husband's death has turned into a murder enquiry.'

'Can *you* do that?' Kirsty pleaded, looking from Peter to Jonah and back again. 'I wouldn't know what to say ... and I'd hate her to think ... well. I mean, it's not very nice to be accusing someone of killing your husband, is it?'

'Don't worry,' Jonah assured her. 'We'll take care of that for you. And,' he added, smiling happily, 'I don't see why we shouldn't do a bit of preliminary investigation – just to keep the trail warm for the official detectives when they arrive.'

'I'm not so sure about–' Peter began, but Jonah ignored his protestations.

'For a start,' he said to Kirsty. 'Tell me more about what you actually saw. You said that Owen was sitting on the wall of the balcony with his feet in the flowers. What exactly do you mean by that? What flowers?'

'The balconies all have like a sort of concrete window box thing on the outside of the wall,' Kirsty explained. 'It's a bit lower than the wall, so Mark Price used to sit on the wall with his feet on the soil around the plants. That's what Owen was doing yesterday. He was sitting right up by the wall between their apartments. I did wonder if he might have got up there so he could talk to Mark, but I didn't see Mark out there at all.'

'Now that's interesting,' Jonah mused. 'You're saying that Owen was sitting on the corner of the wall, next to Mark's apartment? And someone – you don't know who – pushed him with the end of the awing pole, just before he fell?'

'That's right.'

'And whoever it was, they were in Owen Price's

apartment? You're sure of that?'

'Yes. Where else could they have been?'

'I was just wondering if it was possible that, with him being right at the far side of the balcony from you, the person with the pole could have been in Mark's apartment. Could you see which side of the wall the pole came down? Or, put it another way, from where you were looking, was the pole in front of the dividing wall or could it have been behind it?'

'In front – I think – at least … well, maybe not. I honestly don't know,' Kirsty admitted. 'Is it important?'

'It's important to know that you don't know for sure,' Jonah told her. 'The very worst sort of witness is the one who tells you things categorically, when in fact they don't really remember.'

'Don't worry,' Peter told her. 'When the police come to talk to you, just tell them what you remember and don't be afraid to say that you don't know. Jonah's right, I wish I had a pound for all the times I've wasted time following up things that witnesses were completely sure about but which turned out couldn't possibly have happened the way they remember them.'

'Are you a policeman too, then?' Kirsty asked

'Retired,' Peter informed her. 'As Lucy told you, I'm a house-husband now.'

'Well, I'd better be getting back to Lily and Lewis,' Kirsty said, getting up and looking round rather awkwardly at each of them, smiling and nodding nervously. 'Thank you for offering to tell people for me. See you later!'

Bernie leapt to her feet and opened the patio doors for her to leave, closing them firmly behind her before coming back to the table and pouring a second cup of tea for everyone.

'It looks as if we have an explanation for your bloody marks,' she remarked to Jonah.

'Yes,' he agreed, 'but we need to have a look at that awning pole. The way she described it sounds about right, but you never know. We can check it out when we go up to tell Glenys about this new revelation. We ought to secure that pole to avoid any further contamination until forensics can look at it – and the one from Mark's apartment too, for that matter, just in case …'

'Aren't you forgetting something?' Peter asked, smiling at the eagerness with which Jonah was making plans for the investigation of what now appeared to be a murder case. 'As you told Kirsty yourself, you have no jurisdiction here – and hence, no right to go round confiscating people's property. You're going to have to let the Portuguese police decide what needs to be done.'

'I'm not talking about confiscating anything – just keeping it safe until the police get here.'

'Whoever it was has already had overnight to wipe off any fingermarks,' Bernie pointed out. 'And anyway, there are bound to be too many to be much use – all of the Prices for a start and probably lots of previous guests as well. An awning pole isn't the sort of thing you clean regularly.'

'What I can't understand,' Lucy said with a slight tremor in her voice, 'is why anyone would want to hurt Owen Price. He was such a nice man. Everyone liked him. I can't believe anyone wanted him dead.'

'I'm not sure that his brother was that enamoured of him,' Jonah replied, remembering what Owen had told him that morning. 'Apparently he's the older of the two but Owen always outshone him. That sort of resentment sometimes runs deeper than you'd think'

'Do you think Mark did it?' Lucy wanted to know. 'Is that why you asked Kirsty whether it might have been someone on *his* balcony who was holding the pole?'

'No, not really. I wasn't thinking then about *who* did it; I was just trying to cover all the bases, and it occurred to me that, if she couldn't see who was holding the pole, it was possible that she couldn't see where the other end actually was either.'

'Do you think it could be a prank gone wrong?' Peter suggested suddenly. 'Mark Price is just the sort of person who might prod his brother with an awning pole as some sort of joke, never intending to make him fall off. He did look terribly shaken when he saw how badly he was hurt. And the way he insisted on being the one to try to revive him was like ... well, like an act of desperation almost.'

'Yes, Bernie agreed,' seizing upon this hypothesis eagerly. 'That would make a whole lot more sense than the idea that anyone wanted to murder Owen. I agree with Lucy – he got on with everyone. Why would they want to kill him?'

'Who knows?' Jonah said darkly. 'In my experience it's surprising what sinister secrets come out when you start digging into people's relationships. However, there's no point in us speculating. We'd better get off up there to see the widow and let her know that there may be more to her husband's death than we thought.'

18 WE MAY NOT CLIMB

Visiting Glenys in her apartment was easier said than done. There was no lift to the first floor and hence no chance of taking Jonah up in his wheelchair. Peter's initial reaction was to suggest that he and Bernie should go alone, but Jonah insisted that he had promised Kirsty that he would break the news personally. Realising that his friend would not be content to leave it to him to inspect the balcony, retrieve the awning pole and ask all the relevant questions to take forward his unofficial investigation, Peter gave way and offered to carry Jonah up the steep steps at the side of the building.

Jonah drove the electric wheelchair to the foot of the stairs. Bernie went on ahead with the folding chair and positioned it ready on the first floor walkway. Then Peter picked Jonah up from the chair, which conveniently rose to make it easier for him, and positioned him over his shoulder in the traditional fireman's lift. He climbed the stairs and placed him as gently as he could in the waiting chair, which Bernie was holding firmly at the edge of the top step.

'I'm glad you're only a lightweight,' he grunted, panting slightly with the exertion.

'I'll leave you two boys to get on with it,' Bernie said, a little reluctantly because she would have liked to have been present to see the crime scene herself. 'We can't very well all descend on them at once. Lucy and I will wait at the bottom with The Chair.'

Jonah smiled briefly at the way Bernie spoke of his electric wheelchair as if it were the fifth member of their strange family. Then he looked up at Peter.

'Come on then! Let's get on with it.'

Peter pushed the chair along the walkway, past the door to Mark's apartment and on to the second door, which bore the number 512. He looked around and found what looked like a light switch, but which he recognised as the doorbell. He pressed it and heard the sound of a buzzer inside the apartment, followed by children's voices telling Mum excitedly that there was someone at the door. A few moments later, the door opened and Glenys looked out.

She was wearing a towelling bathrobe over pyjamas. Her hair was tousled and she had no makeup on. Her eyes were red and she looked ready to break into tears. She blinked round at them with a confused expression.

'We're sorry to intrude,' Peter began, but before he could explain why they had come, he was interrupted by Freya, who had followed close behind her mother, determined not to allow her out of her sight, and who now pushed past to speak to Jonah.

'Have you come to read *Hairy Maclary and Zachary Quack*?' she asked boldly, grasping him by the knees.

'Sadly, no, Miss Price,' he said solemnly. 'We've got something we need to talk to your mother about. However, I haven't forgotten my promise and I'll be delighted to read your book with you later – perhaps you could come down to our apartment after you've had your breakfast?' He looked up at Glenys, who nodded absently.

'Is there somewhere we can talk in private?' Peter asked, looking down at Freya and then towards her brother and sister, who had come up behind their mother to see what was going on.

'Come out on the balcony,' Glenys said, leading the way down the straight passageway past the bathroom and bedroom to the living area. 'I've been keeping the doors locked and not allowing the kids out there since ...'

'Very sensible,' Peter agreed. He pushed Jonah's chair carefully over the ridge formed by the runner of the sliding door and over to the low wall at the front of the balcony, taking his time over turning the chair round to give Jonah an opportunity to study the crime scene. The white-painted wall was about waist high, with a single rail of tubular steel running along a few inches above and slightly inside the wall to deter residents from climbing on it – something at which it had been singularly ineffective, Peter reflected.

He peered over the wall and saw, as Kirsty had described, a concrete planter stretching the length of the balcony, just at a convenient distance beneath the top of the wall to act as a footrest to anyone who chose to sit there. The wall between the apartments sloped down from about seven feet high at the wall of the living room to join the balcony wall, with the last foot or so being at the lower level. Thus, the corner of the wall where the two balconies joined became a particularly appealing place for anyone wishing to use the wall as a seat. It also made it quite feasible that someone sitting there could be assaulted from behind by someone in the adjoining apartment, as Jonah had speculated.

'I think you ought to sit down,' Jonah said to Glenys. 'I'm afraid that what we have to say may come as a shock to you.'

Glenys obediently slumped into one of the white plastic chairs and gazed languidly at him, as if nothing that they could have to say could affect her any more. Jonah briefly recounted what Kirsty had told them, emphasising that she had not seen who it was who had wielded the awning pole. Glenys looked at Jonah as if she were uncertain whether to believe what he had said, and then at Peter who nodded his confirmation.

'I don't understand,' she said, after a long pause. 'You're saying that someone deliberately pushed Owen off the balcony?'

'I'm afraid so.'

'But why would anyone want to do that?' She shook her head in bewilderment.

'They wouldn't!' Mark's voice stated decidedly from the other side of the dividing wall. 'It's a load of nonsense.'

A moment later, he appeared, sitting on top of the wall, facing away from them. He swung his legs around and dropped softly on to the balcony between Peter and Glenys, who immediately rounded on him, berating him for the bad example that he was giving to the children.

'You surely didn't believe that stupid girl's story, did you?' he demanded, ignoring his sister-in-law's protestations. 'She's obviously just imagining things – or else making it up to make herself seem important. She's probably annoyed because the police didn't interview her yesterday.'

'In my opinion,' Jonah said in the calm, quiet voice that he reserved for dealing with difficult witnesses, 'they ought to have done. If you look at the layout of this building, it's quite clear that the best view of what went on would be from someone on the balcony of Kirsty's apartment.'

'If she was really there,' Mark said scornfully, 'which I doubt.'

'But I still don't understand!' Glenys wailed, looking up with pleading in her eyes. 'How could he have died after such a short fall?'

'It's not for me to pre-judge the post mortem report,' Jonah answered, 'but my guess is that he must have damaged his spinal cord and that was probably what killed him. It was bad luck that he came down head first and then hit the corner between the wall and the ground. It forced his head right back and I'd guess the nerves were snapped somewhere in his neck.'

'But plenty of people break their necks without being killed,' Mark argued, becoming interested in spite of himself. 'You, yourself, for one.'

'Yes. You're right there,' Jonah agreed. 'It's all a matter of how badly damaged the nerves are and, more importantly, *where* the damage occurs. There are eight vertebrae in your neck. The medical people number them from the top: C1, C2 up to C8. If you break the cord anywhere from C3 upwards, it stops you breathing and you'll die if you aren't put on a ventilator immediately.'

'It was just bad luck,' Peter added, 'that he didn't just walk away from the fall the way Gary did.'

'Huh!' snorted Mark. 'Now, that's where you ought to be looking for some idiot who might have played that stupid prank. If Ms Sumner wasn't making it all up then I bet it was one of those students doing it for a lark!'

'Mrs Price,' Jonah said, ignoring this remark. 'You went out yesterday, leaving your husband alone. Can you tell me whether the apartment door was locked?'

'No. It wasn't. It was so hot yesterday afternoon that we'd propped it open to make a through draught.'

'So anyone who came past on the walkway would be able to see into the apartment?' Jonah asked eagerly. 'Right down the corridor and through the patio doors to the balcony?'

'Yes, I suppose so,' Glenys agreed in a listless voice as if she had no idea of the significance of her words.

'And now,' Peter said quickly, before Jonah could continue with his interrogation, 'we ought to be going. We'll have to let the police know about what Kirsty saw and I imagine they'll want to interview you again. We just thought you ought to know beforehand, so that it didn't come completely out of the blue.'

'Before we go,' Jonah intervened, as Peter took the brake off the wheelchair and prepared to leave. 'Can you show us your awning pole? It needs to be kept in a safe place, out of the way of the children and the cleaners, until the police come to take it for forensic examination.'

'Yes, of course,' Glenys answered, looking around vaguely. 'Only, I'm not sure where it is …'

Peter and Mark hastily hunted around the balcony looking for the missing pole, but it was soon clear that such a large and unwieldy object could not be concealed anywhere in that small space. Then they all went back inside the apartment and Glenys questioned the children, who all denied having seen the pole since the previous morning. In the end, Peter and Jonah departed with the feeling that whoever had been responsible for Owen Price falling to his death must have taken away the instrument with which the deed had been done.

As they made their way along the walkway towards the top of the steps, they met the four students, who first stood aside to let them past and then came running after them to offer assistance in taking Jonah back down. Peter tried to argue that he was perfectly capable – and more experienced – but Josh Compton pushed him aside and swept Jonah up in his muscular arms. Almost before they knew it, he was depositing him carefully in the electric wheelchair, which Bernie and Lucy were guarding at the foot of the steps.

'What are they feeding you on?' Joshua asked jocularly. 'You weigh almost nothing!'

'Nine and a half stone,' Jonah told him, resisting the temptation to tell him that this was none of his business and that, in any case, he would have preferred to have been carried by his friend rather than by a comparative stranger. He knew that the lad was trying to be helpful. 'You've got to remember that I'm not in a position to build up my muscles the way you can.'

'No. I suppose not,' Josh said, abashed. 'I was only joking.'

'We know,' Bernie assured him. 'And we're very

grateful for your help. We can do without Peter risking a hernia or a slipped disc!'

'We thought we'd offer to swap flats with Mrs Price and her kids,' Ibrahim told them. 'Ours is the same size as theirs and we thought she might be happier with them on the ground floor – after what happened.'

'That's very thoughtful of you,' Peter said approvingly, setting down the manual wheelchair, which he had carried down the stairs in Joshua's wake. He wondered whether to mention that the police might, in the light of recent developments, want to secure the upstairs apartment as a crime scene and move all its inhabitants out. However, that would involve telling the students about Kirsty's news and he felt that this was something that should not be disseminated further until the police had been informed.

The students headed off on their mission, while Jonah, relieved to be back in the driving seat again, led the way towards Reception to break the news to the manager that it would appear that a murder had taken place in his hotel and to seek his help in contacting the relevant authorities.

19 LO! WHAT A CLOUD OF WITNESSES

'Pittery pattery, skittery scattery, ZIP! Round the corner came Zachary Quack,' Jonah read aloud to Freya, later that morning. The whole family was sitting on the patio with books and maps ostensibly reading or planning excursions, but in reality waiting for the police to arrive and wondering what would happen then.

'Zip!' she repeated, pointing down at the picture book in delight.

'Excuse me,' a voice interrupted politely.

Jonah looked up to see a man and a woman standing together looking down at him from outside the low wall that divided the apartment from the shared area around the pool. They were both dressed smartly in trousers and short-sleeved shirts.

'I am Chief Inspector Eduardo Rosario,' the man told him, holding up an official-looking identification card. 'I am from the Portimão Criminal Investigation Department of the Polícia Judiciária. This is my assistant, Inês Silveira. And you, I take it, are Detective Chief Inspector Jonah Porter?'

'Yes. That's right. And let me introduce you to my friend, Freya Price. I'm sorry, Miss Price,' Jonah added.

'I'm afraid I need to speak with these police officers, so you'll have to go back to your mum now. We'll finish the book later.'

Freya nodded and obediently slipped off his lap.

'I'll see you home,' Peter volunteered, getting up and opening the gate to allow Freya out and the two police officers in. 'Peter Johns,' he added, shaking hands with them as he passed. Inspector Rosario was tall by Portuguese standards, which meant that he was a little shorter than Peter and several inches taller than Bernie. Both he and his companion had the typical Portuguese colouring: black hair, dark brown eyes and olive skin.

'Detective Inspector – now retired,' Jonah added.

'And I'm Bernie, Peter's wife – and this is my daughter Lucy.' Bernie stepped forward to greet them. 'Sit down. Would you like some tea? I was just about to make a brew.'

'No – thank you. We would just like to talk to you all about the incident yesterday. Please – may we all sit down?'

'Yes, of course. I'll fetch some more chairs – or would you prefer to go inside?'

Soon they were all seated around the table on the patio. Peter returned and took his place between Jonah and Bernie, having delivered Freya into the hands of her mother and warned Glenys to expect a visit from the police shortly.

'Chief Inspector,' Rosario began, 'before we start, I would like to say how pleased we are to meet you. You are quite a legend among the police here. We heard your story and very much admire your bravery – an inspiration to us all.'

Jonah reddened at this eulogy and opened his mouth to protest, but Bernie was quicker.

'No more of that, please, Inspector,' she joked, 'Jonah is quite full enough of himself without having comparative strangers heaping adulation on him. Have a heart and remember that we've got to live with him – and his ego –

afterwards!'

'And less of the brave hero stuff,' Jonah added gruffly. 'All I did was to get on with things as best I could. If you asked my two sons, they'd probably tell you that coming back to the job was just self-indulgence on my part and it would save a lot of people a lot of trouble if I would allow myself to be looked after in some nice nursing home somewhere.'

'Nevertheless,' Rosario smiled, 'I hope that you will not object to me saying that I have been very impressed by your work. You have been remarkably successful in your investigations – particularly, I think in cases of murder. Last year, for example – the killing of a member of Oxford University in a hotel. I read all about it.'

'It was nearly two years ago,' Jonah corrected him. 'And it wasn't all down to me. But I have to admit, I was pretty pleased at how quickly we got to the bottom of that one,' he added with a smile of satisfaction.

'And ... in the light of your experience – and bearing in mind that the victim and all the witnesses in this case are British citizens – I was hoping that you might be willing to assist me in this investigation,' Rosario said. 'I suspect that some of them may be more willing to speak to you than to a foreign policeman, and you may well be better than I at noticing ... what is the word? ... at recognising things that they do not say in words. Do you understand me?'

'You mean that I may be more familiar with what their tone of voice and body language mean? Yes, I can probably give you some pointers there.' Jonah became animated at the thought of being part of a criminal investigation once more. 'I'll be delighted to help in any way. Would you like me to start by giving you a rundown of the people involved and our thoughts so far?'

'*Our*?' Rosario's assistant queried, speaking for the first time.

'Naturally I discussed it with my Personal Assistant,' Jonah inclined his head towards Bernie, who smiled in acknowledgement, 'who accompanies me on every case, and with my ex-colleague, who has eight years more experience in murder enquiries than I have, not to mention the lovely Lucy, who is a budding forensic pathologist. You see before you a formidable criminal investigation team!'

'So I see,' Rosario said, smiling round at them all.

'And, to set your mind at rest,' Bernie added, 'we all have alibis for the murder: Jonah and Peter were nearly flattened by the body falling on to this patio while they were sitting there, and Lucy and I were hiking back to Lagos from Ponta Piedade when it happened. The guard on the 14.18, who checked our tickets, will probably remember us.'

'Well, inspector,' Rosario smiled again. 'I can see that I will have some excellent assistance with this case.

'You certainly will,' Jonah affirmed. 'However, since none of us have any official status in Portugal, perhaps we could dispense with this *inspector* stuff and just use first names? I'm Jonah and my backup crew are Peter, Bernie and Lucy – is that OK with you?'

'Very well,' Rosario agreed. 'And I suggest that, in our private meetings, you address us as Eduardo and Inês.'

The sound of voices from the next apartment made them all look up. The students were evidently on their way somewhere, talking and joking excitedly. Peter stood up and looked over the wall.

'Are you leaving?' he asked, seeing the young men with rucksacks on their backs and trolley cases lined up in a row on the patio.

'No, Craig answered. 'We're just swapping apartments with Glenys and the kids. We thought they'd be happier on the ground floor after what happened.'

'A very nice thought,' Rosario intervened, getting up and going over to join Peter. He held up his police identification card above the wall. 'Eduardo Rosario,' he told them, 'from the police criminal investigation department. I have to ask you to delay your move until after my assistant and I have seen the scene of the crime and interviewed the witnesses.'

'What do you mean *the scene of the crime*?' Joshua wanted to know. 'I thought it was just an accident.'

'That was what we all thought – yesterday,' Rosario told him. 'Now, we have reason to believe differently. We need to talk to everyone in these apartments to find out what happened. And it will be best if as little is disturbed as possible meanwhile. So, please – I ask you to delay your move until later.'

'Oh. Right.' Joshua looked from Rosario to Peter, with a puzzled look on his face.

'You'd better do as Inspector Rosario says,' Peter told him. 'He needs to see exactly what things were like when it happened. It will complicate things if people start changing apartments until after he's had a chance to look around. We'll let you know when it's done.'

'And in the meantime,' Jonah called out. 'Stay around here. You'll have to be interviewed later.'

The four students nodded agreement, still looking rather puzzled. They left their bags and cases on the patio and went back inside to confer about this unexpected development. Jonah looked eagerly at Eduardo.

'What next?' he asked, like a child anticipating a treat.

'As your friend said to those young men, we will need to interview everyone and to look at the crime scene; but first, please tell me what *you* think. Is there anyone who might have wanted to kill Major Owen Price?'

'Nobody springs to mind,' Jonah told him.

'He was such a nice person,' Lucy put in earnestly, speaking for the first time. 'Everyone liked him. No one could have wanted him dead.'

Eduardo turned to look at Lucy. He was unsure what to make of her. She was a few centimetres taller than her mother, and yet looked young. On the other hand, she had a mature bearing and spoke confidently and Jonah had described her as training in pathology.

'I agree,' Bernie said. 'He was a very likeable person. I don't have much time for the military usually, but he wasn't what you expect of an army chap at all. He was just a family man trying to have a good time with his children.'

'What about his wife?' Eduardo asked. 'Did they get on? Were you aware of any arguments?'

'No,' Peter told him. 'They seemed a very united couple. She was worried about him being sent off into war zones and wanted him to leave the army.'

'There was just one thing he said to me,' Jonah mused. 'He talked about his brother not getting the same breaks that he did. There could have been some resentment there – but I wouldn't have thought it was enough to make him want to kill him.'

'I see.' Eduardo took out a folder of notes. 'Now can we go over exactly what happened yesterday? You and Inspector Johns – Peter – were sitting here, and Senhora Johns – Bernie – and her daughter were out, when it happened. Is that correct?'

He went painstakingly through the statements that they had made the previous day, getting up to look at the place where Owen Price's body had landed, and going outside into the communal area to look up at the first floor balcony from which he had fallen. The students reappeared, dressed in swimming shorts and carrying towels.

'Is it alright for us to go in the pool?' Joshua asked. 'We'll be around if you want to interview us.'

'Yes.' Eduardo nodded his acquiescence. Then he turned to Jonah again. 'I think I should speak first to this Kirsty Sumner – the lady who told you that she had seen Mr Price being pushed off the balcony. Would you take me to her apartment?'

'Not easily, I'm afraid.'

'It's that one on the first floor,' Bernie explained, pointing. 'There are no lifts, so we can't get Jonah's chair up there.'

'We could ask them to come down,' Inês suggested.

'Ye-es,' Eduardo said slowly. He turned to Bernie. 'Would you mind if we used your apartment as our interview room?'

'Feel free,' Bernie shrugged. 'We are at your service.'

'Before you start your interviews,' Jonah broke in, 'There's something you ought to see.'

He showed the police officers the photographs that he had taken of the marks on Owen's back. Eduardo looked at them with interest.

'Why did you not show these to the local police yesterday?' he wanted to know.

'They didn't ask. And there's this too,' Jonah displayed the picture of the dead man's hand clutching the toy dinosaur.

'Ah!' Eduardo reached into his pocket and produced a plastic evidence bag containing a small plastic model. 'I was going to ask about this. Do you know where it came from?'

'It's one of a collection owned by Owen Price's son, Danny,' Peter told him. 'He must have been holding it when he fell.'

'Thank you.' Eduardo put the toy back in his pocket. 'And now, may we see Senhora Kirsty?'

Peter accompanied Eduardo and Inês upstairs to the flat where Kirsty and Lewis were staying. On the way, they met Mark Price, who was returning from the shops with two baguettes and a copy of the Daily Mail. Just as they were turning in from the open paved area to the narrow path at the side of the building, he rounded the raised flowerbed, planted with low-growing shrubs, which lay between the path to the outside stairs and the path from the driveway.

Eduardo noted mentally that the position of the bed meant that anyone approaching one of the upstairs flats from outside would be visible to watchers from the poolside and from any of the six apartments. It would be difficult for anyone not already upstairs to enter one of them unobserved.

Peter introduced the two men briefly, explaining to Mark that he would be needed later to give his account of the events of the previous day. Mark scowled, but refrained from voicing his opinion that any further investigation was a waste of time. He walked with them up the stairs. Then, when they reached the door of his apartment, he remembered something.

'Wait there a minute,' he commanded. 'I've got something for you.'

He pushed open the door with his shoulder and went inside. A moment later, he was back, with a long wooden pole in his hand. He held it out towards Peter.

'This is the awning pole you and your friend were so interested in. Cameron found it in our apartment. It must have got mixed up with ours. The kids are in and out of both flats all the time.'

Peter took the pole and looked at it. The metal hook and ring looked as if they would exactly match the marks that Jonah had photographed on Owen's back.

'Thanks,' he said. 'Are you sure that this is the one from next door and not the one from your own apartment?'

'Yes. Ours is still on the balcony.'

'Please,' Eduardo intervened politely. 'We need to take them both for examination.'

Mark seemed to hesitate, but then disappeared inside again. Eduardo and Inês took out gloves from their pockets and put them on in readiness for handling key items from the crime scene. Peter passed over the pole that he was holding to Inês, mentally berating himself for having handled it without thinking.

After half a minute or so, Mark returned with another, seemingly identical, pole.

'Here you are,' he said, handing it to Eduardo, who

passed it on to Inês. 'But I don't know what good it will do you. If you're thinking of fingerprints, they'll both be thick with them – all seven of us have had hold of both poles, not to mention the way the cleaners always seem to move things around when they come.'

'Thank you,' Eduardo said evenly, watching Mark keenly. 'As Inspector Johns said, we will need to speak with you later; so please stay where we will be able to find you.'

Mark watched them from his doorway, as the three continued along the walkway, past Glenys' apartment to the far door. He waited until he saw Lewis ushering them inside. Then he stepped back inside his own apartment and went through to the living area to tell Cameron that they were confined to quarters for the time being.

Lewis showed them through to the balcony, where Eduardo prowled around, taking in every detail, in a manner that reminded Peter of Jonah's demeanour in the days before his injury. It did not take long to establish that, from where Kirsty had been standing the previous afternoon, she could easily have seen what she claimed to have witnessed. The L-shaped design of the block meant that apartment 513 had a clear view of the balconies belonging to the other two upstairs flats.

Eduardo declared himself satisfied and they all trooped outside and down the stairs, Kirsty carefully locking the door behind them. Lewis carried Lily in his arms as they descended to the ground and walked round the building. When they reached the apartment, they found Bernie and Lucy waiting outside, while Jonah had retreated to the inside living area.

'If Lily will stay with us, you can leave her out here while you have your chat with the police,' Bernie suggested to Lewis and Kirsty. Lily, however, did not think much of that idea and insisted loudly, in the way that only an obstreperous toddler can, that she intended to go with her parents wherever they went. So Lewis sat on the sofa with her on his knee while Kirsty recounted once more what she had seen the previous afternoon. Eduardo watched her intently as she spoke, and Inês took careful notes.

'I'm sorry I didn't say anything sooner,' Kirsty finished. 'I – I couldn't really believe what I saw. And no one asked. But then, afterwards, I thought maybe I ought to have said something.'

Eduardo remained silent for just long enough for Kirsty to begin to worry that he might be considering what sort of punishment might be available for someone who had thus impeded the police in their enquiries. Then he thanked her briefly and told her that she could go. Bernie, watching from outside, obligingly got up and opened the door for them to leave. Then she looked inside and spoke to Eduardo.

'Would you like me to round up your next witness?'

Eduardo was about to answer when he was interrupted by the arrival of Neil Barrington, accompanied by a young man with straw-coloured hair and blue eyes, dressed in a business suit. Neil introduced him as a member of staff from the British consulate on the Algarve, who had come to assist Mrs Price and her family.

'The consul is away on holiday at the moment,' the young man explained, speaking in what Bernie classified in her own mind as a *poncey public school accent*. 'So, I'm afraid I'm holding the fort. Timothy Lucy-Blythe,' he added, holding out his hand towards Eduardo, who shook it and then introduced Inês, Jonah and Peter.

'As you can see,' he said, hoping to forestall any suggestion that Scotland Yard should be brought in to investigate the death of a British citizen on Portuguese soil, 'we have the good fortune to have two British police officers on hand to help us.'

'So I see,' Lucy-Blythe answered, smiling round. 'I'm sure you have everything well under control. I just thought I ought to pop in to let you know I'm here. Now I'll nip upstairs and see the poor widow – see if there's anything I can do for her. Presumably it'll be a while before you release the body?'

'I'll let you know when we've finished with it,' Eduardo assured him.

'Righty-ho. I'll see you later then.'

'Before you go,' Jonah intervened, 'perhaps Neil could answer a few questions. You were outside when Owen fell,' he went on, addressing the clergyman. 'Please could you tell Inspector Rosario exactly what you saw?'

'Of course.' Neil turned to face Eduardo and adopted the slow, well-enunciated speech that he used when communicating with those for whom English was not their first language. 'I was sitting by the pool, reading. I was concentrating on my book, so I did not see anything until after he fell. The noise attracted my attention and I looked up and saw that something had happened, but I could not see what it was, because the wall prevented me from seeing the body.'

'I see. That all accords with the statement that you made to the local police,' Eduardo said, looking up from his notes. 'And then you went over to see what was going on. You didn't happen to look up at the balcony at all by any chance?'

'No. I was intent on seeing if there was anything I could do to help. I went over and looked in, and then Mr Johns asked me to summon help, so I went straight off to Reception to call the emergency services.'

'Thank you. Now, please can you think back to earlier in the afternoon? You arrived back from your sight-seeing at …?

'About one-thirty. We were hot and tired, so we sat down in the shade by the pool. Then my wife remembered that she needed to do some preparations for our evening meal, so she went back to our apartment. That must have been at about quarter to two.'

'And were you the only people sitting round the pool at that time?' Jonah asked.

'Yes. The place seemed deserted when we got back. We assumed that everyone was either out or else indoors having lunch. We'd already had ours in a little restaurant we know in Silves.'

'Did you see anyone from the upstairs apartment coming or going while you were by the pool?'

'No. No one.'

'And do you think you would have seen them, if there had been anyone?' Jonah persisted. 'I mean – you were facing towards the entrance, weren't you?'

'Yes, I was – but, as I said, I was reading my book; so I couldn't say for certain that nobody came in or out.'

'But if they did,' Eduardo interjected, 'they would have seen you and they might have assumed that you would have seen them?'

'Yes. I suppose so.'

'And when you went off to Reception to fetch help,' Jonah continued, 'did you see anyone outside in the drive – anyone you recognised, or anyone who seemed to be in a hurry to get away?'

'No.' Neil shook his head. 'I didn't notice anyone. I was just intent on getting to Reception as quickly as I could.'

'Thank you,' said Eduardo, bringing the interview to a close. 'I have just one final question. From what you knew of Major Price, can you think of anyone who might have wished him ill?'

'No,' Neil said, very decidedly. 'He seemed a very personable man. As far as I know, everyone liked him. I find the idea of someone deliberately pushing him off a balcony quite inexplicable. My wife said the same, only this morning. It just doesn't make any sense. Now, if that's all,' he went on, turning to Timothy Lucy-Blythe, who had been waiting patiently for the interview to finish, 'I'll show you up to Mrs Price's apartment.'

'Tim Nice-but-dim, I think,' Bernie murmured to Lucy as soon as the two men were out of earshot. 'I don't think Glenys ought to put too much reliance on Young Mr

Lucy-Blythe's help when it comes to organising repatriation of the body and so on.'

'I think I would like to speak to the young men from the ground floor apartment,' Eduardo said, looking at his notes, 'particularly the Indian gentleman who was here when the incident took place.'

'I'll call them in,' Bernie volunteered, getting up at once and going out to call the students in from where they were lounging around the small pool. Only Ibrahim had been interviewed by the police the day before, so the others were excited at the prospect of being part of an official enquiry.

'Senhor Ali,' Eduardo began, 'according to what I have here, you were in your apartment when Major Price fell to his death. Is that correct?'

'Yes,' Ibrahim nodded.

'It says here that you got back at about one fifteen?'

'Yes. It must have been about then.'

'Did you see anyone around the apartments when you came in?'

'I saw Jonah and Peter. We had a few words together and then I went inside.'

'No one else?'

'No.' Ibrahim frowned. 'Should I have done?'

'No, no – I just wanted to be sure. Now, I would like you to think about what you saw and heard while you were inside your apartment. I noticed, when I went upstairs earlier, that it has a window at the side, overlooking the path that leads to the stairs. Did you see anyone going along that path?'

'No.' Ibrahim shook his head. 'But I wouldn't have. I wasn't in the living room. I came in, and then I went to the bathroom to wash, and then I went into the back bedroom where there aren't as many distractions.'

'He means,' Craig interposed, 'that no one can see him bowing and banging his head on the floor.'

Peter flashed an angry look towards the young man,

but Ibrahim grinned, seemingly unaffected by the apparent mockery.

'There's probably a bit of that too,' he admitted. 'Anyway, the main thing is – I wasn't in any position to see people coming and going to the upstairs apartments – sorry.'

'I see.' Eduardo paused for a moment then continued. 'Now please think hard. Did you hear anything while you were in the bedroom? Any noises from upstairs? People running or shouting? Anything at all?'

'Sorry,' Ibrahim shook his head again. 'I was concentrating on the prayers. I wasn't aware of anything happening outside the bedroom until I finished and came back into the living room and saw people rushing around outside.'

'You did not even hear the ambulance siren?' Inês asked, sounding incredulous.

'No – well, yes, subconsciously, I suppose,' Ibrahim answered, struggling to explain. 'I mean – afterwards, when I saw them taking the body away, I sort of remembered that there had been a siren, but while I was praying it didn't register.'

Inês continued to look sceptical, but Eduardo decided to move on.

'Now, I would like to ask all of you,' he said, looking round at the four students. 'You and the Price family have both been staying here for a week now. You must have got to know them quite well. Can you think of anyone who might have borne Major Price a grudge?'

They all shook their heads.

'He was a really nice guy,' Joshua said, speaking for all of them. 'He got on with everyone.'

'Even that brother of his,' Craig added. 'I felt sorry for the kid – Mark's kid, I mean.'

'Yes,' Gary agreed. 'You'd never have thought they were brothers. Owen liked everyone and everyone liked him. But Mark!' He shrugged.

'What about Mark?' Eduardo asked.

'I don't think he liked students,' Joshua told him.

'He complained to the management about us,' Gary added. 'He said we were making too much noise and stopping the kids getting to sleep.'

'Actually, he may have had a point there,' Ibrahim said. 'Things did get a bit rowdy while Mel and her friends were here.'

'But he didn't need to make such a fuss,' Gary insisted. 'And he could have talked to us instead of to the hotel manager.'

'And what was it you were saying about his relationship with his son?' Eduardo asked Craig. 'You said that you felt sorry for him. Why is that?'

'How much time have you got?' Craig said with a shrug. 'Mark was always putting Cameron down in front of other people. He made no secret that he thought he was a wuss.'

'A *wuss*?' Eduardo raised his eyebrows at the unfamiliar term.

'Mark was very athletic,' Joshua explained. 'He was always running and climbing and playing sports. Cameron was the opposite – thin and weedy, and not much good with a ball.'

'I think I understand.' Eduardo leaned back and put his fingers together across his chest, thinking. 'And what about Cameron's relationship with his uncle, Owen? Did they get on?'

'Oh yes!' the students assured him.

'I think Cameron probably wished Owen was his father instead of his uncle.'

'Aah! And how do you think Mark felt about that?'

Nobody said anything, but everyone started to wonder.

'Well, thank you all very much,' Eduardo said, finishing the interview. 'You may go now.'

The students left and Eduardo turned to Jonah.

'What do you think?' he asked. 'You met the two Price

brothers. Do you think Mark could have resented Owen enough to want to kill him?'

'I don't know. I certainly agree with the lads that Cameron preferred Owen to his own father and that he was frequently embarrassed by Mark's behaviour, but ...'

'It isn't just the way his father criticised him openly in front of other people,' Peter added. 'Mark is a thoroughly unpleasant person all round, and Cameron realises it. I could see how uncomfortable he felt the other day when Mark came out with a lot of racist nonsense about black kids and Muslims.'

'I think that I would like to meet Major Price's brother and nephew now,' Eduardo said thoughtfully.

A few minutes later, Mark and Cameron arrived, escorted from their apartment by Inês. Mark looked resentful and belligerent, while his son appeared scared. They sat down on the sofa, facing the four police personnel, who were grouped around the low table.

'Captain Price,' Eduardo began, 'first let me say how sorry I am for your loss.'

He paused and Mark grunted an inarticulate acknowledgement.

'As I'm sure you have heard, we have reason to believe that Major Price's death was not accidental. That is why we need to ask you some questions now. Chief Inspector Porter and Inspector Johns have kindly offered to help us with our enquiries and I hope that we will soon discover who killed your brother.'

'Very well,' Mark answered ungraciously. 'What do you want to know?'

'You were both in the apartment next door when he fell,' Jonah said, having agreed with Eduardo that Mark might respond better to questioning from a British police officer. 'Did either of you hear or see anything that could have a bearing on what happened?'

'No. And I think that girl's story about someone

pushing him is a load of bollocks. She's just making it up to get in the limelight.'

'Cameron?' Jonah asked mildly, ignoring Mark's outburst.

'No. I didn't see anything. I was in my bedroom, getting changed to go swimming.'

'And then you went down to the pool,' Jonah agreed. 'Did you meet anyone on the stairs, or on the path?'

'No.'

'You're sure of that?'

'Yes. I would have noticed.'

'Thank you. That's very helpful. Now, Mark,' Jonah turned back to the boy's father. 'I'd like to ask you again, what you heard and saw immediately before your brother's accident and what brought you to the balcony after he fell.'

'I just told you. I saw and heard nothing until Owen shouted out and I ran out on to the balcony and saw him there.' Mark pointed outside at the patio.

'Thank you. That's better,' Jonah said in the tones of a schoolteacher who had succeeded in bringing a recalcitrant pupil into line. 'You heard a shout. Did you hear any words? Or was it more just a scream?'

'No. There weren't any words.'

'And the tone of voice? Did he sound surprised or frightened or angry?'

'I don't know ... surprised, I suppose.'

'Good. You heard a shout and you ran out to see what was going on and you saw old Peter here giving CPR and then you climbed down over the edge of the balcony to join us.'

'That's right.'

'Which is something that you've been doing regularly ever since you arrived here, despite your sister-in-law's requests that you desist?'

For a moment, Mark looked embarrassed. Then he launched into a defence of his actions.

'Glenys always made such a fuss about things. I knew

what I was doing. It was quite safe. That's what I don't understand,' he added, turning suddenly from anger to confusion. 'It was such a short fall. How could it have killed him?'

'Bad luck, probably,' Jonah answered. 'And, of course, *you* always made sure that you landed on your feet. Whoever pushed him off the wall saw to it that he didn't have that option.'

Thank you,' Eduardo said, taking up the questioning. 'I think we are clear now of the sequence of events. Now I need to ask you to think: is there anyone who might have wanted to kill your brother?'

'No, of course not!' Cameron said before his father could answer. 'Everyone liked Uncle Owen. He didn't have an enemy in the world.'

'Captain Price?'

'Well, there are … no, Cameron's right. Everyone got on with Owen.'

20 THE WIDOW AND THE FATHERLESS

'Lunchtime!' Bernie announced, putting her head in through the patio doors as soon as Mark and Cameron had left. 'We nipped round to the panadería and got some bread, she added, holding up two large rustic loaves, 'and there's plenty of cheese and ham in the fridge.

She bustled in and started laying the table.

'You will eat with us, won't you?' Peter invited Eduardo and Inês.

'It won't take long,' Jonah added, 'unless you'd rather press on with the investigation?'

'They can do it without you, in that case,' Bernie warned from the kitchen where she was mixing a salad.

'We would be delighted to join you,' Eduardo replied, inferring from Bernie's tone that there was some underlying reason why lunch should not be delayed but sensibly not enquiring further. 'And while we eat, I would very much like to hear your opinion about what we have been told so far.'

'I can't help thinking,' Peter murmured, 'that I wouldn't be at all sorry if it turned out to be Mark who pushed his brother off the balcony in a fit of jealousy.'

'That's not like you, Peter,' Bernie commented. 'Usually you have time for everyone.'

'I have to confess to a lack of fondness for bigoted racists, and I would get a certain degree of satisfaction over seeing Mark Price given a life sentence.'

'I know what you mean,' Jonah agreed, 'but aren't you forgetting the kids in all this? They've already lost their dad. Seeing their uncle sent down for murder is hardly going to help them – even if he isn't a very good uncle.'

'I suppose you're right,' Peter admitted. 'In fact I know you are. I think that Danny, in particular, is probably quite fond of his uncle. I suppose, from their point of view, the best thing would be if it turned out to be some stranger that they don't know.'

'From their point of view,' Bernie said, decidedly,' it would be better if it somehow turned out to be an accident – the way it looked as if it was – but Kirsty's evidence looks conclusive, doesn't it?'

'OK then,' Jonah brought them back to the nub of the matter. 'Who have we got in the frame?'

'Not many suspects to choose from,' Peter said, reviewing in his mind what they had heard in his usual systematic way. 'It has to be someone who was already up there *before* Cameron came down for his swim – otherwise he would have seen them.'

'Yes. I agree,' Eduardo nodded. 'So, we have: Kirsty Sumner and her husband, Mark Price and, of course, Cameron himself. He could easily have slipped into the apartment before going downstairs.'

'Plus anyone who sneaked upstairs earlier,' Bernie added. 'Is there anywhere up there that they could have hidden?'

'There's a storage room at the back of the third apartment,' Peter told her. 'It's where the cleaners keep brooms and mops and things. Someone *could* have gone up and hidden there, waiting for Glenys Price to take the children to the Kids Club.'

'Yes,' said Lucy eagerly, keen to have the spotlight moved off Cameron, for whom she felt sorry. 'And they could have gone up there any time after the cleaners finished. What time did the maid come round on Tuesday?'

'Dunno,' Peter shrugged. 'It was while we were out. But that means, sometime before eleven thirty in the morning.'

'That is something that I can check with the manager,' Eduardo said, noting this down. 'We are making progress.'

As soon as lunch was over, Bernie was dispatched to find Glenys and bring her to the interview room. She found the whole Price family, including Mark and Cameron, sitting around the table in Glenys' apartment with the remains of their meal in front of them. Glenys immediately agreed to come down to speak with the police, but Mark intervened, insisting that he should accompany his sister-in-law, 'to make sure those foreign police agents don't try to intimidate you'. Glenys looked daggers at him, but seemed too tired and despondent to argue. Instead, she looked helplessly round at the children in a wordless appeal to know what to do with them while she was being interviewed.

'Bring the kids with you,' Bernie suggested. 'Lucy and I will keep them occupied down by the pool, where you'll be able to see that they're OK.'

Danny raced on ahead, delighted to be free to roam after spending the morning cooped up in the apartment. Freya carefully collected all her books together and Bernie helped her to pack them into a small rucksack to take with her. Holly clung to her mother and insisted on walking hand-in-hand down the stairs to the ground floor. Bernie surmised that perhaps she had a better understanding than her younger siblings of what had happened to her father.

When they reached the apartment, Holly at first refused

to be separated from her mother. Eventually Bernie persuaded her to sit on one of the chairs on their patio, where she could watch the interview without hearing what was said. Freya was disappointed that Jonah was not available to read to her, so Bernie offered to sit with the two girls and try her hand at this important duty. Lucy and Cameron meanwhile did their best to keep watch over Danny, who was running around like a mad thing pursuing imaginary murderers and shooting at them with his water pistol.

Glenys had little to add to the testimony that they had already heard. She confirmed the timings of her departure with the children to the Kids Club and her return – which, in any case, had been witnessed by Jonah, Peter and the ambulance crew. She confirmed the identity of the plastic triceratops that Owen had been clutching at the time of his death and appeared nonplussed when asked if she could suggest why he might have been holding it. When asked about any potential enemies that her husband might have had, she shrugged her shoulders and gazed around as if bewildered by the question.

'I honestly can't think of *anyone*,' she said earnestly. 'He got on with everyone. He even managed to make friends with some Taliban prisoners that he had charge of. That's the sort of man he was.'

'Of course, there *are* those who think that anyone in the forces is a legitimate target,' Mark said darkly. 'That's where you ought to be looking, in my opinion – that is, if you can't see that it's probably all a load of nonsense made up by that stupid girl. She told me they were pacifists,' he added in tones of deep disgust. 'Maybe she just wants to make trouble for anyone in the military.'

'Don't be silly, Mark,' his sister-in-law protested. 'I'm sure she wouldn't do anything like that.'

'Alright then,' Mark shrugged. 'In that case, I suggest you ask that Muslim boy what he was doing on Tuesday afternoon. They all hate the British forces.'

'Mark! Please!' Glenys begged, looking more and more uncomfortable.

Eduardo decided to bring the interview to an end. They seemed to be gaining nothing beyond deepening the rift between Glenys and her brother-in-law.

Peter let them out on to the patio and closed the doors behind them. Holly immediately flung herself at her mother, sobbing her relief at being reunited. They went to join Danny at the poolside, finding him engaged in a wrestling match with his cousin. Bernie, watching them from her patio, thought that Cameron looked more happy and relaxed than she had seen him up to now and wondered how the dynamics of the Price family would develop in the coming weeks and months.

21 I CANNOT TELL

Eduardo closed his notebook and put it away in the pocket of his jacket, which was hanging on the back of his chair. Inês, following his cue, stowed her own notes in a leather bag, which she slung over her shoulder. They both got up to leave.

'Before you go,' Jonah said, 'can you tell me where things are up to with the post mortem? Have you established cause of death yet?'

'We have a preliminary report,' Eduardo told him, 'but it is confidential. We have rules that this is not disclosed publicly until the Public Prosecutor's enquiry is completed. However …'

'I assume that we can take it that Peter's favourite theory – that he had a heart attack which made him fall off the wall – won't wash?'

'There is no evidence that he died before hitting the ground,' Eduardo agreed carefully.

'And the way he cried out as he fell bears that out,' Jonah added.

'You're right,' Peter agreed. 'It just seemed like a plausible explanation at the time – before we had any reason to suspect foul play. And less upsetting for the family.'

'I'm assuming that he must have broken his cervical spinal cord when his head hit the wall,' Jonah said to Eduardo. 'Does that fit with your preliminary report? I'd say he must have severed it somewhere above C4—'

'The fourth cervical vertebra,' Peter added, helpfully, seeing the blank looks on the faces of their Portuguese colleagues.

'— which is why he wasn't breathing when Peter got to him,' Jonah concluded.

'Yes,' Eduardo nodded. 'That assessment accords with our findings so far. However, I must emphasise that you should not talk about this to anyone — except as your own personal theory. The doctor's report, as I said, is confidential until it has been officially established whether or not there is any criminal activity involved.'

'We understand.'

'And, on the same subject,' Eduardo continued, 'the police investigation is also confidential. We have rules about waiting until we have results before talking to the press or to the relatives of the victim. I think this is rather different from the way you do things in Britain. It is a matter of protecting the privacy of witnesses and preventing unhelpful speculation.'

'We understand,' Jonah said again.

The Portuguese police left and Bernie and Lucy came back in and closed the door.

'Time for a brew, I think!' Bernie declared, predictably, going into the kitchen and filling the kettle.

'I know you can't tell us what everyone said,' Lucy said, sitting down opposite Peter and Jonah and looking at them keenly, trying to assess whether they looked as if they had made a breakthrough in the case, 'but do you think you're any nearer finding out what really happened?'

'I'm not sure that we are,' Peter told her. 'It all boils down to: who could have got into the apartment between when Glenys left to take the kids to the Kids Club and when Owen fell.'

'And, now that we've thought of the store room as a hiding place,' Jonah added, that means anyone not accounted for between when the maid finished the cleaning and when Cameron came down for his swim.'

'Except that you'd have seen if anyone went up while you were sitting out, wouldn't you?' Lucy pointed out. 'So they must have been up there already by then.'

'I'm not so sure about that. I was dozing in the sun and Peter was sitting by the wall with his back to the path. We could easily have missed someone coming in and going upstairs.'

'But didn't you say that Neil Barrington was outside when it happened?' Bernie asked, bringing in the tea and sitting down next to Lucy. 'He'd have seen, surely?'

'He wasn't there for that long,' Peter told her, 'and he was reading.'

'But what I still don't get,' Lucy complained, 'is *why* anyone would *want* to kill him in the first place.'

'And, if they did,' Bernie added, having given the incident much thought during the day, 'why did they use such a stupid method. It was a pure fluke that he *did* die. The chances were that he would only be slightly injured – and quite possibly be able, therefore, to identify his attacker.'

'Perhaps you're right there,' Peter agreed. 'Put like that, it does look more like an act of impulse than premeditated murder. Could it be that someone lost their temper and gave him a push, never intending him even to fall off, never mind get himself killed?'

'In that case,' Jonah said thoughtfully, 'we'd be talking about someone who would have been there in the flat as a matter of course – either Mark or Cameron, probably.'

'Or even Glenys?' Bernie asked.

'No,' Peter said with conviction. 'She didn't get back until it was all over.'

'Ye-es,' Jonah mused. 'Yes, I think you're right, Peter.

The obvious solution is that either Mark or Cameron had words with Owen and poked him with the awning pole in frustration – or even just as a joke – and knocked him off balance by mistake. And now they're afraid to admit what happened.'

'If it was Cameron,' Peter added, 'Mark may know and be lying to protect him.'

'And if it was Mark,' Jonah agreed, 'he could have done it from the comfort of his own balcony, without having to go next door at all.'

'Those poor kids!' Bernie said with feeling, giving a sigh. 'The way you two put it, it looks very much as if they're going to have to face either their uncle or their cousin being convicted of manslaughter, if not murder, as well as having lost their father.'

They all sat in silence for several minutes. Nobody quite knew what to say after that. Then Lucy gave a little gasp and looked up from her iPad, on which she had been carrying out her own investigation on the internet.

'Oh Mam!' she exclaimed in a small voice, holding it out to Bernie and pointing at the screen. 'Look at this!'

Bernie looked down and saw some figures displayed.

'I was researching spinal injuries to see how likely it was Owen being killed outright like that,' Lucy explained, 'and I found this website where you put in the details of someone's injury and their age and it comes up with their life-expectancy.'

Her mother struggled vainly to think of something to say. Peter reached out and snatched the tablet computer from Bernie's hands. While he studied the figures on the screen, Lucy looked round at each of the adults in turn. When she came to Jonah, she caught his eye and he smiled back at her sheepishly.

'You knew about this, didn't you?' she said in a voice half accusation and half anguish. He nodded.

'I assumed you would too,' he said quietly. 'Didn't anyone tell you?'

Lucy looked towards Bernie, who put her arm around her daughter.

'I'm sorry, love. I suppose I thought it was too much for you to take in when you were younger – and then, well, I suppose I just didn't think about it later.'

'But I never thought ... 'Lucy tried to explain her feelings. 'I mean – I always knew Jonah needed to be careful about infections and things, so I suppose I knew he probably wouldn't live to be a hundred or anything like that, but ... but it says here fifteen years! And that's from the date of his injury, so he's already had seven of them!'

'Lucy love,' Bernie repeated, hugging her close. 'All this is just statistics. *Life Expectancy* is just that. It means how long you can expect to live *on average* after a spinal injury of a particular kind. That means that some people will live longer – maybe a lot longer – and some will live for less long.'

'And *anyone* can be accidentally killed or develop an incurable disease at any time,' Jonah added. 'Take Margaret, for example. Her life expectancy before she got cancer would have been much longer than it turned out.'

'But in eight years I'll only be twenty-four,' Lucy argued. 'I won't even have qualified by then.'

'Well, for a start, stop talking about eight years,' Peter said forcefully. 'Look here! You've put in Jonah's age when he got shot.'

'Yes. That's what it says to do,' Lucy argued.

'But, the life expectancy *then* will include all those people who die shortly after injury because of complications,' Jonah put in eagerly, seeing a way of mitigating Lucy's anxieties, 'and the ones who develop problems during the next few years – you know, chest infections, diabetes, all sorts of things – and I haven't got any of them yet.'

'That's right,' Bernie agreed. 'So it would make a lot more sense to put in Jonah's age *now*, because he's at least as fit as he was when he was shot.'

Peter entered some new figures into the online calculator and looked at the result. He handed it back to Lucy.

'There you are,' he said triumphantly. 'Look! I've just added four more years to Jonah's life!'

Lucy and Bernie looked down at the figures.

'And see there,' Bernie pointed out. 'It gives the life expectancy for a man of the same age in the general population. Jonah's is only eleven years less.'

'That seems like an awful lot to me!' said Lucy, thinking that it was more than half her lifetime.

'Well,' Bernie said, trying to shock Lucy out of her misery with a joke, 'look on the bright side. I'm already living on borrowed time: both of my parents were already dead before they got to my age! I could be the one to go first.'

'And I'm older than the lot of you,' Peter joined in. 'It could be me!'

'But the chances are,' Bernie continued, 'that at least one of us will live for long enough to need you to look after us for years and years while we develop dementia and all sorts of other diseases of old age. You be careful what you wish for!'

Lucy giggled in spite of herself and started looking a little more cheerful.

'And there's something else,' Jonah said, more seriously. 'You know how you accused me of not believing in things?'

'I didn't *accuse* you of anything,' Lucy protested.

'Whatever. Anyway, I've been thinking. There's something important that I *do* believe in: the Communion of Saints and the Life Everlasting.'

Lucy looked puzzled, so he continued.

'I'm afraid that I can't get quite as worked up about my life expectancy as you seem to have done, because, although I enjoy life – and you are responsible for a lot of that enjoyment, I should add – it isn't the thing of greatest importance to me, especially since Margaret died. Do you understand what I'm getting at?'

'Yes. I think so,' Lucy said slowly. 'You mean you're not so bothered about dying because you can look forward to being with Margaret again?'

'Something like that – not that I'm not hoping for a long and happy life *before* I join the Church Triumphant, you understand!'

Peter reflected silently that it must be nice to be so sure of being reunited with one's loved-ones after death. He wished that he could believe that Angie was waiting for him *just beyond the river*, as she had been so fond of singing during her lifetime. He wondered whether Jonah was really as confident as he sounded.

There was a knock at the patio door and they looked round to see the stooping figure of Neil Barrington looking in. Bernie got up and opened the door to admit him.

'I hope I'm not intruding,' he said apologetically. 'I saw that the police had left and I thought I'd pop round to see how you were and if there was anything we can do to help.'

'Come in!' Jonah called to him. 'Take a pew. We were just discussing the Resurrection of the Body and the Life Everlasting. Perhaps you would like to give us your professional opinion on the matter.'

'I'll do my best,' Neil said, a little nervously, taken aback by this surprising demand. He had been expecting to offer counselling after the shock of Owen Price's sudden death and had come unprepared for a theological discussion. 'Was there anything in particular?'

'Well,' Jonah said, smiling blandly, 'there's one thing that has always puzzled me. You remember the raising of Lazarus?'

'Well, not personally,' Neil sniggered nervously, 'but I know the story, yes.'

'I've got two questions about that: what was the point

and why would nobody ever believe in it happening today?'

'I'm not sure I understand what you're getting at?'

'Well, regarding the first question: what's the point of reviving a man when he's going to die again eventually anyway?'

Neil thought rapidly.

'I think perhaps your two questions are related,' he said in the end. 'The raising of Lazarus was a sign of Jesus's messiahship. So, in a way, it wasn't for Lazarus's benefit, but for the people around him. And we wouldn't expect it to happen like that today, because Jesus is no longer on earth.'

'A bit hard on Lazarus,' Peter muttered, 'dragging him back and making him die twice!'

'Ah yes!' said Neil. 'And that's another aspect of it. The raising of Lazarus happened under the old dispensation – before Jesus rose from the dead. It was different in kind from Jesus's own resurrection. As you rightly point out, Lazarus died again, whereas, when we talk about the resurrection of the body we mean resurrection to eternal life. So, again, we wouldn't expect another Lazarus, because we now anticipate the resurrection of all believers. St Paul said that Jesus was the first to inhabit the new life in a heavenly body, while Lazarus was simply brought back to his old earthly body.'

'So,' Jonah pressed him, smiling mischievously, 'you wouldn't expect to be able to raise the dead at one of your healing services?'

'No. Of course not.'

'Have you, in fact,' Jonah persisted, 'ever had anyone being cured at one of them?'

'That rather depends what you mean by that,' Neil said cautiously.

'I once was blind, but now I see,' Jonah suggested. 'That sort of thing.'

'I think,' Neil answered slowly, thinking on his feet,

'that perhaps you are confusing the concepts of *cure* and *healing*. 'Very often, what people need is not so much a cure for their bodily ailments as healing of their spiritual ills. They need to gain inner peace – and peace with those around them. And I can certainly testify that there are people who have experienced that. And, sometimes, when they become spiritually well, they experience bodily healing too.'

'In other words,' Bernie suggested, 'people get better when what was wrong with them was probably psychosomatic in the first place.'

'If you want to put it that way,' Neil admitted, 'but through the grace of God.'

'So, you don't really believe in miracles?' Lucy asked. 'Not real ones.'

'It all depends what you mean,' Neil answered, beginning to feel rather beleaguered by this inquisition. 'I believe that God intervenes to change and heal us, but not necessarily in such way as that you could say: *that must be supernatural.*'

'It strikes me,' Peter observed, 'that you're really telling us that it's all in the mind. I can just see Richard Dawkins and his like saying that you don't need God to explain the sort of things you're talking about.'

'But that's just it! Jonah exclaimed suddenly, interrupting Peter's flow. 'We don't need God to explain anything. That's just precisely where the militant atheists have got it all wrong. Saying that you don't need God to explain some potentially supernatural phenomenon is like … like … it's like … When I announced that I was marrying Margaret, if you had said to me, "you don't *need* her to cook your meals and clean the house, you can do all those things yourself, or else pay someone to come in and do them." If you'd said that sort of thing, I'd have told you to take a running jump, because that's not what marriage is all about. And that's what I'm trying to say. I don't *need* God to explain things that science doesn't understand yet.

That's where this idea of *the god of the gaps* is so ill-conceived. I don't need God to fill in the gaps; I need him to pull me up short when I'm behaving badly, and to prod me into doing the things I know I ought to but don't want to, and .. and ... don't you see? It's the difference between a – a *force*, if you like, and a *person*. That's why we're stuck with calling God *he*, whatever the feminists may think, because *it* doesn't express that personal aspect properly.'

He paused for breath and then turned to look at Lucy.

'And I think, Lucy, that answers your question from the other day. I don't expect God to step in and cure me miraculously, because that's not what he's all about. And I wouldn't want him to anyway, because ... because it would be too much like, when Margaret sometimes used to do something specially nice for me and I'd know that it meant that she was angry with me about something and was building up to explaining exactly what it was that I'd done that was particularly idiotic and crass. If that's not being irreverent,' he added, looking towards Neil, who was sitting rather bemused, hoping not to be asked to make any further contribution to the discussion.

'No, no,' he said hastily. 'Not at all. I like your analogy. I may use it myself sometime.'

'Here endeth the first lesson,' Bernie declared, getting up and collecting together the mugs, which were still on the table. 'And now, to bring you all back down to earth with a bump, isn't it time someone thought about what we're going to eat this evening?'

22 YOUR CAPTAIN GIVES THE WORD

There was a kerfuffle outside and Jonah looked up from his computer screen to see the four students once more engaged in taking all their belongings out of the apartment next door and depositing them on the paved area around the pool. Excited young voices signalled the arrival from upstairs of the Price children. Jonah was surprised to see that they were accompanied by a woman whom he had not seen before. She looked to be in her sixties – or perhaps well-preserved seventies – with white hair cut in a bob and dark brown eyes, which reminded Jonah of Owen and made him suspect that she was Mrs Price senior.

He was proved right in this deduction when Freya ran across to where he was sitting just outside their patio area.

'Granny Wendy has come to help Mummy,' she told him, holding out a new book for his inspection. 'She brought me this book; will you read it to me?'

The older woman hurried over to apologise.

'I'm so sorry,' she said. 'I'm afraid my granddaughter can be very demanding at times. Wendy Price,' she added, holding out her hand towards him.

Lucy, who was sitting, perched crossways on a sun lounger next to Jonah, reached out and intercepted the hand.

'Good evening, Mrs Price,' she said, shaking hands very formally. 'My name is Lucy Paige, and I'm sure Freya will have told you all about DCI Jonah Porter.'

'And please don't apologise,' Jonah added. 'We've enjoyed sharing Freya's books and we'll be delighted to have another one to read.'

'We're moving,' Danny told him, pushing past his grandmother to speak to Jonah and Lucy. 'We're going to be next door to you now.'

'So I gather,' Jonah said solemnly. 'We've been looking forward to it ever since the lads broke the news to us this morning. Why don't you leave Freya with us,' he added, looking up at Wendy Price, who was trying to persuade the children to come with her into their new ground floor apartment, 'while you get settled in?'

'If you're sure she won't be a nuisance,' Wendy said doubtfully.

'Don't worry,' Lucy assured her, 'we'll hand her back if she is.'

'Very well then,' Wendy agreed. 'There you go, Freya. You can stay with Inspector Porter while we bring everything down. Be a good girl, now.'

She turned away and continued with her task of managing the move. Jonah watched, with admiration and some amusement, her skill in organising everyone concerned. This was clearly a woman used to being in charge. She soon had the students engaged in carrying down the heavy suitcases from the apartment above, supervised by Mark, while Danny helped by stowing various beach toys in the cupboards in the living room and Cameron was tasked with unpacking a box of foodstuffs and putting them into the fridge

Glenys stood at the entrance of the apartment, looking on with a bemused expression on her face, as if she were not sure exactly what was happening, while Holly clung to her hand determined not to allow her mother out of her sight. Wendy sized up the situation and dispatched them to the kitchen to prepare refreshments for the workers. Then, after looking round to check that everyone else was usefully employed, she set off to negotiate with the hotel management for fresh sheets and towels to be provided in both apartments and for the change of tenure to be formally registered.

Jonah watcher her go, mentally filing away everything that he was learning about the inner workings of the Price family. Granny Wendy was clearly a matriarch who was used to taking charge and seeing that things got done. Her efficient handling of the situation contrasted starkly with the way her daughter-in-law appeared to have been completely prostrated by her bereavement. Jonah wondered whether Glenys welcomed or resented her intervention – or if she was simply too stunned by her husband's death to notice or care one way or the other.

Without waiting to be invited, Freya climbed on to Jonah's lap and held up the book for him to see the cover.

'It's your turn Roger,' he read out.

'I had that when I was little,' Lucy exclaimed. 'Look, Peter!' she called, seeing her parents coming out of the apartment to join them. 'It's your turn Roger. Do you remember reading that to me?'

'I certainly do,' he answered with a grin. 'I think I could probably still recite most of it by heart.'

Peter sat down on another sun lounger and Bernie lay down on it with her head in his lap.

'Why do you call your daddy *Peter*?' Freya asked.

'Because it's my name,' Peter told her.

'But you call your mummy *Mam*,' Freya argued, with unanswerable logic.

'It's because Peter isn't my real dad,' Lucy explained. 'My real dad died a long time ago. Peter was my godfather and then he married my mam, so now he's my stepdad as well.'

'Will *my* mummy marry someone else now that Daddy's

died?' Freya asked anxiously.

'I shouldn't think so – not for years and years, anyway. My mam didn't marry Peter until nearly seven years after my dad died.'

'What made him die?' Freya wanted to know.

'Don't you want Jonah to read your story,' Peter intervened, hoping to divert the little girl from what might turn out to be a painful subject for her.

'Afterwards,' Freya insisted. 'I want Lucy to answer my question first.'

'He fell off a roof.'

'Why?'

He was a policeman. He was chasing a suspect, and they got into a fight and he fell off. Peter and my dad and Jonah were all policemen together years ago.'

'Why did my daddy fall?'

'We don't know. That's what the police are trying to find out,' Jonah told her firmly. 'Now, are we going to read this book or not? I'm itching to find out what happens.'

'Granny Wendy says that my Daddy is in heaven now, with Grandpa Mark,' Freya said, refusing to be diverted. Now that she had the attention of three adults who might be willing to satisfy her curiosity as to what was happening around her, she did not intend to give up. 'But Cameron said that he's at the hospital, and Mummy was talking to a man about bringing him back to England. So where is he really?'

'I suppose,' Jonah said slowly, trying to think of the best way of explaining things, 'it all depends what you mean. You see ... when you die, your body stops working and it isn't any use any more; but that isn't the real you – the bit that really makes you, you. That's different. That's what people call your *soul*. And that bit goes on, but not the same way. So, your daddy's body is in the hospital, in a special place called the mortuary where they keep dead bodies safe until the people's families take them away; but his *soul* is in heaven, with your grandpa. Does that make sense?'

'Yes,' Freya nodded. 'Will we take Daddy's body back with us on the plane?'

'No. There'll be special arrangements for that. It might upset the other passengers having a dead body on the plane.'

'When *I* die, will I go to heaven and meet Grandpa Mark too?' Freya wanted to know.

'Yes, but you don't want to be thinking about that. It'll be years and years before that happens.'

'I don't remember Grandpa Mark. He died when I was a baby.'

'Was he your Daddy's daddy?' Jonah asked, unable to resist the opportunity of getting more information about the family of the murder victim.

'Yes,' Freya nodded. 'And I've got Grandpa Rhodri and Grandma Pauline, but we don't see them very much because they're very, very busy.'

'Was your Grandpa Mark a soldier like your dad?'

'Yes, he was a colonel,' Freya nodded proudly. 'But he wasn't killed fighting,' she added quickly. 'He got ill and died.'

Jonah sat staring into space, thinking. He was beginning to get a feel for what it must have been like for the Price brothers growing up. He pictured the scene in his mind's eye. Mark, the firstborn, named after his father and expected to follow in his footsteps and to fly high, but destined to disappoint. And Owen, his mother's favourite perhaps, outshining his brother in everything they did, following him into the regiment – and being promoted over his head.

And then marriage. Mark got in first on that one. Was he pleased to have something that Owen did not have – for a while? Or could it have been quite different? Was there a reason why Mark had only the one child? And why he sometimes seemed almost resentful even of that one? Perhaps it had been a case of being compelled by straight-laced parents into marrying Cameron's mother after they discovered that Mark had *got a girl into trouble*, as they used to say. And so, he married a woman whom he did not love and they had a son who could not have been more different from Mark or any of the rest of the Price family. And, in due course, his younger brother also embarked on matrimony, but (of course!) everything went well with him. He had a string of children, all the spitting image of their father, and all bright, spirited youngsters of the sort that Mark would have wanted his own offspring to be.

And now his wife had left him – presumably it was *she* who had left *him* – and he had been forced to fight for access to his son, who seemed determined to be everything that Mark despised and disliked, and who was apparently only having anything to do with his father at all because he was required to do so by law. What had their mother thought of his divorce? Jonah suspected that she would probably have viewed it as a family disgrace and that she would not have been reticent in expressing her views. Very probably, she had made comparisons between Owen, the golden boy who could do no wrong, and her fistborn who failed at every turn. Small wonder then, if Mark felt little affection towards his brother. But was sibling rivalry and resentment sufficient to make him stoop to murder?

'Aren't you going to read?' Lucy interrupted his reverie. 'I want to hear it again, even if nobody else does.'

Freya obligingly opened the book and held it on her lap where Jonah could read the words. He forced himself to concentrate on the text, pushing to the back of his mind all the thoughts that kept trying to crowd in. Thoughts of motives (not many of those!), means (the instrument of death was clear, and available to anyone who entered the apartment) and opportunity (two clear suspects, two possibles and potentially many more, if you accepted the *hiding in the broom cupboard* hypothesis).

The book starred Roger the pig, who, trying to avoid the chores, visits neighbouring pig families to find one that suits him better. Jonah did his best to add interest by giving each pig family a different regional accent. Freya giggled as she recognised an exaggerated form of her mother's Welsh lilt.

'I loved the way all the families were different colours,' Lucy said, when Jonah reached the end of the book and Freya gleefully snapped it shut between her two hands. 'I used to think that they'd missed one though. I wanted to see a family with different breeds living together – maybe a pink pig and a black pig and lots of little grey piglets.'

'Time for your bath, Freya!' They all looked up to see Mrs Price senior standing before them, her arms full of fresh towels. Behind her, standing to attention, were two of the hotel maids in white aprons, bearing clean sheets and pillowcases. In the background Joshua and Ibrahim stood, clutching inflatable beach toys, clearly awaiting their orders as to where to put them.

'Yes, Granny Wendy,' Freya mumbled, sliding off Jonah's lap.

'And what do you say to Inspector Porter and his friends?'

Freya turned and favoured Jonah with a wide smile.

'Thank you for having me.'

'It has been delightful, Miss Price.' Jonah inclined his head gravely. 'I hope that we shall have the pleasure of your company again very soon.'

Wendy Price gave Jonah and his friends a brief smile before turning abruptly and leading her small brigade of helpers at a brisk marching pace into the apartment, with Freya trotting at her heels.

Mark emerged, standing aside to let his mother's procession pass. Jonah was surprised to see that he was accompanied by Gary and that they seemed to be having an animated conversation. The two men walked over to greet Jonah and his companions. Mark appeared more relaxed than Jonah remembered seeing him since they arrived.

'Thank you for keeping Freya occupied,' he said pleasantly. 'We've been trying to keep the kids on the go to stop them thinking too much about what's happened. I'm glad my mother managed to get out here to give us a hand. It's hit poor Glenys for six and she doesn't seem to know what day of the week it is at the moment. Freya's questions were really getting on her nerves earlier, so it's great that she's taken such a shine to you. She's usually shy with strangers.'

'Always happy to help', Jonah replied to what was the longest speech that he had heard Mark make. It was also the first time that he had spoken without sounding either critical or resentful. Jonah wondered what had prompted the improvement in his mood.

Cameron came out of the apartment, having finished his assigned tasks and been dismissed by his grandmother, who was now fully occupied in putting the two younger children to bed. He closed the gate behind him and turned to go upstairs, back to his own room. Jonah gained the impression that he was deliberately attempting to avoid his father's notice. However, in this he was unsuccessful.

'Hi Cam!' his father called to him, waving. 'Come over here and have a chat.'

For a second, Cameron continued walking away from them. Then he stopped and turned. His face bore a sulky expression, which changed to surprise and enquiry, as he took in the unfamiliar sight of his father in the company of the black youngster. He started over towards the group near the pool.

'Gary's been telling me that he's studying on an army bursary,' Mark told him. 'It gives him a thousand a year while he's studying and another three K when he completes his officer training. Why don't you apply?'

'Because Mum says she doesn't want me going into the forces,' Cameron growled, his face clicking back into sulk mode.

'It's up to you to decide, isn't it?' Mark's good humour

evaporated at the mention of his ex-wife. 'You shouldn't allow other people to rule your life.'

'It's good fun,' Gary put in eagerly. 'I'd been in the cadets before I went to uni, but the Officers Training Corps is much better.'

'Cameron's in the cadets, aren't you Cam?' Mark said, trying to engage his son in the conversation.

'No. I dropped out. I've got better things to do.'

'Like what?' Mark was beginning to sound angry now.

Cameron did not reply. He knew that his father would have no time for the things that interested him.

'Like what?' Mark asked again. Gary looked around and gratefully spotted two of his fellow-students passing.

'I'm sorry, sir,' he said to Mark, 'I've got to go. It's been nice speaking to you.'

'Like what,' Mark repeated, taking hold of Cameron's elbow and shaking it.

'If you must know – not that it's any of your business,' Mark retorted at last, finally goaded out of his habitual taciturnity towards his father, 'I've joined an amateur dramatic society and I've been volunteering with hospital radio. I want to do something creative with my life. I'm not interested in tramping for miles with a ton of kit on your back or target practice or endlessly going through the same drill over and over. You can stuff the cadets!'

He strode off round the corner of the building, heading for the stairs. Mark stood watching him for a moment then turned briefly towards Jonah and his friends.

'I'm sorry. Excuse me,' he muttered before heading off after this son.

'Don't you think–?' Peter began mildly, but Mark was gone.

'I would say, Peter,' Jonah remarked drily, 'that you have hit the nail on the head. Captain Price appears not to be in the habit of thinking – or at least not on the same wavelength as those around him. Now, let's go inside. I'd like to talk a few things through with you where we won't be overheard.'

23 WHO IS HE?

'Is it OK for us to stay?' Lucy asked. 'Or is this a hush-hush police investigation meeting?'

'Oh, you can certainly stay,' Jonah assured her. 'I don't think we'll be discussing anything you don't already know, and I'd like your opinion – as a witness.

Peter closed the door firmly and they all sat down round the table looking expectantly at Jonah.

'I know old Peter thinks I tend to rush ahead of myself with theories and don't take enough time to weigh the evidence first,' he began.

'I've never said anything if the sort!' Peter protested.

'Nevertheless, that's what you think. So this time, I want to run a hypothesis by you all to see what you think, before taking it any further.'

'Go on then – fire ahead.'

'We're agreed, aren't we, that one big difficulty is finding a motive for anyone wanting to kill Owen?' Everyone nodded. 'Well, seeing Mrs Price senior mustering her troops this evening made me start thinking about the internal workings of the Price family, and in particular the relationship between Owen and his brother. It set me thinking that there might be quite a build-up of resentment there.'

He looked round to check that he had their full attention before going on. Peter noticed the move and bit back an impulse to urge his friend to *stop grandstanding and get on with it*. He found Jonah's tendency towards the dramatic irritating.

'Owen himself told us that Mark got up people's noses –'

'Hardly surprising,' Peter growled, 'considering the way he went on. He'd got it in for everyone. He was racist, homophobic, bigoted, and the way he treated poor Cameron!'

'Precisely!' Jonah agreed. 'But what made him like that? In particular, how come he was like that when Owen was so different? It couldn't have been parental influence or why didn't his brother exhibit the same prejudices? I imagined them growing up together: Mark the older brother always in the shadow of his younger sibling. Perhaps his parents made it plain that they preferred Owen. So then he tried harder to get their attention, but it always backfired and he ended up in trouble while Owen continued to be the apple of their parents' eye.'

Jonah looked round at his audience again, checking that they were still attending to his story.

'He followed his father into the army – probably to please them – and then, so did his hated rival, Owen. He got promotion – but not as fast as Owen, who soon leapfrogged over him – maybe even spent some time as his commanding officer. And perhaps even the way that happened may have seemed unfair to Mark. Suppose Owen is one of those irritating people who manage to break rules and take risks and they always pay off.'

At this point, Jonah broke off and looked towards Peter, who returned his stare expressionlessly. He had no intention of acknowledging that this was very much the scenario that had played itself out when they were both detective sergeants.

'In home life as well,' Jonah resumed, 'Owen has all the luck. It comes home to Mark on this holiday. There is Owen surrounded by his doting wife and three delightful children who all adore him – while Mark's wife has run off and his son is a sulky teenager who isn't interested in any of the things that Mark thinks are important. And he starts to think how much nicer it would be if there was no Owen for everyone to be comparing him with all the time. Well – what do you think?'

'I think that you'd never get it to stick without a whole lot more evidence,' said Peter. 'It's all supposition.'

'But, Mark is one of the very few people who were upstairs at the time and so *could* have done it,' Bernie pointed out. 'And Jonah's story does provide some sort of motive – even if it doesn't seem entirely logical.'

'I must admit – I'd *like* it to be Mark,' Peter said, 'but we mustn't let that get in the way of the evidence. And you don't have any real evidence for this deep-seated resentment that you say Mark had towards Owen. From what I saw, the two brothers seemed to get on pretty well. Remember the way Owen leapt to Mark's defence when we criticised him?'

'That's a point,' Bernie said, thoughtfully. 'The way he spoke, it was as if Mark had been alright until things started to go wrong for him – his experiences in Afghanistan and his wife leaving him.'

'OK then,' Jonah conceded. 'Suppose it *wasn't* Mark who tipped Owen off the balcony, who do you suggest it was? Cameron? From what I've seen, he'd have been more likely to target his father than his uncle.'

'Yes!' Lucy exclaimed suddenly. 'She had been keeping quiet, unsure whether she was supposed to be contributing to the discussion. 'Couldn't that be the answer? I don't mean that Cameron did it – I mean, couldn't whoever did it have been aiming at Mark, rather than Owen? After all, they do look fairly similar from the back.'

'You know, Lucy,' Jonah said eagerly, 'I think you may

have something there. 'After all, it was Mark who made a habit of climbing on the balcony wall, not Owen.'

'Yes, Bernie agreed, 'and the brothers are remarkably similar in many ways: same hair, same build, both sun-tanned and freckled. Anyone could be forgiven for getting them muddled if all they saw was a back view.'

'Right,' Jonah said briskly. 'So let's assume for the time being that Mark was the intended victim. Who might have a motive in that case?'

'Practically anyone,' Peter observed, making no attempt to hide his hostility towards the older Price brother. 'Cameron, for showing him up in public all the time; Glenys for the way he behaved in front of the children; anyone from an ethnic minority or any other kind of minority group; pretty well anyone who met him, I would think.'

'Hmm,' Jonah grunted. 'Aren't *you* in danger of hypothesising ahead of the evidence now? Just because you don't like the fellow ...'

'I'm not hypothesising,' Peter defended himself. 'All I'm saying is that there could be a lot of people who wouldn't have been particularly sorry if it had been Mark and not Owen who was in the hospital morgue now.'

'Why don't we make a list?' Bernie suggested. 'Of specific suspects, not generic groups. And top of the list has to be Cameron, because he had motive and opportunity.'

'But, he must have known that it wasn't Mark sitting on the wall,' Lucy objected, 'because he'd just come out of the apartment where Mark *really* was.'

'I don't know,' Jonah thought this through. 'We'll have to think about that one. Let's put it to one side for the moment and think about who else could have wanted to get rid of Mark.'

'The kids – Holly and Danny, I mean – told me that Glenys doesn't like Mark because he's been unfair to his ex-wife,' Bernie contributed. 'And we've all seen the way she keeps criticising his behaviour. But she didn't get back from the Kids Club until after it happened.'

'I'm afraid we have to include Ibrahim,' Peter said, reluctantly. 'I don't believe for a minute that he did it, 'but he had been the target of Mark's bigotry and *might* have been resentful. And, the worst of it is that he was on hand when it happened.'

'But he couldn't have got upstairs without going past you and Jonah and the Barringtons,' Lucy said quickly. 'Everyone agrees that he was inside the apartment when it happened.'

'I'm sorry, Lucy,' Jonah said gently, realising that what he was about to say would be very unpopular, 'but there's a window on the side of his apartment, so he could have climbed out of that, gone up the outside stairs, pushed his victim off the balcony and nipped back down and back through the window.'

'But he wouldn't' Lucy insisted. 'He's not like that.'

'I agree,' Bernie added in support, 'and his motive is very weak. I mean, why would he care that much? He's not going to see the man again after they go home. Surely it's much more likely that it would be one of the Price family who've got to put up with him for life.'

'I don't know,' Peter sighed. 'The thing is: we don't know what may have gone on between them in private, and some people do get very het up if they think someone is insulting their religion.'

'Sorry, Lucy,' Jonah nodded in agreement. 'I don't like the idea any more than you do, but the fact remains: Ibrahim was there and he does have a motive of sorts – assuming that he thought it was Mark, and not Owen, sitting on the wall.'

'But how could he have known that he was there?' Lucy wanted to know.

'He might have seen him from below, when he came in – or,' Jonah went on excitedly, 'he might have actually seen Mark sitting there, but by the time he got upstairs the two brothers had swapped places.'

'OK,' Bernie agreed grudgingly, 'we will put Ibrahim on the list, but now let's think who else ought to be there. We've got Cameron, who has both motive and opportunity, and Glenys who has motive but also appears to have an alibi. Are you two *sure* she couldn't have slipped back without you noticing?'

'I *think* so,' Peter answered, 'but I was facing the other way.'

'And I have to admit that I was dropping off to sleep some of the time,' Jonah added. 'However, it would be a bit risky for her to assume that she hadn't been noticed, and she did actually arrive back later. So she'd have had to have sneaked in and sneaked back out again without being noticed, before making her grand entrance after it was all over.'

'Hmm,' Bernie sounded reluctant to drop the idea altogether. 'Let's keep her on the list but with all those caveats that you've just mentioned. She certainly had no love for her brother-in-law and if she thought he was endangering the kids ...'

'I suppose,' Peter said reluctantly, breaking the long silence that followed, 'that we ought to put Gary down. 'Mark certainly had it in for him and the feeling could have been mutual.'

'But he was out with Josh and Craig,' Lucy objected.

'No, he wasn't – not quite. They went out on the banana boat, but he wasn't allowed because of the plaster on his arm, so he was just watching. If we accept that Glenys could have slipped past us twice, then so could he.'

'But like Mam said about Ibrahim, why would he bother killing someone that he was never going to see again after this week? You might just as well say that Wayne and Dean did it!'

'Indeed we might,' Jonah agreed. 'Sorry Lucy, but we'll have to add them to the list, now that we're working on the assumption that Mark was the intended victim. He'd made no secret of his dislike of their lifestyle. In fact he'd even suggested that they were a danger to his son.'

'How about Kirsty and Lewis?' Bernie suggested, hoping to divert the conversation from this line of reasoning. 'I can't think of any motive for them, but they were upstairs at the time.'

'We'll come to them in a moment,' Jonah refused to be deflected. 'We haven't finished considering Wayne and Dean yet. Does anyone know where they were yesterday afternoon?'

'I seem to remember Dean saying something about surfing,' Peter said, trying to remember. 'I think he knew somewhere that he could hire a board. But I've no idea whether he actually went.'

'Wherever they were, they'd be together,' Bernie said, still determined to keep their young friends out of the frame. 'So it would have had to be a conspiracy, which doesn't seem likely.'

'Not if Dean was surfing,' Lucy said miserably. 'Wayne doesn't like to admit it, but he's afraid of the sea. He can only just about make it across the swimming pool and waves terrify him. So he'd find some excuse not to go, if Dean was surfing.'

'Well, you're surely not expecting me to believe that someone the size of Wayne could slip past two trained observers — twice — without being noticed?' Bernie exclaimed. 'Still, I suppose they'll both have to go down on the list — until we can find out where they really were. Now, back to Kirsty and Lewis. They could easily have gone round from their flat and pushed Owen off the wall.'

'True, but why then would Kirsty make such a point of telling me that it wasn't an accident?' Jonah asked.

'Attention seeking?' suggested Peter. 'Or could Lewis have done it without Kirsty realising that it was him?'

'But why would he want to?' Jonah asked. 'I know we all said that it would be a lot easier to find someone who wanted to get rid of Mark than Owen, but the more I think about it, the more I conclude that we don't really have *any* plausible motive for killing *either* of the Price brothers. It's a long way from not particularly liking someone to pushing them off a hotel balcony.'

'I agree,' said Bernie, getting up. 'We're getting nowhere fast. Let's sleep on it. It's time we were getting off to bed anyway.'

24 THE MOURNFUL MOTHER WEEPING

Sleeping on the problem failed to produce the hoped-for breakthrough. As he chewed the breakfast cereal that Lucy spooned diligently into his mouth the following morning, Jonah pondered on the events of the day before.

'Did you notice how much happier Mark seemed to be yesterday evening?' he asked between mouthfuls. 'I mean, when he was talking with Gary – before Cameron annoyed him.'

'I don't know about happier – he was certainly different,' came Bernie's opinion. 'The mere fact that he was talking to Gary, for a start.'

'And I was wondering whether it could have been anything to do with Owen not being around any more,' Jonah continued. 'I was wondering whether that cat-on-a-hot-tin-roof demeanour that he used to have could have been because he was always anxious about what Owen might say to him – or about him.'

Peter opened his mouth to answer, but he was interrupted by a tap on the patio doors. They all turned to see who it was calling at such an early hour. They saw

Glenys standing outside, dressed in yellow pyjamas with flip-flops on her feet. Her face looked pale beneath its tan and her eyes were red. Bernie got up and opened the door for her to come in.

'I'm sorry to intrude on your breakfast,' Glenys apologised. 'I wanted to see you without the kids trailing along. They're still in bed. Wendy said she'd get them up and dressed for me, so I thought I'd come round.'

'Sit down,' Bernie urged. 'Have some tea. I'll get another cup.'

'Thanks.' Glenys took the chair that Bernie had vacated on Jonah's left.

'What can we do for you?' he enquired, smiling kindly at her.

'I wanted to know … I mean: I was hoping you'd tell me …'

'Yes?' Jonah prompted encouragingly.

'I need to know how this investigation's going on – into Owen's accident, I mean. Will they be finished soon? Will we be able to go home next Tuesday, like we planned? The kids have to go back to school next week, and I've got my job to think about, and …' She looked into Jonah's eyes with an expression of confusion and hopelessness.

'I'm afraid that all of that is up to the Portuguese authorities,' Jonah told her gently. 'I have no jurisdiction here. They just took me along for the ride in case I could help with the investigation – with it involving mainly British people – but I can't tell you anything about what has been going on. It's all very confidential at the moment – until the Public Prosecutor certifies the cause of death. I gather that's a bit like our coroner's inquest. That's what determines whether or not the police investigation goes any further.'

'So they haven't definitely decided that it's murder?' Glenys asked. 'That policeman yesterday seemed so certain – I can't think why. It seems obvious to me that it must have been a simple accident.'

'Why do you say that?' Jonah asked quietly.

'Well, it stands to reason. I mean – who would want to harm Owen? Everyone liked him.'

'We did wonder,' Peter said cautiously, 'if someone could have mistaken him for Mark.'

'You mean, whoever it was meant to push *Mark* off the balcony?' Glenys sounded surprised, but then seemed to see the attraction in this idea. 'I suppose … yes, that could have been what happened. But who?'

'We were wondering if *you* could suggest who might have wanted Mark out of the way.'

Lucy put down the spoon, seeing that Jonah was intent on watching Glenys' face to see her reaction to this remark.

'I see.' Glenys thought for a moment. 'Well, I admit there have been times when I wished there was something *I* could do to get him out of my hair, but it never got to the point where I'd have tried to kill him. And that goes for everyone else I can think of. I mean, it's not something you do, is it?'

'Someone did,' Jonah observed drily. 'But never mind that. I was also wondering whether Mark could possibly have been responsible for the death of his brother. They often didn't see eye-to-eye about things, did they?'

'Oh, no – never!' Glenys declared decidedly. 'They were very close, even if it didn't always look like it. Mark would never have done anything to harm Owen, I'm sure of it.'

'He didn't resent the way Owen had done better for himself?' Jonah probed gently.

'You mean getting promoted quicker? Oh no! He was quite alright about that. Maybe years ago – when their dad was still alive – it might have been an issue, but not now. Colonel Price was a bit hard on both of them,' she went on, becoming expansive as she talked about a world with which she had become very familiar. 'He was from a different era – when promotion was all about who you knew and who your parents were. He didn't understand that it's much more structured now. So he was disappointed – and he made it clear to the boys that he was disappointed – that they didn't get to senior ranks as quickly as he expected. It was no good trying to explain to him how it could have been that a little cockney from a comprehensive school might have risen from the ranks and overtaken his boys! But he was hard on both of them equally – not just Mark.'

'I see.' Jonah paused to think and Lucy took the opportunity to feed him with another spoonful of cereal. While he masticated it, Glenys returned to the subject of the police enquiry.

'So you said that it hasn't been decided that it *wasn't* an accident?' she asked.

'Not officially,' Peter confirmed. 'But, with the evidence from Kirsty Sumner, they can hardly decide that it was.'

'Don't you think she might have been mistaken?' Glenys asked hopefully. 'I mean, she can't have got a proper look from that distance, can she? I really think an accident is much more likely, don't you?'

'Getting back to your brother-in-law,' Jonah said, carefully evading Lucy's spoon and turning his head towards Glenys. Lucy replaced the spoon in the bowl and sat watching for another opportunity. 'I rather get the impression that he could be a difficult person to live with.'

'You can say that again!' Glenys agreed. 'He denies it, but he used to knock his wife about. And the way he talks to Cameron sometimes, makes me want to slap his face. I know he had a hard time in Afghanistan, but there's no excuse for the way he treated poor Julie after he came back from his last tour of duty. God knows I've tried to understand what he went through, but however bad it was he's got no business taking it out on his wife and kid like that.'

'Are you suggesting that his behaviour changed?' Peter

asked with interest. 'That he wasn't always …' he hesitated, not quite liking to describe Glenys' brother-in-law in the terms that had sprung to his lips, 'well, not always quite so decided in his opinions, perhaps,' he finished tactfully.

'You mean, not such a ranting, racist homophobe?' she asked, giving a brief smile before her features snapped back into an expression of mixed sadness and bewilderment. 'Oh yes. When I first met them both, he was the nicest guy you ever met – well, apart from Owen, of course. I remember when I was expecting Danny, I was quite ill and Mark did a lot to help out. That's when I really got to know Julie properly. They looked after Holly while I was in hospital. Wendy couldn't help, because she had the boys' dad to look after – he was in the final stages of lung cancer, you see. It's only these last few years – since his second time in Afghanistan – that he's been such a …' Her voice trailed away and she looked round rather helplessly at them all.

'How do you think his son feels towards him?' Jonah asked. 'We've seen the way Mark puts him down, but Cameron seems to put up with it better than a lot of teenagers would.'

'I don't know. I suppose he knows he'll be going back to his mum next week.'

'So you think he may have been bottling up all the resentment that he must feel?'

'Yes – no! I don't mean that he might have tried to kill his father, if that's what you're getting at. Oh! This is all just so awful.' Glenys pulled a tissue out from her sleeve and started dabbing her eyes as tears welled up. 'I don't understand. How did he die? That other boy only broke his arm.'

'It's all just a matter of chance,' Peter said, taking her hand in his in an effort to comfort her. 'You can't predict these things.'

Glenys nodded. For a few moments they all sat in silence.

'So it *was* an accident really, wasn't it?' Glenys said at last. 'You just said, nobody could have predicted ... why does there have to be all this police investigation?'

'There would have to be an investigation into the death, even if it *was* an accident,' Peter told her gently. 'People need to know *why* it happened – I mean how it wasn't prevented.'

'The tourist industry is very important to the local economy,' Bernie added. 'They can't risk headlines in the press. *DEATH ON THE ALGARVE: UK holidaymaker falls from unsafe hotel balcony.*'

'It wouldn't be *UK holidaymaker*,' Jonah said glumly. 'It'd be *British war hero*. Bernie's right, they have to get to the bottom of what happened so that they can be seen to be doing something to stop it happening again.'

Glenys nodded again.

'Well, I'd better be getting back,' she said, pushing the tissue back up her sleeve and getting to her feet. 'Will you be seeing that policeman again? Could you ask him about when we'll be able to go home? I'd like to try to keep the kids as much in their usual routine as possible.'

25 BROTHER, SISTER, PARENT CHILD

'So brother Mark isn't such a bad egg as we all thought,' Peter remarked, once Glenys was safely out of earshot.

'Or that's what she would like us to think,' Jonah commented. 'But is she just trying to convince us that she didn't really have it in for him, despite all the appearances to the contrary?'

'Even if she is, that doesn't mean that she's guilty – only that she's realised that you think she might be,' Peter pointed out. 'And to be fair on him, he did seem to have got over his prejudice against Gary last night.'

'Yes,' agreed Bernie, 'I think he's one of those people who carries around a load of stereotypes in his head, but then when he actually gets to know someone, he forgets about them.'

'He's the sort of person who says *when I talk about coloured people, I don't mean you, Gary – you're just like a white man*,' Peter said scathingly. 'And he thinks he's paying a compliment.'

'Gary seemed to be getting on alright with him yesterday too,' Bernie pointed out. 'So either he wasn't aware of the things he'd said about him or he was willing to bury the hatchet.'

'Or he was being deliberately friendly in order to avoid anyone suspecting him of having a grudge against Mark,' Jonah suggested.

'We've been through all that,' Lucy complained. 'Gary wasn't even there when it happened and he would have been bonkers to want to *kill* Mark, whatever he'd heard him say.'

'If you ask me,' Bernie chipped in, 'it was a pretty bonkers way of trying to kill someone anyhow. What were the chances of even succeeding, never mind getting away with it?'

'You know – you're right,' Jonah said excitedly. 'Is that where we've been going wrong all this time? It wasn't intended to be murder. Glenys is right, in a way, it was an accident that he died, but it wasn't accidental that he fell.'

'You mean, whoever it was pushed him off, thinking he'd just break his arm or something, like Gary?' Peter asked.

'Precisely! And that throws the field wide open again. We couldn't think of anyone who might have wanted to kill Owen – or even his unlikeable brother, Mark – but someone who just wanted to teach one of them a lesson? That's a completely different ball game!'

'It needn't even have been vindictive,' Bernie added. 'It could have been a bit of horseplay gone wrong. Mark, for example: he's just the sort of person to prod you with a seven-foot pole to attract your attention, instead of coming up and tapping you on the shoulder! You can imagine it, can't you? *Hey bro! I thought you were forbidden to sit up there. You'll catch it from the missus when she gets back!* And then, poke, poke – whoops!'

'And he pokes a bit harder than he intends – or else he makes Owen jump and he tips forward and loses his balance – and down he comes,' Peter added. 'You're right – it could have been unintentional that he fell.'

'I'm not sure,' Jonah mused. 'I don't like Mark any more than you two do, but I can't help feeling that, if it had just been a bit of larking about, he'd have owned up. I don't rule out the idea that he pushed Owen off to teach him a lesson – and then got scared when it turned out to be fatal – but if the fall was an accident, I think he'd probably have come out with an explanation right away.'

'That's all pretty academic anyway,' Peter sighed. 'There's poor hopes of ever proving *who* it was, never mind *why*. It seems to me, we're right back at square one again. As you said just now, it could be anyone who wanted to teach either of the Price brothers a lesson or who was on silly-knockabout-antics terms with them.'

'We'll just have to hope the police come up with some convincing forensic evidence,' Bernie sighed.

'Not very likely.' Jonah was sceptical. 'All the most likely suspects – Mark, Cameron, Glenys – have perfectly legitimate reasons for their fingermarks and DNA to be all over both flats and, most importantly, all over the murder weapon.'

'It'd tell us something if there were other prints,' Peter suggested. 'One of the students, for instance.'

'Still not definitive,' Jonah shook his head. 'Unless you could be sure their prints were the most recent – which is unlikely seeing as we know that Mark Price, for one, handled the awning pole *after* Owen's death – they could argue that they'd touched it earlier in the week. Don't you remember Mark saying that they'd been friendly with some girls in the end flat upstairs – who used to climb over the wall into the Price's apartment? I bet those awning poles got switched around pretty frequently and it'll be impossible to say who touched what when.'

'Hi Lucy! Are you coming out?'

Their deliberations were interrupted by a shout from outside. The students were on their way down to the beach and they were wondering whether Lucy would like to join them.

'Go on, love,' Bernie urged her. 'You might as well go and have some fun. We'd better stay around here in case there's anything we can do for Glenys and the kids – or in case the police want to see us again, but there's no reason why you can't try to salvage something in the way of a holiday.'

The four young men stood in a huddle, just outside the low apartment wall, waiting while Lucy went into her bedroom to collect her swimsuit and a towel. They were surprised to hear Cameron calling down to them from his balcony.

'Are you going to the beach?' he shouted, sounding unusually self-assured. 'Can I come with you?'

'Course you can,' Gary called back. 'Come on down. We're just waiting for Lucy.'

Peter and Bernie exchanged glances.

'I wonder what Mark's reaction will be to that,' Bernie murmured. 'Do you think he's come round to the idea that students are not all bad?'

Seemingly not. A few minutes later, Lucy and Cameron both joined the little group waiting in the paved area around the pool. Joshua greeted them warmly and the group of youngsters started off. Lucy waved and called out that she would be back at lunchtime. However, when they came to the corner of the building they found their way barred by Mark Price, standing with his legs apart and arms outstretched.

'Not so fast,' he said firmly. 'Cameron – you're needed here. You can't go off enjoying yourself. Think of your Aunty Glenys and the kids.'

For a moment Cameron wavered. He was fond of his aunt and did not want to upset her further. On the other hand, he did not think that his presence was likely to help her much. He tried to think of a way of explaining that he was trying to keep out from under her feet at this difficult time – and then he considered changing his plans and staying at home after all – and then his father, impatient at his lack of response, went on.

'And I've told you before: I'm not having you going off

alone with –'

'With what?' Cameron retorted, going very red. 'With a load of students? With a couple of *coloured boys*? With a Muslim who's probably plotting to blow us all up?'

'With lads three or four years older than you,' Mark said, thinking on his feet for an argument that would not antagonise his son further. He regretted having been quite so outspoken in expressing his opinion of the students whom, he had to admit, had shown commendable concern for his sister-in-law. 'It stands to reason that they'll want to do things that aren't suitable for –'

'You said it was up to me to decide what I do,' Cameron argued, remembering his father's words from the previous evening, 'and I've decided to go to the beach with Josh and his mates.'

'Well you can just *un*-decide it. You're needed here and here you are going to stay.'

'Bollocks!' Cameron exclaimed rudely, deliberately using one of his father's favourite expletives. He stepped forward, intending to skirt round Mark and make for the slope down to the driveway, but Mark darted sideways and blocked his path. Cameron tried to dodge, but Mark was there before him. Cameron changed direction again and Mark reached out to grab hold of him – and fell to the ground as Lucy neatly tripped him with her foot. She took Cameron by the arm and hustled him out of the gate.

'Now – run for it!' she said to him in a low voice.

All six young people raced off down the drive, while Mark lay on the ground, too stunned for a moment or two to attempt to follow. Bernie went over to help him up.

'I'm afraid my daughter is a bit of an anarchist,' she apologised, trying unsuccessfully to suppress a grin. 'She doesn't approve of an authoritarian approach to parenting.'

'Don't you worry about Cameron,' Peter added, as Mark scrambled to his feet and brushed himself down. 'Lucy will see he doesn't come to any harm.'

Mark grunted something that might have been thanks to Bernie for her assistance and nodded towards Peter.

'I'd better see how Glenys is getting on,' he mumbled, pushing open the gate to his sister-in-law's apartment. 'See you later.'

'That was neat footwork,' Craig said admiringly to Lucy when they slowed to a walk, convinced that they were not being pursued.

'All part of making sure I keep getting picked for the first team,' she grinned back at him. 'And you never know when it may come in handy off the pitch as well!'

They reached the beach and saw, stretching out before them, a wide expanse of smooth sand. Lucy immediately proposed building a sand castle. Cameron looked at her dubiously.

'Isn't that a bit childish?' he asked.

'Of course!' Lucy laughed. 'That's part of the fun. Come on! The tide's just right and with all these civil engineers about, we should be able to design a magnificent fortress.'

She put her rucksack down on the ground and took out a small plastic spade with which she proceeded to mark out a large rectangle in the damp sand. Ibrahim immediately took off his own rucksack and got down on his hands and knees to help her.

'That's cool,' he declared. 'What's the plan? Are you going to dig a moat right round the edge?'

'That's right – and we always put the drawbridge at the back, so it'll be the last thing the sea reaches, otherwise it collapses before the moat fills up properly.'

'How do you know the tide's coming in?' Craig wanted to know.

'I downloaded the tide tables off the internet,' Lucy explained. 'Now are you helping or what?'

They were soon all busily engaged in the building. Even

Cameron overcame his inhibitions and joined in.

'I'll take a photo of you,' Lucy said as she watched him carefully patting the sand down to compact it and make the structure stronger, under directions from Craig. 'Then you'll have evidence to show your dad that we haven't been leading you astray into anything unsuitable for someone of your tender years.'

'I don't know,' Cameron answered, grinning up at her. 'There's no pleasing him sometimes. He'd probably think there was something pervy about grown men making sandcastles.'

Eventually the castle was finished and the little group looked down with satisfaction at the fruit of their labours. Lucy had to admit that it was the most magnificent that she had ever built. The keep stood three feet high and it was surrounded by a wall with towers at each corner and a tall gatehouse at the back, guarding the drawbridge. Gary, whose broken arm had limited his digging capacity had collected shells and interesting pebbles with which to decorate the edifice and Ibrahim had revealed his artistic skills by using some of the smaller stones to fashion a mosaic Liver Bird on the front face of the keep. Lucy clapped her hands in delight when she recognised the familiar shape.

'I *must* take a picture of that,' she declared. 'My mam will be dead chuffed when she sees it.'

Leaving Gary to guard the castle, the others went for a swim to while away the time until the tide reached the moat. Then they returned and lay drying in the sun as the water crept slowly up the beach towards them. Lucy looked at Cameron's red face and peeling nose and offered him some sunscreen.

'We always carry some factor 45 around with us,' she told him,' because Peter burns so easily. It's his red hair that does it. Mam and I are lucky; we tend to go brown instead of red.'

'Like my dad,' said Cameron, accepting the proffered

tube. 'That's just another of the things that annoys him about me. He's always wanting to get out into the great outdoors and Mum's there telling him to make sure I wear a hat and cover up if the sun comes out.'

'How does your mum feel about the divorce?' Lucy asked. Divorce was something outside her personal experience and she was interested to know how it came about. 'I mean – does she regret it at all, or is she just glad to get out?'

'Dunno. For a while I knew they weren't getting on, but they tried to hide it all from me, so it came as a bit of a bombshell when they told me they were splitting up.'

'That must have made it hard for you,' Lucy suggested. Cameron shrugged.

'I dunno. Dad and I never hit it off, so in a way it was a relief not to have him around being disappointed in me. And mum let me drop things like the Army Cadets and boxing and rugger. So …'

'That's rather sad,' Lucy said thoughtfully. 'I don't mean the boxing and rugby; I mean it's sad that you and your dad had so little in common. Isn't there anything that you're both interested in?'

Cameron thought for a while, then shrugged. 'Nope.'

'What about your uncle Owen? How did you get on with him?'

'Oh, he was alright.'

'And did they get on OK – your dad and his brother, I mean? Some brothers are always fighting.'

'They got on OK – hey! What *is* all this?' Cameron suddenly realised that he was being pumped for information. 'Are you interrogating me?'

'In the nicest possible way,' Lucy said coyly. 'Aren't you flattered that I'm taking such an interest in your family?'

'Not if it's so you can report it all back to your policeman friend.'

'Don't you want to find out who pushed your uncle off the balcony?'

'Not if it means my dad or Aunty Glenys going to jail.'

'Glenys wasn't there,' Lucy pointed out. 'She didn't get back until later. So ...' she paused, wondering whether to go on or to let things drop, 'so, at the moment, it's not looking that good for your dad. Which is why I wondered if they got on. I mean – I wondered if he could have pushed him off by accident – you know, playing around, pushing and shoving the way some people do.'

Cameron did not answer. Instead, he stood up and started to roll up his towel.

'Oh Cameron! I'm sorry,' Lucy said, pulling his arm so that he collapsed on the sand next to her. 'At least stay until the sand castle falls. The sea's nearly here now.'

As she spoke, a wave, closer than any that had come before, raced up the beach and dribbled into the moat.

'Not long now,' Ibrahim said excitedly. 'Let's dig a trench to let the water in.'

He picked up Lucy's spade and started excavating a V-shaped gully to funnel the advancing sea towards the castle moat. Craig and Joshua joined in, digging with their hands, while Lucy, Cameron and Gary looked on.

The sea was coming in fast now. They retreated up the beach and deposited their bags and towels above the high water mark. Then they went back to watch as the castle gradually sank beneath the waves. Cameron tentatively put out his arm and took Lucy's hand in his. She looked up and smiled at him.

'I think maybe it's time I was getting back,' she said. 'I promised I'd be in for lunch.'

The four students decided to have lunch in one of the beach cafés, so Lucy and Cameron walked back alone together.

'My mum told me that she went out with Uncle Owen before she started seeing my dad,' Cameron told Lucy. 'Then he – Uncle Owen – got posted to Germany and she started going out with Dad.'

'How did Owen feel about that?'

'Dunno. I wasn't born then, was I? All I know is, it was about ten years before he got hitched to Aunty Glenys. Mum and Glenys always got on, but Glenys never liked my dad and Dad blamed her for Mum asking for a divorce. I don't think he wanted Mum to leave. So, now you know it all. I'm sure Dad wouldn't have pushed Uncle Owen off the balcony and I'm even more sure that Aunty Glenys wouldn't have. And I know for certain *I* didn't – so I hope your policeman can think of someone else, or else that Kirsty woman changes her mind about what she saw.'

26 FOLD TO THY HEART THY BROTHER

'Kids! Eh?' Jonah said to Mark, manoeuvring his chair into the space between the sun lounger upon which Mark was reclined and one of the raised flower beds in the pool area. 'My two boys both went through various stages of rebellion, but they both turned out alright in the end.'

Mark looked up and acknowledged Jonah's presence with a slight movement of his head. His mother had shooed him away when he called in to offer his support, telling him that she had plenty to do with getting three children up, dressed and breakfasted, without having a man around the place getting under her feet. Mark did not fancy going back upstairs to his own empty apartment, so he settled down in the early morning sun, choosing a position from which he could monitor the return of his son – whenever that might occur.

'Mind you,' Jonah went on conversationally, 'there must be different pressures when you've only got the one. Our two used to be at each other's throats one minute and ganging up against us the next!'

'Are you divorced?'

'No – a widower.'

'I'm sorry. How long?'

'Just over two years.'

'So not until after you were shot?'

'That's right. She was diagnosed with cancer four years after it happened.'

'That's bad luck.'

'Yes. I was very lucky to have our Bernie and old Peter to fall back on, so to speak.'

'Yes. I was wondering about that. How come …?'

'Peter and I were in the police force together for years,' Jonah explained. 'You'll understand how it is – not quite comrades in arms, but the same sort of thing.'

Mark nodded.

'And Bernie's first husband – that's Lucy's father – was our commanding officer when we were both just striplings. That's what brought us all together after he died. And then, I got myself shot and they rallied round and, well – here we all are!'

'I thought maybe your marriage might have broken up because of what happened to you – if she couldn't handle it, I mean,' Mark said, after a short pause. 'You don't think about … I mean, these days that's how most marriages end, isn't it, divorce?'

'Was that what happened with your wife? Did she find it hard being an army wife? I've heard some people just can't cope.'

'I don't think it was so much the army as such – more the baggage that comes with being out on active service. I guess she got used to it being just her and Cameron and then it was difficult having me back and expecting her to understand about all the things I'd been through. She could have tried harder though. It's not much to ask – just to listen – but she just wasn't interested.'

'You must have envied Owen,' Jonah suggested, hoping to prompt Mark to talk about his relationship with his brother. 'Glenys seemed to me to be a hundred percent behind him all the time.'

'Yes,' Mark agreed. 'But she wasn't happy. Julie had been working on her – turning her against the army – she'd been on at Owen to jack it in and find a civilian job.'

'And how did he react to that?'

'I guess you'd say *politely*, but I don't think he ever seriously considered it. He was a fucking good officer and he knew it. And he wouldn't have wanted to let Dad down.'

They sat in silence for a moment or two.

'Owen was due to go out to the Middle East next week,' Mark said suddenly. 'It was all very hush-hush, but, whatever the official line was, we all knew that meant Syria. Glenys was *not* happy at all about that, but she'd no right to complain because, it was his job to obey orders – not to mention the fact that *officially* he was going to be a military advisor in Iraq. I think she was giving him a hard time about it, though.'

'I suppose it must be difficult for her being left at home with three kids.'

'She knew what she was signing up for when she married him.' Mark was uncompromising. 'She got what she wanted: escape from that pokey little flat above her dad's ironmonger's. But, to be fair, she never used to complain. It's just now that Julie's got her claws into her.'

'Or perhaps she was just worried that he might be in real danger,' Jonah suggested mildly. 'A top secret mission to Syria sounds risky to me.'

'Yes. It's ironic isn't it? After so much time out in war zones, fancy him getting himself killed on holiday with the kids in Portugal!'

'How do you think your sister-in-law will manage? I suppose, she must have been ready for it in a way – with him having been out on the front line so many times – but nothing ever really prepares you for it when it comes.'

'Oh Mum'll take over and sort everything out for her. She's a great organiser.'

'What about her own parents?'

'Like I said, they've got this little shop in Swansea. They'll be far too busy with that to help Glenys with the kids, and there's no room for them to go to stay there. No. Mum will move in and manage everything.'

'It sounds as if you speak from experience.'

'Too right I do. She's been managing me ever since Julie left – and she managed Dad to death before that.' Mark smiled and Jonah reflected that it was the first time that he had seen any evidence that the older Price brother possessed a sense of humour. 'Now, look who it is! Your queer friends have arrived.'

Jonah looked up and saw Wayne and Dean coming up the path from the driveway. They waved at him and hurried over. Wayne addressed Mark seriously.

'We wanted to say how sorry we were to hear about your brother.'

'We came round to see if there's anything we can do,' Dean added.

'Thanks.' For a moment or two Mark did not know what to say. 'But, as I was just telling Jonah, now that my mother has arrived, everyone else is surplus to requirements.'

Wayne grinned. 'My mum's a bit like that.'

'No she isn't!' Dean protested. 'You just don't like the way she tries to make you tidy up your mess. If you weren't such a slob, she wouldn't need to keep on at you.'

Mark smiled, in spite of himself. He could not help being reminded of the banter that he and his wife used to exchange, before everything had turned sour and her light-hearted complaints about Wendy's interference in their affairs had changed to become part of the portfolio of evidence to justify her demand for a divorce.

'Why don't you two go in and rout out Peter and Bernie?' Jonah suggested. They *said* they were just going to tidy the flat, but they've been long enough to spring clean it from top to bottom.'

'You don't think we might be interrupting something,' Wayne said, winking. 'You know: kids off elsewhere, couple on their own for the first time in ages …'

'Much more likely to be old Peter agonising over whether he's got all the ingredients for a really authentic Portuguese something-or-other recipe. He seems to be turning into some sort of culinary connoisseur!'

'Don't knock it,' Dean laughed. 'I remember his Jamaican patties – they're something to write home about alright!'

'*They* are a labour of love,' Jonah said gravely. 'You never knew Peter's first wife, did you? Neither did I, but I wish I had.'

The two young men went inside and Jonah turned back to Mark.

'I owe a lot to those two,' he observed. 'Over the years they've made things a lot easier for me and those around me. It's amazing some of the things they come up with – and, as you can see, they're always ready to go the extra mile.'

'I've been surprised how many people keep offering to help *us*,' Mark remarked. 'The Barringtons are taking Glenys out this afternoon to organise repatriation of the body – once it's released, that is – and even those students! Fancy them thinking about Glenys being more comfortable with the kids on the ground floor!'

'Yes,' Jonah agreed. 'It is remarkable the way people rally round in a crisis. In fact, people are generally a lot nicer than we tend to think.'

27 A LITTLE CHILD MAY KNOW

That afternoon, Glenys left the children in the care of Claire Barrington while she and Neil went off to complete the various formalities associated with arranging for her husband's body to be returned to England. Wendy insisted on going with them. She clearly did not trust Neil to take proper care of her daughter-in-law or to be capable of dealing appropriately with foreign officials. Neil assured her that he had assisted holidaymakers in similar situations before, but Wendy remained unconvinced.

'At least they're not relying solely on Tim the stand-in consul,' Bernie whispered to Jonah as they departed. 'He very much had the appearance of a chocolate teapot when he came round.'

Claire had come armed with a variety of craft activities to keep the children occupied. She sat them all down around the plastic table on the patio of their new apartment and showed them how to make a pot by rolling modelling clay between their hands and then winding it round in a spiral. Holly soon got the knack, but Freya could not make the layers balance on top of one another and Danny completed his pot very quickly and then smashed it flat with his fist. Claire patiently suggested that he might like to make something different – what was he interested in? Eventually he settled down happily moulding a family of fearsome dinosaurs while Freya contented herself with rolling out clay sausages and handing them over to her sister to be made into ever more elaborate designs of plates, bowls and vases.

Bernie stood watching over the wall as Claire expertly managed her small class. Then she turned to Peter, who was sitting in his accustomed place on the shady side of the patio reading a book.

'What shall we do this afternoon?' she asked. 'It seems rather callous to go off sight-seeing as if nothing had happened, but there doesn't seem to be anything much we can do to help at the moment.'

'It's too hot for anything as energetic as your sort of sight-seeing,' Peter replied without looking up. 'I vote we stay around here until tea time and leave off the route marches and hill walking until the cool of the evening!'

Bernie had to admit that Peter was right. The temperature had risen during the day and was now a sizzling thirty-two degrees. By common consent, they took drinks and books out and set up camp around the pool in the shade of the umbrellas. Lucy and Bernie splashed around in the pool while Peter and Jonah contented themselves with reading. After a few minutes, Cameron and Mark appeared, dressed in swimming trunks and carrying towels, which they put on sun loungers at the opposite side of the pool from where Peter and Jonah were sitting. The small pool suddenly felt very crowded and Bernie climbed out and went to join her husband in the shade. A few minutes later Lucy followed her.

'Is it OK for me to go with Cameron to the big pool?' she asked. 'This one is too small for serious swimming.'

'Good idea,' Mark called out, having overheard her question. 'I'll race you there.'

'Actually,' Peter put in hastily, 'I was hoping you might stay around here and give us a hand.'

'You go on, love,' Bernie urged Lucy. 'Make the most of it. You know what time to be back.'

'Sure,' Mark answered, turning to face Peter. 'What is it you need me to do?'

'Er ...,' Peter struggled to think of an excuse for asking Mark to remain with them instead of accompanying his son to the other pool.

'Hydrotherapy!' Bernie said, with sudden inspiration. She had understood immediately that Peter was trying to arrange for Lucy and Cameron to have some time together away from parental supervision. 'This small pool is just perfect for Jonah, but of course he would need lifting in and out.'

'Of course I'll help. No problem.' Mark sounded pleased to have been asked.

'Come along,' Bernie said to Jonah. 'Come inside and I'll get you changed into your swimming things.'

Jonah said nothing, but made his way into the apartment and down the corridor to the bedroom. He hated people to see his wasted limbs and normally insisted on dressing in long trousers and long-sleeved shirts in public. Even on this holiday, he had only agreed to wearing shorts for brief periods of time and within the confines of the private patio.

'Couldn't you have thought of some other favour for Captain Price to do for us?' he complained, as Bernie stripped him and dressed him in a pair of Peter's swimming trunks.

'Sorry! It was the only thing I could think of on the spur of the moment.'

'The things I do for this family!' Jonah grumbled. 'I hope young Lucy is suitably grateful; that's all I can say.'

'You have *my* undying gratitude, even if she doesn't care,' Bernie assured him. 'Now do your best to pretend to enjoy it and we'll get you out as soon as we can, OK?'

Half an hour later, Peter and Mark lifted Jonah out of the pool and deposited him gently on one of the sun loungers. Bernie stepped forward with a towel and started to pat him dry.

'Thank you,' Peter said gratefully. 'We really appreciate your help.'

'Any time.' Mark answered with a shrug. He seemed unused to being thanked and unsure how to react.

As soon as he was dry, Jonah asked to be taken inside and dressed again. Mark offered to lift him into his chair, but Bernie assured him that it was unnecessary. She demonstrated how easy it was for a single person – even someone as slight as Lucy, say, to transfer Jonah from the sun lounger to the chair by adjusting it into a reclining position, lowering it to bring it level with the lounger and then rolling him on to it.

'Very impressive,' was Mark's verdict. 'I've never seen anything like that before.'

'It's all down to Wayne and Dean,' Peter told him. 'They designed the whole thing.'

'I suppose you think that means I ought to approve of their lifestyle,' Mark muttered.

'Not at all. The two things have nothing to do with each other.'

'You're entitled to your views,' Jonah added to Peter's reply, 'but you can't expect us to share them.'

He brought the chair back into its upright position and headed off for the apartment with Bernie following.

'Doesn't it worry you, having your wife dressing and undressing another man all the time?' Mark asked Peter.

'Why on earth should it? My first wife was a nurse. She was doing intimate things to male patients every day in her work. If I was going to have hang-ups about that sort of thing, I'd have gone barmy years ago! It's just a job.'

'Do you think so?' Mark sounded sceptical.

'Well,' Peter smiled, 'I suppose with Jonah it's a bit more than that, but no – it really doesn't bother me.'

'Where's my triceratops?' A wail from Danny interrupted their conversation. The boy had got out his dinosaur collection to provide models on which to base his own clay figures and had now discovered that it was incomplete. 'Holly,' he went on accusingly, 'have you taken it?'

'No of course not!' his sister replied indignantly. 'I don't want your stupid dinosaurs. I expect you dropped it.'

Peter got up and walked over. 'If I may butt in,' he said, looking over the wall to where Holly and Danny were still busy with the clay, 'I may be able to clear up this little mystery for you.'

'Have *you* got my triceratops?' Danny asked belligerently.

'No, but I know who does. Your dad was holding it when he fell, so it's an important piece of evidence and the police are keeping it safe.'

'Really?' Danny opened his eyes wide at the thought that one of his toys was in police custody.

'Yes. And they'd be really interested to know *why* he was holding it,' Peter went on. 'Do you have any idea?'

'No.' Danny shook his head. 'I put them all lined up on the balcony, so they could look out for us coming back from the Kids Club, but Mum wouldn't let them. She put them all away in the cupboard before we went.'

'Do you think she could have missed one and your dad was tidying it away for her?' Peter asked.

'No,' Danny was adamant. 'She picked up the triceratops first. I saw her put it in the box and put the box in the cupboard.'

'Where's Jonah? I want him to read to me.' Freya pushed her brother out of the way and looked up at Peter. She had tried clay modelling, colouring and French knitting in rapid succession and now, tired of them all, had decided that it was time that one of the adults did something to entertain her.

'He's just getting dressed after his swim,' Peter told her. 'Will I do? I'm an expert at reading bedtime stories. Lucy will vouch for me, if you don't believe me. That's the only reason our Bernie married me. What would you like us to read?'

'I don't believe you,' Freya said, after considering for a minute.

'That I'm good at reading stories?' Peter asked, his eyes twinkling. 'Why not try me and see?'

'No. I meant that's not why she married you. That would be silly.'

'What would be silly?' Jonah asked, reappearing dressed in cream-coloured long trousers and a light green open-necked shirt. Bernie followed him out through the gate and sat down next to Peter.

'She won't believe that Bernie chose me because I was so good at reading bedtime stories to Lucy when she was younger,' Peter told them. 'You tell her Bernie.'

'He's quite right,' Bernie told Freya solemnly. 'That and the cooking and the shopping and the cleaning,' she added with a grin.

'I think you're both being silly,' Freya declared, frowning at them from beneath her thick fringe. Then she turned to look at Jonah. 'Will you read to me now?'

'Of course! Climb aboard. I've got something to show you. It's called an e-book.'

Freya climbed on to Jonah's lap and he showed her how he could display pages of a book on the screen attached to his chair.

'My little granddaughter, Carolyn, is about your age,' he told her. 'I've got some books on my computer for when she comes to see me. *I* can turn the pages of these ones – look!'

Freya watched, fascinated, for a little while. Then she became bored and slipped off his lap.

'I like proper books better. Wait here!' she commanded, disappearing into the apartment in search of one of her own books. She nearly collided with Holly, who was bringing out a tray loaded with her pottery masterpieces to show them. Claire Barrington followed her out and stood behind her ready to catch the tray if she appeared to be about to drop it. They all looked at the bowls, cups and vases and made suitably admiring remarks about Holly's handiwork. She smiled with pleasure at their compliments, then suddenly appeared to remember something and became serious.

'It was Mummy's fault that Daddy fell off the balcony,' she said unexpectedly, her bottom lip starting to tremble. 'If she hadn't made us go to the Kids Club, it wouldn't have happened.'

'Why's that?' asked Jonah, trying to sound casual but in reality burning with curiosity.

'We wouldn't have let it!' she was nearly crying now. 'And Mummy wouldn't have let him get up on the wall. She always got very cross about that. She kept on and on telling Uncle Mark off about it,' she added, giving Mark a hard stare.

'It was *your* idea to go,' Danny pointed out.

'No it wasn't. You said you wanted to be a pirate.'

'You said it first.'

Freya returned, carrying a pile of books, which she put down on the sun lounger next to Peter and Bernie. Then she took the top one and climbed with it on to Jonah's lap. He hardly seemed to notice. He was much more interested in the argument between Holly and her brother.

'I *did* want to go,' Holly conceded, 'but not after I found out Karl Blomberg was going to be there. I said I wanted us to go to the beach instead, but Mummy said it was too late and I had to go.'

'*I* didn't want to go either,' Freya added. She was not sure what this was all about, but she wanted to make sure that everyone knew that she had not been part of a conspiracy to go to the Kids Club, now that Holly had suggested that there was something wrong about it.

Holly started to cry and the tray wobbled dangerously in her hand. Claire stepped forward and took it gently from her.

'I'll put that down,' she said kindly but firmly. 'And then I need you to come with me to the bar and help me carry back an ice cream for everyone.'

'I can do that for you,' Danny volunteered eagerly.

'Thank you Danny. I'm going to need you both.'

Claire carried the tray back into the apartment and came out with her handbag over her arm and a packet of tissues in her hands. She took one out and wiped Holly's nose and face.

'What about you, Freya? Are you happy to stay with Inspector Porter while we get you an ice cream?'

Freya nodded. She had already opened her book was wondering when everyone would stop talking and allow Jonah to read it to her. He was staring straight ahead, thinking about what Holly had said. He wondered why Glenys Price had been so determined to send the three children to the Kids Club on Tuesday afternoon. Did she have something planned to do with Owen while they were alone? Or could she have been making an opportunity to confront Mark? Or was it a simple case of trying to impress upon Holly that she could not expect everyone around her to change their plans according to her personal whims?

'Come on!' Freya interrupted his reverie. 'Read!'

Jonah forced himself to turn his attention to the adventures of Dilly the Dinosaur and his annoying big sister. They had not got far when there was another interruption. The students were back. They had met Claire, Holly and Danny outside the bar and had insisted on helping to carry back ice creams for everyone. Now the two children were each licking giant cones piled high with multi-coloured scoops of ice cream while the students carried two each and Claire was left empty-handed. There was some confusion as everyone settled down and the ice creams were handed out.

Mark looked very surprised when Ibrahim handed a cone of chocolate-flavoured ice cream to him, but he took it graciously and sat down on the edge of one of the raised beds to eat it. There was a moment of embarrassment when Craig, without thinking, held out his spare cone towards Jonah. Bernie deftly intercepted it and prepared to hold it for him to eat. Then, looking round, she spotted Ibrahim sitting with his hands clasped in his lap.

'Hi Ibrahim!' she called to him. 'Seeing as you can't eat with us, do you think you could make yourself useful and hold this for Jonah?'

The young man looked up, smiling and came across eagerly to help. Jonah was not best pleased at having a stranger feeding him, but forced himself to smile back and mumble some words of gratitude.

Danny demolished his ice cream within a few minutes and, seeing that everyone else was still engaged in eating, he leapt to his feet and began his favourite game of pretending to be a sniper on a mission to pick off enemy fighters. He hid behind a palm tree, emerging briefly every so often to fire imaginary bullets at members of the party. Then he dashed across to take cover behind a large terracotta pot containing a shrub with clusters of pink flowers. When he emerged from this vantage point and took aim again, Gary, who had just finished his ice cream, obligingly clutched at his heart and subsided into a clump of yellow daisies in the raised bed behind where he was sitting.

Danny crowed with delight and came over to look down on his vanquished foe. Gary opened his eyes and looked up at the boy, grinning broadly.

'I'm dead,' he announced, lying back and assuming a ghastly expression with his eyes wide and staring and his mouth open in a grimace.

Danny grinned back. Then he looked from Gary up to the balcony above and back again and his face became first serious and then puzzled.

'Why *aren't* you dead? You fell just as far as Daddy did.'

There was a sudden hush as the various conversations

that had started up came to a sudden halt. Everyone looked towards Danny. For a few moments, nobody knew what to say.

'Your daddy was very unlucky,' Peter said at last. 'He fell awkwardly and we think he must have broken his neck. Nobody could have known that he would be badly injured. The chances were he would have just got away with a few bruises.'

Nobody could have known Jonah repeated silently to himself.

'Not even the person who pushed him off?' Danny asked boldly.

'Who told you someone pushed him off?' Claire asked sharply. 'We don't know that. It was probably just an accident.'

'You've all been talking about it,' Danny protested. 'Mum and Uncle Mark and that policeman. Everyone!'

'Well, we're not going to talk about it any more,' Claire said firmly. 'Now, if you've finished your ice creams, let's all go to the playground and run off some of that energy before your mum gets back.'

Nobody could have known Jonah mused again as Freya slipped off his lap and trotted after her siblings. *Is that the answer to what's been going on here?*

28 FORWARD INTO BATTLE

'You wanted to see me?' Eduardo Rosario said as Peter let him in through the patio doors that evening. 'Do you have more evidence to tell me about?'

'Not evidence, exactly,' Jonah admitted. 'More a bit of a hunch. But I'd like to see what you think. Sit down and I'll tell you how my mind's been working.'

Eduardo took a seat on the sofa and looked towards Jonah expectantly.

'I'm coming to the conclusion,' Jonah said, 'that we're not looking at a murder at all.'

Eduardo raised his eyebrows questioningly.

'I don't mean he wasn't pushed. I just don't think whoever did it intended to kill him.'

'And why is that?'

'Well, I think we're agreed that whoever it was, it was most likely one of the people staying in this block of apartments. A stranger coming in would have been sure to be noticed by me or Peter or the Barringtons.'

'Unless he – or she – came earlier and hid in the store room,' Eduardo pointed out.

'Do you have any evidence that anyone did that?' Jonah asked with interest.

'No. I merely remind you that we agreed that it was a possibility.'

'A possibility,' Jonah agreed,' but not very likely. And even if they came earlier, they would still have had to get past anyone who was sitting round the pool or on any of the apartment balconies. So I think we can assume that it's much more likely that it was someone from within this small group of people, *all of whom* knew that a young man had fallen off one of the balconies a few days earlier and done very little damage to himself. That being the case, it doesn't make sense for any of them to push Owen Price off the balcony wall with a view to killing him, but they might have done it intending to teach him a lesson or even as a joke.'

'And who would have wanted to do that?'

'The obvious candidates are family members. I'm glad the children were all undeniably at the Kids Club – otherwise I'd have had my money on it being one of them. Danny, for instance, could so easily have done it, pretending the awing pole was a lance and he was a knight fighting in a tournament or something. However, with them safely out of the way, we're left with Mark, who might well have wanted to take his brother down a peg or two, and Cameron –'

'Not Cameron!' Lucy interrupted indignantly. 'Why would he want to hurt Owen?'

'I wasn't thinking so much of Owen as that he might have mistaken him for Mark,' Jonah explained, wishing that he had approached the possibility of Cameron's guilt with greater caution. 'The sort of thing I had in mind was a row with his dad, after which he sets off down to the pool, but then he thinks of something more to say and comes back – or, better, maybe he goes to see his Uncle Owen to ask for advice. Then, when he looks in at their apartment, he thinks he sees his dad on the balcony wall and –'

'I don't believe a word of it!' Lucy declared emphatically. 'But don't let that stop you. Go ahead. Tell us what you think happened.'

'Actually,' Jonah said quietly, 'as it happens, I don't think it was Cameron who did it.'

'Who then?' asked Lucy grumpily.

'I think the most likely person was Glenys.'

'But she didn't get back until after Owen fell,' Peter pointed out.

'Ah, now there's something I want to show you on that score,' Jonah said mysteriously. 'Come with me.'

He led the way outside and round the corner of the building to the path that led to the staircase. Part way down he stopped and gestured with his head towards the raised bed that separated this path from the one leading down to the gate and the driveway beyond.

'Look at that,' he said, looking towards a clump of herbaceous plants with small green leaves and spikes of blue flowers. Between those blue flowers and those bushes – there! Do you see? It's almost like a path.'

They looked and saw that there was indeed a track through the low-growing bushes. Several people had walked across the bed, compacting the earth and crushing some of the smaller plants.

'It's a shortcut,' Bernie said. 'If you don't want to go all the way round the bed, all you have to do is climb up, walk across here and then jump down on the other side.'

'And, if you did that,' Peter agreed, 'you wouldn't be seen coming in from the road and going up the stairs.'

'Precisely! Jonah said triumphantly. 'And that's what I think Glenys Price did when she came back from the Kids Club on Tuesday afternoon.'

'However, this does not prove that it was she who did it,' Eduardo said thoughtfully. 'Someone else could have used this path – and escaped this way again afterwards.' He sighed. 'We ought to have seen this before – when we came to look at the crime scene yesterday. Now it is too late to look for footprints or other signs of who may have passed this way.'

'I'd say it was already too late on Wednesday,' Peter commented. 'It was probably even too late by the time the police came on Tuesday. We'd had the ambulance crew and the hotel manager, not to mention all of us tramping around all over the place by then. Unless someone completely unexpected walked across that patch of ground and left traces it wouldn't tell us anything much. After all, for all we know, the Prices used that path on a regular basis.'

'I bet Danny knew about it and used it,' Bernie agreed. 'It would be just the sort of place he'd like to hide and jump out at people.'

They turned to go back inside and almost collided with the Barringtons who were on their way out. *Of course!* Jonah thought with a pang of guilt. *They are on their way to the Healing Service.* He looked towards Lucy, who seemed oblivious to this oversight.

'I'm sorry, Lucy,' Jonah said, in a low voice. 'I completely forgot about the service – honestly. I wasn't trying to get out of it. Really I wasn't.'

'I told you before,' she whispered back. 'It's no big deal.'

Peter closed the door firmly behind them. They all sat down and looked round at one another.

'So your theory is that Senhora Price killed her husband accidentally by pushing him off the balcony?' Eduardo said to Jonah. 'May I ask what reason she had for doing that?'

'Presumably we're still working on the idea that Glenys thought that it was Mark sitting on the wall,' Peter said. 'I can see what you're getting at. She comes home – using the shortcut that she often uses – and sees Mark sitting there, where she's told him, time and time again, not to sit, and she decides to show him how dangerous it really is.'

'Perhaps,' Jonah nodded, 'but actually, I think it was more premeditated than that. Do you remember what Holly said about Glenys insisting that they all went to the Kids Club, even though Freya didn't want to go – and I remember now, she said as much to me that very morning – and Holly had changed her mind? I think she wanted all the children out of the way because she'd already made plans to give Mark his comeuppance.'

'I think you're reading too much into that,' Peter argued. 'When our kids were young there were lots of times when Angie and I would have been grateful for a chance to get them out of the way so we could have some time to ourselves.'

'The way the kids talked, I got the impression that this was something unusual,' Jonah insisted. 'If you remember, the whole point of the holiday was for them to have time with Owen before he went off on active service again.'

'You know, you may be right,' Bernie said slowly. 'In fact, I wonder … could it have been a conspiracy between Glenys and Owen? They were both clearly embarrassed by Mark's behaviour. Could the plan have been that Glenys would get the kids out of the way while Owen sorted Mark out? And then, when she gets back, she looks into the apartment and see, as she thinks, Mark sitting up there on the wall, bold as brass, and Owen nowhere to be seen. She assumes that Own has bottled out and decides to take things into her own hands. She picks up the awning pole and pushes him off. Then, when she hears the commotion below, it suddenly dawns on her that she's pushed a man off a balcony and she could be charged with assault or even attempted murder. If Owen had done it, it was highly unlikely that Mark would press charges, but would he feel so inhibited when it came to Glenys? So she runs down, flinging the awning pole inside Mark's flat as she goes, and goes back across the flower bed ready to come round the corner as if she'd just got back from delivering the children to the Kids Club.'

'I have one objection to that scenario,' Eduardo said. 'We have examined both of the awning poles that were found in the apartment of Senhor Mark Price. What we found was surprising.'

'Tell me more,' Jonah urged, as Eduardo paused.

'They had both been cleaned very thoroughly and very recently,' he told them. 'Our forensics team tell me that they have been washed and scrubbed using detergent and water. Consequently, the only fingerprints on them are those of Senhor Mark Price, from when he handed the poles to you,' he looked towards Peter, 'and your prints from when you took them from him. They did, however, find microscopic traces of blood on the metal hook at the end of one of the poles.'

'Does it match Owen Price?' Jonah asked eagerly.

'We do not know yet. With such small traces, we are awaiting the result of another test. However, the point I wish to make is that whoever used the pole must have kept it in their possession for long enough to effect this cleaning. That is why I dispute your suggestion that Senhora Price put it in her brother's apartment as she was leaving.'

'Point taken.' Jonah thought for a moment. 'But that doesn't make any difference. Nobody looked for the pole until the following day, so Glenys could have cleaned it up later on Tuesday – after the kids were in bed, I expect – and then slipped it into the next-door flat on Wednesday morning, or even overnight.'

'Yes, agreed Bernie. 'And what the cleaning of the pole *does* suggest is that it must have been someone with ongoing access to both apartments. I'd say that definitely rules out the stranger-lurking-in-the-store-cupboard theory. It *has* to be one of the Price family.'

'But not Cameron,' Lucy said firmly. 'Mark watches him like a hawk. He'd never have been able to go round scrubbing down the awning poles without his dad wanting to know what he was up to.'

Eduardo sighed. 'I think that you are right when you say that Mark or Cameron or Glenys must be the guilty one, but I do not see how we will *prove* which of them it was. The evidence is all circumstantial.'

'Our best hope is to get the culprit to confess,' Peter opined. 'They might be persuaded – if we can convince them that we accept that they weren't trying to *kill* anyone.'

'It's not something I'd normally suggest,' Jonah said tentatively, 'but on this occasion I'm wondering if our best chance mightn't be to set up an Agatha Christie-type finale to try to bounce them into an admission of guilt. You know the sort of thing?' He added, looking at Eduardo. 'We gather all the suspects together in the drawing room and go through the evidence, pointing the finger at each in turn and in the end the miscreant realises that the detective is on to him and confesses. Glenys, in particular, might well be bounced into a confession if she thinks that otherwise someone else will be accused of a crime that *she* committed.'

'I am not sure,' Eduardo said doubtfully. 'There is always the risk of a false confession to protect the real killer.'

They sat together for several minutes without speaking.

'What a mess!' Bernie said at last. 'Those poor children! If you're right, Jonah, they'll have lost their mother *and* their father.'

'Even if he's wrong,' Peter agreed gloomily, 'the only other possibility seems to be that it was their uncle who killed their father.'

'I think we ought to go ahead with Jonah's idea,' Lucy said. 'That's the only chance there is of getting it all over with. It's the not knowing that's the worst bit and it could drag on for years if you're waiting for concrete evidence to turn up.'

'Lucy's right,' Bernie backed her up. 'They're bright kids and it won't take them long to realise that the people in the frame are all members of their family. I even think that may be part of what Holly meant when she said that it was her mum's fault that her dad died.'

'What do you say?' Eduardo asked sharply. 'The little

girl accused her mother?'

'No – not like that,' Peter cut in hastily. 'She just said that, if her mother hadn't insisted on the children going to the club that afternoon, their father wouldn't have fallen off the balcony.'

'I see.' Eduardo sat for a few moments thinking. 'Very well,' he said at length, getting up and turning to face Jonah. 'Let us try your experiment. I will come again tomorrow morning at … shall we say ten? Will you see to it that everyone is present?'

'Better make it ten thirty. I don't want to be getting folk out of bed. But, yes, I'll see that everyone's there.'

29 WITH CONTRITE HEART

'I feel I ought to be handing out hymn books,' Bernie said as she ushered the students into their places the following morning. She and Lucy had arranged chairs (brought out from each of the downstairs apartments) in a wide circle, leaving a gap for newcomers to enter and another for Jonah's wheelchair. Peter had gone round as early as he dared, informing the occupants of each apartment that they were required to attend a meeting with the police inspector. Now there was a hum of excited chatter as everyone speculated on what this could be about.

'Is everyone present?' Eduardo asked, arriving in the company of Jonah, who had been waiting for him at the gate.

'All except Kirsty Sumner and Lewis Best,' confirmed Peter, ticking off names on a list.

'And the children?' Eduardo enquired in a low voice, looking round the circle and seeing the three Price youngsters sitting on the ground on front of their mother's chair. Danny had brought his toy dinosaurs and was staging a fight between a tyrannosaurus rex and a stegosaurus. 'Is there somewhere we can send them while we talk?'

'We suggested the Kids Club,' Peter whispered back, 'and Bernie and Lucy volunteered to take them to the playground, but they won't leave their mother.'

'It will make things very difficult having them here.'

'I know, but short of physical restraint I don't know what else we can do. They know something's up and they don't want to be excluded.'

Claire Barrington squeezed past them carrying a pile of colouring books and a box of crayons. She went over to the children and knelt down to talk to them. Danny and Freya each selected a book and started colouring, but Holly sat unmoved, staring towards Jonah and Eduardo, waiting for the proceedings to begin. Claire laid one of the books down in front of her before stepping past and taking her own seat.

'Sorry we're late!' Lewis called, hurrying across the paving with Lily in her buggy. Ibrahim and Craig moved their chairs to make room for the buggy, and Lewis and Kirsty sat down with Lily between them.

Eduardo cleared his throat and Bernie clapped her hands to call the meeting to order.

'I would like to thank you all for coming here today,' Eduardo began, 'and for your patience in answering our questions. I know that you are all very anxious to know what happened to make Major Price fall from the balcony. Inspector Porter has some ideas about that, which he would like to share with you all. I must emphasise that the police investigation is still ongoing and may not be finished for some time, but we thought it was time that you were given some more information about progress so far. Inspector Porter ...'

Jonah inclined his head towards Eduardo in acknowledgement of his introduction. Then he looked slowly round at the assembled company.

'I suppose I'd better start by telling you that we are almost certain that whoever pushed Owen off the balcony must have been one of us here.' He looked round, trying to gauge the reaction to this statement. 'We've been able to establish that some of you could not have done it. Neil, Peter and I were all down here and visible to one another when it happened. The three Price children,' Jonah noted that Danny looked up at this point and both he and Holly watched intently as he continued, 'were at the Kids Club. The time of their arrival is documented in the register.'

Danny returned to his colouring, apparently satisfied that he was not under suspicion. Holly continued to stare at Jonah with a look that might have been anger or perhaps fear. Glenys looked down at the children and then back at Jonah with a strange blank expression that he could not decipher. Was she aware that she was under suspicion? Or did she think that the children's alibi extended to her too? Or was she past thinking about such things?

'Mrs Barrington was inside their apartment,' Jonah continued. 'I saw her go inside shortly before Major Price fell and she would have had to walk across in front of where I was sitting in order to get up to the first floor. I've checked and the wall is too high for anyone to climb over and get round the building the other way. In addition, she came out of her apartment again afterwards, which means that for her to be the perpetrator would have involved crossing the pool area without being noticed *twice*, which seems pretty well inconceivable. Continuing with the ground floor residents, we now come to the occupants of apartment 501. I think you have some information about them, Inspector Rosario?'

'Indeed,' Eduardo agreed, standing up to address the group. 'We have established that Senhor Craig Jenner and Senhor Joshua Compton were out in the bay, riding on the banana boat when the incident occurred. Senhor Gary Knowles was awaiting their return in a café by the marina. We have testimony from the staff there confirming this.'

'What about the other one?' Mark asked belligerently, as Eduardo paused briefly. 'The Muslim. He was here in his apartment, wasn't he?'

'Yes,' Eduardo answered calmly. 'He returned at about one fifteen. He met Senhora Price and the children as they were leaving, and he was seen arriving back by Inspector Porter and Inspector Johns. Indeed, he spoke to them. He had come back for his prayer time, which was due to start at one thirty-five.'

'But you only have his word that he stayed inside praying,' Mark pointed out.

'That is correct,' Eduardo admitted. 'However, it would have been impossible for him to come out through the door of his apartment without being seen by at least three people. We have carried out a minute examination of the side window of his apartment and there is no sign of anyone having climbed through it.'

'That doesn't mean he didn't,' Mark argued. 'And he is by far the most likely person to want to kill a British soldier. He's a fucking Muslim for God's sake!'

'Let's just set that aside for the time being, if you don't mind,' Jonah intervened. 'The police have good reasons to believe that Ibrahim was not responsible for your brother's death, so now I'd like to move on to consider the upstairs flats.'

'Be quiet Mark!' his mother reproved him. It was not clear whether this was because she disagreed with his sentiments, was shocked by his use of such language in front of the children, or was merely disapproving of his bad manners. 'Let the inspector finish.'

'Kirsty Sumner and Lewis Best were both in their apartment on the first floor,' Jonah resumed. 'On the face of it, there is no reason why they might have borne Owen Price any ill-will and, since they were both together, if either of them was involved they must both be. There is also the question of why, when the incident appeared to have passed off as an unfortunate accident, would they then draw attention to him having been pushed?'

'Attention-seekers,' Mark muttered.

'More significantly,' continued Jonah, ignoring the interruption, 'it is unlikely that either of them could have gone into and out of the next-door apartment without being seen either by Glenys Price and the children when they went out or by Cameron when he went down for his swim. Moreover, we know for a fact that the awning pole that was used to push Owen off the balcony ended up in Captain Price's apartment, having been cleaned of fingermarks. It would be very surprising if anyone other than a member of the Price family would have been able to do that.'

'One moment, please,' Wendy Price interjected. 'Am I to understand that you are accusing one of our family of deliberately pushing my son off the balcony in order to kill him?'

'No, Mrs Price. I don't think they intended to do more than inflict a relatively minor injury. A week earlier, this young gentleman,' Jonah looked towards Gary and inclined his head to direct his audience's gaze, 'fell off a similar balcony and merely fractured his arm. I believe that the person who pushed Owen expected him to sustain similarly inconsequential damage.'

'But why?' demanded Mark. 'What would be the point?'

'Ah!' Jonah smiled. 'Now that is where things start to get interesting.'

He looked round to check that he had everyone's full attention before continuing. His eye lighted on Holly Price who was staring earnestly at him with open mouth. She was evidently taking in his every word. He turned back to Wendy Price.

'Mrs Price, I really do think it would be better if you could take the children away now.'

'Yes. Yes, of course.' Mrs Price senior immediately understood. 'Holly, Danny, Freya! Come with me. It's far too hot for you out here in the sun. Come inside with me.'

Recognising the urgency in her voice Danny and Freya scrambled to their feet, but Holly did not want to go.

'No Granny Wendy,' she said stubbornly, 'I want to stay and hear what Jonah says.'

'Mummy will tell you all about it later,' Wendy promised. 'Right now, I want you to come with me. Bring your colouring book with you – you can carry on with it indoors. No arguments!'

Such was the force of Wendy Price's personality that Holly gave in. She bent down and picked up her book, grabbed a fistful of crayons out of the box and followed her grandmother into the apartment, scuffing her feet as she went and wearing a sulky look on her face. Jonah watched them go, waiting until he heard the click of the patio doors closing before he continued.

'I would like you to put yourself in the position of someone looking in through the open apartment door and seeing, beyond the bedrooms and living room, the balcony with the bright midday sun – remember it's summer time, so at one thirty the sun is more or less at its highest and brightest – shining directly in. On the wall of that balcony, sits a man with his back towards you. You know that Captain Mark Price habitually takes up this position, while Major Owen Price has never been known to do so. You see, as I said, a man sitting on a wall, facing away from you with the light behind him. You could be forgiven for not recognising Major Price in this unaccustomed position and for assuming that it is his brother Mark, who has been seen sitting there so often before.'

You could have heard a pin drop, as everyone listened intently to Jonah's description of the scene on the balcony three days earlier. However, it was not the dropping of a pin that interrupted his narrative – it was the sound of footsteps on the cobbles and a low murmur of voices, which announced the arrival of Wayne and Dean, intent on discussing arrangements for travelling home the following day.

'Sorry! Is something going on?' Dean asked when he saw the assembled group. 'We'll come back later.'

'No. Sit down and listen to a fairy story,' Mark growled. 'It should suit you, shouldn't it?'

The two young men looked towards Jonah, who deferred to Eduardo.

'You are Wayne Major and Dean O'Brien?' They nodded. 'Then I think it is better if you stay. I have on record a statement from Captain Price, in which he names you both as potential suspects for the killing of his brother. Therefore, it is appropriate that you should hear what we believe actually happened.' Eduardo turned to address Mark. 'If you do not wish to make enemies, Captain Price, I would advise you in future to be more circumspect in the way you speak.'

'That's telling him!' Lucy whispered to Bernie with a grin.

Wayne and Dean pulled up a sun lounger and sat down on it together.

'For the record,' Eduardo continued, 'we did consider the possibility that Senhor Major or Senhor O'Brien could have been responsible for the death of Major Price. They knew the apartments and they were known to everyone here. It would have raised no suspicion had they been seen here. However, we have irrefutable evidence that they were elsewhere. They took a beginners class in surfing that afternoon. The instructor remembers Senhor Major very well.'

He paused and looked towards the pair with a twinkle in his eye and the suggestion of a smile playing on his lips. Dean grinned and nudged Wayne in the ribs.

'I told you he'd never seen anything like it!' he chortled. 'Talk about incompetent! How anyone can be quite as useless with a surfboard as you, I don't know!'

'So, as you see,' Eduardo went on, 'we are forced to assume that the perpetrator was one of those staying in these apartments. Now, Inspector Porter, perhaps you will continue.'

Jonah looked round to check that everyone was

listening and then resumed his story.

'As I was saying: imagine that you are outside the apartment, looking in and seeing, as you think, Mark Price sitting on the wall of the balcony. Imagine further that you have just had a blazing row with him. He has been criticising you and your friends and has humiliated you in public.'

Jonah paused and looked across the room towards Cameron. Their eyes met and Cameron flushed deep red and looked away.

'You are burning with rage and indignation – and yet, here he is, sitting calmly on the balcony wall as if nothing had happened. He has always made you feel small and powerless and now, for perhaps the first time, you are in a position – literally – to knock him off his perch. It must be very tempt –'

'Stop!' Glenys Price shouted. 'Stop this at once! I can see where this is going and it's all nonsense.'

All eyes turned to look at her, sitting very upright and very rigid, looking straight at Jonah.

'I can see that you're trying to make out that Cameron pushed Owen off in mistake for his father,' she went on, speaking in a tight staccato voice as if she were having trouble getting the words out. 'But you've got it wrong.'

'Too right he has!' Mark interrupted. 'Pure fantasy – that's what it is! Who does this guy think he is, coming here and making wild accusations? And, just because he's in a wheelchair, everyone is too polite to tell him to his face that he's lost it. He may have been –'

'Mark!' Glenys spoke sharply and urgently. 'Just you stop it too.' She took a deep breath and appeared to be bracing herself in readiness for an unpleasant duty. 'Inspector Porter – and Inspector Rosario,' she added, looking towards Eduardo, 'I was the one who pushed my husband off the balcony using the awning pole from our apartment. Afterwards, I went outside, intending to go downstairs, and I realised I was still carrying it, so I stuffed it in through the door of the other apartment because it was closer.'

'But you weren't there,' Mark said. 'You didn't get back from the Kids club until later. Go on!' He looked at Peter and Jonah, 'Tell them! You saw her get back after Owen was already on the floor.'

'Mrs Price,' Jonah said quietly, 'would you like to explain how it was done?'

'When I got back from taking the kids to the club, I didn't come in round the path. I climbed up into the flowerbed and cut across to the stairs that way. The kids often went that way. Danny liked hiding in the bushes. I went up to the apartment, pushed Owen off, and then came back down and went back across the flowerbed. Then I came round the outside of the bed, as if I'd just got back.'

'And we have photographs of footprints in the raised bed that I am confident will match the shoes that you are currently wearing,' Eduardo added. 'Although, of course, we cannot be sure that they were made on that occasion.'

'But why?' Cameron burst out. 'Did you hate Dad that much, that you wanted to kill him?'

Glenys sighed. Suddenly she felt very weary.

'I didn't hate anyone. And I didn't want to kill anyone. I just wanted to stop Owen being sent to Syria.'

There was silence – apart from the persistent song of the warblers in the trees.

'I'd been trying to persuade him to leave the army for months – years now – and he took no notice. And then he got orders to go out to the Middle East. It was supposed to be as a military advisor in Iraq, but then it was "northern Iraq" and everyone knew it was really Syria. He knew how unhappy I was about it, but he couldn't disobey orders and he wouldn't resign his commission. And then I saw this boy,' she pointed towards Gary, 'with his arm in plaster and I suddenly thought: if Owen got injured before he was due to fly out, they'd have to send someone else instead. And I started thinking about how to make him have an accident that would stop them sending him out there.'

Glenys broke off and looked directly at Jonah.

'You've got kids. Can't you imagine what it's like, day after day, wondering if you're going to hear that their dad has been killed – or worse! Captured and tortured, maybe. Or shot in the back like you. I don't know how you manage to keep going the way you do. I'm sure Owen wouldn't have been able to cope – he's – he was so active. That's why I pushed him off the balcony. I thought he'd maybe break an arm or a leg or perhaps his collar bone – and then he'd have to stay at home until it healed up, and that might give me time to convince him to come out of the army and start putting his family first. You do believe me, don't you? I never meant to hurt him seriously. I was trying to keep him safe!'

Her voice cracked and she subsided into soft sobbing. Claire got up, came across to her and sat down in the chair that Wendy had vacated. She put her arm round Glenys and pressed a tissue into her hand.

'Don't take any notice of her!' Mark's voice sounded strident in the stunned silence that had followed Glenys' confession. 'I don't know why you're doing this,' he went on, addressing his sister-in-law, 'but you don't have to lie about what happened. I suppose you're trying to protect Cameron, but it isn't necessary. He didn't do it. And neither did she,' he added rounding on Jonah.

Jonah raised his eyebrows interrogatively, but said nothing.

'*I* pushed Owen off the wall,' Mark said baldly. 'You were right about one thing – I never meant to do him serious damage. I'd been going up and down from the apartment that way all week. It's hardly any distance down – seven, eight feet at the most. Our mother will tell you things always worked out for him and always went wrong for me. And what made it worse was the way he was always so nice about it! I'm sure that he and Glenys encouraged Julie to leave me – and to go for custody of our son. And then, on Tuesday, there he was! Sitting up on the wall of the balcony, in just the same place that Glenys had told me off time and time again for. And I thought about how Glenys would come back and find him there and she wouldn't tell *him* off. It would be alright for him to be there, because Owen could do no wrong. And I thought: *she's so sure it's dangerous sitting up there, I'll show them how dangerous it is!* So I got hold of the awning pole and just gave him a little nudge and he fell off.'

'I see,' said Jonah quietly. 'And now, please can you explain the triceratops?'

'The what?' Mark exclaimed in bewilderment.

'The plastic toy that your brother was clutching when he fell. Danny was playing with his collection of dinosaurs shortly before he went out. Glenys made him take them off the balcony wall and she tidied them all away in a cupboard. I'd like you to explain how Owen came to be holding one of them when you pushed him.'

'How would I know? I suppose he must have found it somewhere and picked it up. Danny was always leaving his things about.'

'Mrs Price?' Jonah looked towards Glenys.

'I don't know how you knew,' she replied, sniffing and wiping her eyes. 'Yes. That was how I was planning to get him up on to the wall. I put all Danny's dinosaurs away before we went out, except for one. I threw that one as far as I could along the planter, so that it was out of reach from our balcony. The idea was that I would pretend to find it, after I got back from taking the children to the Kids Club, and I'd ask Owen to climb up and get it and then …'

'And then?' prompted Jonah gently.

Glenys took a deep breath and continued.

'When I got back, I saw he was already up on the wall. I suppose he must have spotted the dinosaur and got up to get it back. I never realised he'd got it. I forgot all about it after ... everything. I was afraid he'd get down again before I could get to him, so I grabbed the awning pole and stabbed at him to make him fall. I was surprised how easy it was. I was expecting to have to push really hard, but he just toppled off. Then, like I said before, I went down to find him and I pushed the pole into Mark's flat as I was passing. And that was it.'

For several minutes nobody spoke. Even the warblers in the tree fell silent. Nobody wanted Glenys Price to be found guilty of killing her husband, but nobody could think of any way that it could be avoided now that she had confessed. Kirsty looked down thoughtfully at Lily, calmly chewing a plastic toy and staring, apparently enthralled, at the sight of her own bare toes wiggling on the footrest of the buggy.

Glenys looked towards Eduardo.

'What happens now?' she asked in a scared voice.

'Hang on!' Kirsty called out, jumping to her feet. Lily, detecting the urgency in her mother's voice started to cry. Lewis lifted her out of her buggy and cradled her on his lap, rocking her back and forth in an attempt to calm her.

'I want to say something,' Kirsty said, looking towards Eduardo. 'I'm really sorry, Inspector Rosario, but I want to withdraw my statement about seeing someone push Owen Price off the balcony. I've been thinking about it and I'm not sure any more. I mean – I thought I was, but, well, I wouldn't feel comfortable about swearing to it in a court of law. The sun was in my eyes and the more I think about it, the more I think I was mistaken.'

'I see,' Eduardo said calmly. 'Thank you for telling me now.'

He got to his feet and looked round slowly, taking in everyone's expression. Then he looked directly at Glenys Price and then down at the toy dinosaurs scattered on the ground in front of her chair. Everyone waited for him to speak. High up above, the warblers resumed their song.

30 TIS MERCY ALL

'Mrs Price,' Eduardo said at last, 'I would like to suggest what really happened. It is my belief that, after you returned from taking your children to the Kids Club – cutting across the flowerbed as you often did to save time – you decided to pull out the awning to shade your balcony from the sun. It was particularly strong that day, as others have reminded us. I have examined the awnings in these apartments. I have observed that they can be difficult to adjust. Using just the pole, it is easy to get them jammed. I think that you struggled with the awning and your husband offered to help by climbing up on the wall and pulling it with his hand while you continued to push with the pole. As he started to climb, he noticed your son's Triceratops and picked it up, intending to put it away after you had fixed the awning. He was in a sitting position and was about to stand up when the pole slipped in your hands and struck him on the back, knocking him off the wall. What a disaster! You do not know what to do. For some time you remain unable to do anything. Then you run out of the apartment to go down to help your husband. You fling the pole into the next-door apartment – as you told us. When you reach the bottom of the stairs, you see your nephew ahead of you. Rather than pushing past him, you return across the flowerbed and approach along the other path.'

He paused and looked at Glenys, waiting for her to respond, but she said nothing.

'Yes,' came Mark's voice, tentative at first and then more certain. 'That's exactly how it must have been. I noticed the extra awning pole, but I didn't think anything of it until Jonah came round the next morning with that story about someone using one to push Owen off the balcony. I got rattled in case someone from our family got blamed for what must have been just an unfortunate accident, so I washed both the poles down to remove any traces there may have been of Owen's blood or anything. I had to wash them both because I didn't know which one it was that had been involved.'

'And you very nearly succeeded,' Eduardo told him. 'Our forensic scientists only found minute traces of blood on one of the poles. However, it was a risky thing for you to do, because they also found traces of the shower gel that you used to clean the poles and it matches the brand that you have in your bathroom.'

'And if I say that your version of what happened is true?' Glenys asked, 'what will happen to me?'

'I will need to take fresh statements from everyone,' Eduardo told her, looking round at the attentive audience. 'And then I will write my report for the Public Prosecutor. In it, I will set out the evidence and my opinion that the death was an unfortunate accident and a recommendation that the hotel takes steps to advise guests more strongly not to climb on the balcony. It will be for the Prosecutor to decide, but I would be surprised if there were any criminal proceedings.'

'So I'd be free to go home? With the kids?'

'As I said, it is not my decision, but that is what I would expect.'

There was a low murmur of sound, almost as if

everyone had been holding their breath and had now released it.

The party broke up at that point, with a collective sigh of relief that the investigation was, or so it appeared, over and that nobody, or so they all hoped, would be charged, much less convicted, of murder or even of manslaughter. Glenys, walking as if in a dream, retired to apartment 501 to play with her children and to relate to her mother-in-law the outcome of the meeting.

Eduardo retreated to apartment 502, where he set up an impromptu interview room for the purpose of re-examining each witness and obtaining fresh statements. Bernie made a pot of tea to refresh them all and to while away the time while they waited for Inês to arrive to take notes of the interviews. The students, the Barringtons and Kirsty and Lewis all returned to their respective apartments, having been instructed by Eduardo to remain on hand pending his summons.

Only Mark and Cameron remained by the pool. They sat, looking rather awkwardly at one another, neither knowing what to say. Eventually Cameron plucked up his courage and addressed his father in a rather awe-struck tone.

'That was very brave what you did.'

'I didn't do anything.' Mark, spoke without looking at Cameron. He was unaccustomed to praise from any source, least of all his son.

'You did though.' Cameron insisted. He hesitated, wondering whether to go on and ask the question that he was burning to have answered. 'She did do it – Aunty Glenys, I mean – she did push him off deliberately, didn't she? And you told that policeman that it was you, so that she wouldn't go to jail.'

Mark turned towards his son and looked him in the eyes.

'If that's what you think,' he said, speaking very deliberately, 'I can't stop you. But you must never, *never*, say that – or even hint it – in front of the kids. Do you understand?'

Inside apartment 502, others were also expressing surprise at the way in which Mark had come to the defence of his sister-in-law.

'Who would have thought it?' Peter said incredulously. 'He never even seemed to like her. Some of the things he said to her – and things *she* said about *him*, come to that!'

'He was thinking of the kids,' Jonah said with quiet confidence. 'Like the rest of us.'

'But if we'd believed him, he'd most likely have been convicted of murder,' Peter pointed out. 'That must have taken a lot of bottle.'

'I think we probably all misjudged Captain Price,' Bernie observed, setting down the tea tray on the table. 'Owen kept trying to tell us that he was more sinned against than sinning, but we didn't listen.'

'Well, Eduardo, I'm certainly glad you managed to come up with a more satisfactory solution than mine,' Jonah said heartily. 'I must say I was in two minds about trying to get a confession out of Glenys. But I always think that even the worst possible knowledge is better than uncertainty and continuing suspicion, so I decided it was better to go ahead even though it would most likely land her in jail when she didn't really deserve it – and when the children certainly didn't deserve to lose their mum.'

'I would never have managed it without your help. I had completely ruled Mrs Price out in my own mind – both because she was not there and because I was convinced that she truly loved her husband.'

'She did,' Bernie interjected. 'That was obvious to everyone. That's why nobody's going to break ranks and go to the press or start accusing you of a cover up. Mind you,' she added, 'I think I'll make a point of impressing on the students the importance of discretion – you never know what they might say to their mates when they get home. This will have been quite a holiday for them!'

'And so,' Eduardo continued, looking ruefully towards Jonah and Peter, 'it was only when I thought of the possibility of an accident that I could believe that she was responsible. I only wish we could have found this solution earlier. Now I have so much paperwork to do!'

31 HOME! WEARY WANDERS, HOME

When Lucy and Bernie emerged from the apartment the following day, intent on putting the luggage in the car ready for the journey back to the airport, they found a large party of well-wishers waiting to see them off. All the occupants of the six apartments in their block had come to see them on their way.

'Let us help you with those,' Josh offered, stepping forward and trying to wrest one of Lucy's two trolley cases from her hand.

'No thanks. We can manage.'

The young man shrugged and turned towards Bernie, who favoured him with a smile but continued on her way, without giving up either of her own burdens. Peter, carrying only a case small enough to be classed as cabin baggage, slipped past them and hurried on ahead to unlock the car.

After stowing the cases in the back of the car, Bernie ran back up the cobbled slope to conduct a final check of the apartment for things left behind. While she peered inside cupboards and drawers and under the beds, Peter, Lucy and Jonah waited outside, watching for Wayne and Dean, who were to join them. They were all booked on the same flight home and, although it would be a bit of a squash, they would all manage to fit in the spacious hire car. Cameron sidled up to Lucy.

'I've sent you a friend request on Facebook,' he told her, speaking low in the hope that his father would not hear.

'Oh. OK,' Lucy answered, taken aback.

'And I wondered if maybe we could meet up sometime,' Cameron went on, still speaking in an undertone and flushing red. 'We live in Gloucester, which isn't all that far from Oxford.'

'I don't know,' Lucy mumbled, unsure what to say. 'I'm going to be very busy, with my A' levels and things.'

'Not in the summer holidays. You won't have started them then.'

'I don't know. I think we've got plans for the summer.'

'You don't have to come to Gloucester,' Cameron persisted. 'I could visit you in Oxford. Mum said she'll take me round to see universities. Oxford Brookes do a Drama and Film Studies degree I night put on my UCAS form.'

'I don't know,' Lucy repeated. She was not sure whether she wanted to encourage Cameron Price. She did not have anything in particular against the boy and she felt sorry for him and did not want him to feel that she was giving him the brush-off. On the other hand, she did not wish to lay herself open to accusations of having led him on, and she did not herself feel any desire to prolong or develop their relationship. 'Let's just stick to Facebook for the time being, shall we? See how things go.'

'Sorry we're late,' Wayne called out as he and Dean approached round a corner of the drive. 'Dean insisted on stripping the beds to save the maid a job when she comes. I told him not to bother, but some people just won't listen to reason.'

'Is there someone else?' Cameron asked Lucy, a new possibility suddenly dawning on him.

'No. Well ... um ... I suppose there probably is,' Lucy

murmured vaguely, making a conscious effort not to allow her gaze to be drawn towards Jonah, who was on his way down the cobbles, the wheels of his chair resonating loudly on the rough surface. She forced herself to ignore her instinctive desire to follow him down to the car and supervise his passage up the ramp to ensure that he made it safely inside without mishap. Instead, she looked up at Cameron and held out her hand. 'I think we're ready to go now. I'll accept your Facebook request as soon as I log in when we get home.'

They shook hands formally – something that Cameron could not remember ever having done with anyone before – and Lucy turned quickly away to join Jonah, Wayne and Dean in the back of the car. Peter climbed into the driving seat and Bernie wound the window down on the front passenger side and waved enthusiastically at everyone as they drove away.

'Making progress?' Mark asked, breaking into Cameron's thoughts as he watched the car disappear along the drive. 'Or was she giving you the old heave-ho?'

Cameron shrugged and turned to go. Then he hesitated and turned back and looked at his father.

'I don't know,' he confessed. 'Like I told you – she's weird.'

Mark started to formulate a reply, then, with uncharacteristic perceptivity, decided to remain silent and wait for his son to elaborate.

'She's like – the only thing that matters is that guy in the wheelchair ... well, that and getting wonderful grades and going to Oxford uni.'

'I suppose she must admire the way he keeps on in spite of being paralysed,' Mark suggested. 'Don't you?'

'Yes, but it's like she really *cares* about him? And he's old ... older than you.'

'Thanks!'

'Like, the other day, she was going on about how awful it was that his injury probably meant he wouldn't live that long. I mean, so what? OK, it's not great for him, but ...'

'You don't want to play second fiddle?'

'I think Lucy probably thinks I'm only fit for the triangle!' Cameron replied, with an unusual burst of humour. 'She says she'll friend me on Facebook. I suppose that's a start.'

'Welcome back,' Becky greeted them as Pedro wheeled Jonah on to the plane. 'I heard you had problems with your wheelchair. I hope they got sorted.'

'Yes, thank you,' Jonah assured her. 'And we've taken steps to protect the workings better going home, so all being well it'll survive intact this time round.'

'I do hope so. We're all very sorry you were inconvenienced. I've been told to serve free drinks to you and your friends as a goodwill gesture; so just let me know what you'd like – any time during the flight.'

Peter and Wayne carefully lifted Jonah out of the wheelchair provided by the airline and settled him into his seat. Bernie produced an inflatable cushion and positioned it to make him as comfortable as possible. Lucy squeezed past and sat down on his left.

'I hope you had a relaxing holiday,' Becky said conversationally.

'It was very *interesting*,' Jonah hedged.

'We don't really do *relaxing*,' Bernie told her, settling down on Jonah's right.

'Well, so long as you had a good time.'

'Bit of a roller-coaster really,' Jonah concluded, 'but things worked out in the end – more or less.' He paused for a moment, thinking about how different life would be for the Price family when they returned home. 'Anyway,' he added, cheering up, 'it's back to the grindstone on Monday. I wonder if they'll have a nice juicy murder case for me to get my teeth into!'

THANK YOU

Thank you for taking the time to read DEATH ON THE ALGARVE. If you enjoyed it, please consider telling your friends or posting a short review. Word of mouth is an author's best friend and much appreciated. Thank you,

Judy.

MORE ABOUT BERNIE AND HER FRIENDS

Bernie features in five more books.
- **Awayday:** a traditional detective story set among the dons of an Oxford college.
- **Changing Scenes of Life:** Jonah Porter's life story, told through the medium of his favourite hymns.
- **Despise not your Mother:** the story of Bernie's quest to learn about her dead husband's past.
- **Two Little Dickie Birds:** a murder mystery for DI Peter Johns and his Sergeant, Paul Godwin.
- **Murder of a Martian:** a double murder for Peter and Jonah to solve.

Read more about Bernie Fazakerley and her friends and family at https://sites.google.com/site/llanwrdafamily/

Visit the Bernie Fazakerley Publications Facebook page here:
https://www.facebook.com/Bernie.Fazakerley.Publications

Follow Bernie on Twitter: https://twitter.com/BernieFaz.

ABOUT THE AUTHOR

Like her main character, Bernie Fazakerley, Judy Ford is an Oxford graduate and a mathematician. Unlike Bernie, Judy grew up in a middle-class family in the South London stockbroker belt. After moving to the North West and working in Liverpool, Judy fell in love with the Scouse people and created Bernie to reflect their unique qualities.

As a Methodist Local Preacher, Judy often tells her congregation, "I see my role as asking the questions and leaving you to think out your own answers." She carries this philosophy forward into her writing and she hopes that readers will find themselves challenged to think as well as being entertained.

Printed in Great Britain
by Amazon